I0772598

From Her Ashes

Tina Bonilla

FIC044000   FICTION / Women

ISBN (Hardcover): 9798990202603
ISBN (Paperback): 9798990202610
ISBN (EPUB): 9798990202627

Cover design by Anna Kavanagh

Printed in the United States of America

To

Those Who Made Her Strong

AB BR BW HS TH TS

And

Those Who Made It So

AK EA

PROLOGUE

Elizabeth Catherine Stevens glanced in the reflective glass as she stepped into the curved space of the revolving door. Impeccable. It was a word her father had used often to describe his "Beth." He never referred to his daughter as Elizabeth. Not even when he summoned her into his walnut paneled study to scold her about one transgression or another. A lesson in brutality, he would call it. His words burned into her head while his hand seared across her face. She would gaze beyond him during these trials, looking out at the New York City skyline perfectly framed by the study's windows. Pretending to be a princess wounded by a fire breathing dragon. Her knight in shining armor was coming to rescue her from the beast. She could see him just past the garden's gates, galloping toward her on his white stallion, a silver sword raised in his hand and a gold cross affixed to his breastplate.

She never cried. Not once. Despite the many years of torture he had inflicted upon her, loving her one minute, loathing her the next. To an outsider, their relationship was that of a protective father watching closely over daddy's little girl. They both relished their image in a world where image mattered most. Behind closed doors, Elizabeth Stevens adored her father. She knew from an early age that she was his favorite. He revealed his honest interior to her, and no one else. Not to her mother, and certainly not her brothers. Elizabeth's oldest sibling, Edward "the Fourth," had the burden of being the first-born son. And Miles did what middle children tend to do. He succumbed to his role as jester. Comic relief. Not good enough to ever hold the role his older brother played, and not cherished like his baby sister. But if he had been asked as he grew into adulthood, Miles would have readily admitted that he was content with his position. He was his mother's child. And that was his saving grace. Backed further by an ample supply of handsome good looks, Miles saw life as one great, big quest. For what, he wasn't quite sure.

Elizabeth's parents had more than disapproved when she announced her intention to live in California. "How could you," her mother yelled. It wasn't a question. Beth was reminded daily that her mother had not sacrificed the better part of 24 years to give her daughter lessons in manners and fashion from the finest House of So-in-So, only to leave the civility of the East for the waywardness of the West. "You stupid girl," her father followed. This was not what he wanted. She was to be near his side at the firm. Not necessarily to use her newly graduated skills as an attorney. But to reel the clients in with her light blue eyes, dark brown hair, and everything that followed. She was part daughter, part colleague, and part therapist. She was the glue which held the family together. Of course, they all looked to Edmund as a provider, but they all looked to Elizabeth for peace.

Edward was furious. Not only with his daughter, but with himself for spending emotional collateral combating his beautiful Beth. He had always been able to carefully control her, to steer her ever so gently toward his intended direction. And although he and his wife of 32 years endured a joyless marriage, on this mad declaration by their child to move to California, they did agree. They united in a stronghold. They were not having it. What followed were less than subtle suggestions that Elizabeth should escape to Europe for a while. She should have a rest. After all, completing a bachelor's degree in economics, followed by law school and the accompanying Bar exam would deplete anyone. Elizabeth was equally stubborn. Yes, she needed a rest. On the West Coast where it was warm, but not too warm.

Where you could drive your own car, rather than being escorted everywhere in the back of a black sedan. A place where the ocean, forest, desert, and mountains coexisted beneath an open sky. The disagreements continued for weeks. Elizabeth completely shut down, knowing that in doing so, she would finally win. She would be the knight in shining armor and rescue herself.

He, on the other hand, had failed. Mr. Edmund Anthony "the Third," had failed. "Christ," he would say aloud to no one, except himself. He knew it was common for recent college grads to run as far from their parents as opportunity would allow. But Edmund certainly didn't consider his family to be "common." Prestige was built upon decades of toil. Tradition continued to have its place in a society where AI and Instagram had become paramount to the young with their new money ideals. Edmund knew Beth's decision would reflect poorly upon his wife at her Wednesday bridge matches held in their Central Park South sky-rise. She would probably avoid her tennis matches in Southampton altogether, giving various reasons for having stayed in Manhattan over yet another weekend. He didn't care about her, but he was gravely concerned about the gossip which undoubtedly would follow these women back to the security of billionaire's row, across the thresholds of their towery apartments, and to their final resting places at dinner with their husbands.

He could picture it now. His family would be the focus of an entire evening's conversation. Assholes. He never really thought of any of these men as peers. They were boring souls placed in his path to serve his needs. Someone to smoke cigars with at a nauseating cocktail party. Someone to hold court with at the club to emit the air of success. No. He never confided in these men. He wouldn't dare. Too much was at stake. His capital ventures. His family's wealth. Even his whoring.

These men were all the same. They all lived careful lives. Isolated lives. They talked about everything, yet nothing at all. The Yankees. The Jets and the Giants. Cars. Women. The same conversations they'd been having since university, only with money as the overarching theme. It was his Beth who brought light into his darkness.

Edmund was hard on her, he knew. He thought about her birthdays. They were always special. Elizabeth's mother created themes which were fun and appropriate. Although jet setting to Paris with classmates for a weekend was financially a reality, Elaine wanted to have parties filled with games and friends and warmth. After every child had gone, and the decorations were removed, Edmund would call his delicate Beth into his study where a gift had been carefully wrapped and placed in the center of his desk. Every year, father and daughter played a game. "Take it. Open it. This gift belongs to you," Edmund would tell the child. "Or don't. Leave it, and wonder." It was a test. Beth often imagined that the box contained nothing. In her heart of hearts she hoped that her father had indeed carefully selected something for this magical day. She would never defy his wishes by opening the gift. The real present was in seeing the pleased look on her father's face and in his deep green eyes when she refused. When she demonstrated her restraint.

"Silly," Edmund thought. He felt abandoned. Betrayed. For the first time, he felt the very sting he had so often bestowed upon his Beth. It was her turn now. She was moving forward without him by her side. "Payback," he wondered. He didn't give the thought much recognition. He knew Beth did not live her life in that realm. No, his daughter wanted to escape. From him? It was too painful to imagine. From her mother? Edmund doubted it. While they were not of the traditional mother-daughter relationship set about in fairytales, Elaine and Beth were comfortable with one another. It certainly wasn't the closeness that his wife shared with Miles. Oh no. Those two were inseparable. Laughing until they cried. Sharing secrets. Traveling to the far ends of the earth, returning to tell fabulous stories of the people they'd met, the food they had eaten, and the occasional trouble they had gotten themselves into and then back out of again. Elaine always, always took away her son's pain. The pain of being forever stuck in the middle.

She had never told anyone that, had Miles been born Melanie, his younger sister would never have been conceived.

And then there was his successor, Edmund Anthony the fourth, Elizabeth's oldest brother. He was a good son. Not brilliant. Not witty. But not a trouble seeker. He would dutifully carry the weight left behind by the First, the Second, and eventually himself, the Third. The Fourth had checked every box, completing the required tasks. Boarding school. Check. Water polo. Check. Columbia. Check. A semester in Italy. Yale law. Jesus! The only thing missing was a wife. And children. He was approaching his thirty-second birthday and dating a so-called supermodel, not from Paris or the States, but rather Australia. Edmund Anthony the Third cringed. She was beautiful, but her accent cheapened her entire persona. It was well, so *not* British. She traveled extensively but seemed to have nothing to say. She did, however, have new wealth, so that was something. And the Fourth had been able to maintain her interest for nearly two years. Still, a committed relationship between the two was laughable. Their connection seemed based in excess. The St. Moritz Polo World Cup. The Formula 1 Monaco Grand Prix. The Wimbledon Tennis Championships. And most recently, New York and Paris Fashion Weeks.

Edmund knew his son was drowning. Oh, he could handle the pressure from the Saudis and Chinese. His reputation was most definitely that of the top producing international attorney at his father's firm. He was six feet and one-half inches tall and looked the part of a successful lawyer in his Brioni suits. But Edmund the third knew all too well the anguish. Did anyone really want to walk a step behind in their father's shadow? Edmund certainly hadn't. God, the miserable years he himself had spent at Switzerland's Le Rosey school. The endless studying for the Bar. The countless rounds of golf with his father, the Second. The "boys will be boys" attitude that his grandfather boasted about until, at 23, Edmund had finally lost all respect for the patriarch of the family. He hadn't shed one tear when his grandfather passed. Instead, he was grateful. Maybe the sickening feeling in his stomach would die alongside the wretched old man, forever closed in a coffin buried far beneath the ground.

The revolting feeling Edmund had come to know did not disappear until he finally found himself standing before his own father, the Second, as he lay in a silent coma. Edmund the third was older now. He had a wife and three children of his own. He was making his mark at the firm, both in the States and abroad. He didn't despise his father, the way he had his grandfather. But he did not love him, either. This time, though, Edmund chose the path of least resistance, lying to his hushed father in the final hours before his dying. Thanking him again and again for the life his father had given to him. The Third had approached death with great intensity. He had been present when both patriarchs took their very last breaths upon this earth. Edmund the third was finally free.

Edmund's father had been a prick. Pure and simple. He had hurt his mother. In turn, Edmund had now hurt Elaine. Why had his wife stayed by his side for these 32 years? Once upon a time, she had been "the one." She was sharp. Well-spoken. They met at Yale. He was a law school student. She was an undergrad. Her pale skin, brunette hair, and pouting lips had sealed the deal. That, and the fact that she walked down the aisle pregnant with the Fourth. Why had she stayed with him as he continually lied and ignored her. Of course, he knew the answer. It came in the form of a private jet, friends on Capitol Hill, and a wardrobe full of clothes that she would never wear. It was a marriage backed by a photograph at a gala opening and having the family name recognized as it spread across a building.

In fairness, she was a wonderful mother. She loved her children very much. While it was obvious that Miles was her favorite, she never ignored the Fourth or Beth. She encouraged their activities and made certain she shared quality time with them. She knew her children's friends in more than a passing manner, listening to them talk about their teachers, fellow students, and especially their enemies. She played video games and listened to their favorite music. It was exhausting. But it had given her purpose, when she wasn't occupied with being Mrs. Edmund Anthony the third's wife.

Edmund knew his daughter, from a very early age, had been placed in the position of referee between himself and Elaine. Truthfully, the only thing keeping Elaine in check when it came to staying in her marriage, was their daughter. That, and an iron clad prenup. It wasn't right to put a child in that position, but Elizabeth accepted it. Even as a little girl, Elizabeth recognized that she did not want to be the product of a divorce. To prevent arguments from escalating, she played interventionist. She knew how to lighten a heated conversation before it became a war of words between her parents.

Now, Beth was going to leave her father to sit in misery. With Elaine and Miles and the Fourth becoming his only sources of entertainment. There weren't enough escorts in all of Manhattan or DC or halfway around the world to take away the sorrow. Edmund felt empty. That three o'clock in the morning emptiness that he experienced after fulfilling his church-like rituals. The late night check-in at the luxury hotel. The room service supper. The Highland Park scotches to the bottom of the bottle. The last glance as yet another girl took the money from his clip and laid it on the table, turning out the lights and leaving him alone in the darkness. He had learned long ago that money wasn't enough to satisfy himself. And at 59, even the women no longer filled the void. The longing for his authentic self. No, that was lost. And now, he was losing his last hope. His only daughter. His Beth.

Edmund Anthony the third had begun to spin the story very cautiously. His daughter's move to San Francisco must appear as a welcomed adventure. He and Elaine would throw a party and wish their daughter well. Colleagues from the office. Friends from the clubs, and a few celebrities to ensure Page Six attention. Hell, Elaine would probably turn the whole thing around into some sort of fundraiser. Great. He could simultaneously appear philanthropic and give his child a lavish sendoff.

Elaine, of course, would discuss Beth's plans with her judgmental friends in broad, simple terms. The sky-high apartment in the City by the Bay. The endless phone calls with the decorator to make certain their 24-year-old felt comfortable and safe. New wardrobe choices. But the why. How would he and Elaine explain it? He thought about this incessantly, as he paced the study's navy carpeting. It had to be a simple story. Not something that could be researched or reviewed in this Meta filled universe. Something that made sense as he watched his daughter walk out the door. He didn't know if he would ever see her walk back through it again.

After weeks of preparation, it had been decided. Beth and her parents had agreed. She was going to San Francisco to consult on behalf of the firm. That was it. Done. Not something anyone would question. After all, she had followed in the footsteps of the Fourth, the Third, the Second, and the First. She had attended law school out of a sense of duty. She never actually intended to practice law, but not one of their friends knew that. It was the perfect explanation. And old money didn't ask. Because they had their own secrets they never wished to share.

The party was to be an opulent affair. Edmund wanted to hold it in their apartment. Elaine wouldn't think of it. It had to be Michelin-starred. It had to be Ren's. At $1,000 per plate. Before any alcohol was served. Elaine arranged to have the entire restaurant. The guest list was fastidiously selected. Invitations were hand delivered in glossy blue boxes, tied with silk ribbon. It didn't matter that the delivery would be made to a concierge or member of the office staff.

The restaurant was known for its classic modern style, boasting prominent red fabric panels along its corridors and offering long banks of seating. The red didn't suit Elaine's color scheme for the party, so she convinced Ren Kimura himself to change the panels out to blue, with no concern for the added expense. Special dishes were created for the evening, along with signature cocktails which had become expected at these affairs. News media were supplied with a complete guest list, and influencers were enticed to attend with the promise of a pose-worthy gift.

The party was ultimately unimaginative in Edmund's mind. Too much rich food. Definitely too much alcohol. Even the second tier actors and athletes appeared bored. The congressmen looked around, standing shoulder to shoulder with the state senators. Feeling "bigger" with their federal careers, knowing all the while that the real power sat with New York and California. It had been a night filled with small talk, phony laughter, and a speech he hadn't delivered until half past midnight. With exhaustion fully set in, the evening finally came to an end.

CHAPTER 1

It was all one great piece of fiction. Elaborate in every detail, the narrative provided her with reassurance that she could be of that pedigree. She could dismiss the truth for her intensions. She envisioned herself as the beloved daughter from a prominent line of Manhattan attorneys. Tucked carefully away. A member of a family institution, which flaunted its considerable financial position. With offices in the nation's capital and clients across the world. She wished to be the girl in the freshly pressed white dress who ran barefoot along the beaches near Sagaponack in her childhood, while the ocean's salt water splashed across her legs in a carefree breeze. She imagined what sorority parties smelled like at Yale. A mix of perfume, beer, and boys. Tennis. Dinners. Conversation. Even the wood paneled study lodged in the stately New York City apartment. She saw herself as she was taunted in that room with the navy carpet. Never shedding a tear. Waiting for her knight in shining armor as a child. Refusing to unwrap the birthday gift set out before her, so that she might please her father. Yes, these details kept her calm and safe.

The story was a million miles from the truth. She did have those gorgeous blue eyes, stunning dark brown hair, and a body to match. And she used those looks to her full advantage. She *was* impeccable. And the money, impressive. In the beginning, she felt she had sold her soul so that she might embody Elizabeth's wealth and presence. In hindsight, she realized she never had a soul. She had been born into a lower middle class lifestyle that few ever climbed out from. Not poor enough for a free ride, but rather just enough to survive. It was an always wanting existence. Not painful but exhausting.

The only bright spot was the fact that she had been raised by her mother in Pacific Grove, California. Perfectly situated between Monterey and Carmel-By-The-Sea, she had watched as the wealthy enjoyed their patio lunches, sunset strolls, and cocktails with carefully positioned olives balanced against the glass. People didn't need to prove their wealth or worth here. They had it. In subtle ways. A black cashmere sweater from Scotland. A magnificent watch. An almost nondescript pair of buttery leather shoes. Casual and comfortable, but oh so expensive.

Elizabeth was a character. Make believe. Her given name was Sarah. It had been among the most popular names for girls in the late 90s. It made Sarah feel so completely ordinary. In fact, she was known during her elementary school years as Sarah J., because there had also been a Sarah F. and a Sarah R. in her class. A wealthy, East Coast girl would have an old money name. One that allowed her father to lovingly call her as he chose. Beth. A name with a family history dating back centuries, maybe even to a line of royalty. And so, Sarah had her name legally changed to Elizabeth Catherine Stevens as a gift to herself on the occasion of her 21st birthday. Quietly. Secretly. Not that anyone cared. But it made her feel more a part of her own fraudulent tale.

Sarah and her mother, Lynda, had survived on her mother's job as a housekeeper at the famous Inn at Spanish Bay in Pebble Beach, where visitors oftentimes would leave a little something extra for the help. If a big tournament were in town, the players would hand out stacks of hundred-dollar bills to thank housekeeping for their discretion. After all, the housekeeping staff cleaned up every broken glass, returned every forgotten cell phone, and changed the sheets. The "extra" left behind allowed Lynda to buy birthday gifts and Christmas presents.

It helped keep Sarah feeling a little more normal in a town where nothing was ordinary.

Sarah had been born when her mother was only 19. They helped to raise each other. The summers were glorious in Sarah's eyes. Sunsets so orange the sky turned red. Hunting for seashells among the tourists. Feeding the seagulls bits of stale bread at the far end of the beach where tourists never bothered. Racing the waves in the wintertime when the air was still and crisp. However, Sarah knew deep inside herself that her life was far from middle class. Her mother scrimped and saved what little she could. Lynda paid the bills. She made sure Sarah got to school, and even though she had stopped being able to help her daughter with her homework, she insisted that Sarah share it with her every night. Sarah had no idea who her father was, and she never asked. She knew better.

Sarah got her looks from Lynda. Her mother had become tired around the eyes by the time she was 25, but they were the same pale blue color that Sarah inherited and looked through to see the world. Lynda also had a great pair of legs, shapely but not too athletic. She had been propositioned many times over her years at Spanish Bay, but she never succumbed. She couldn't risk losing her job. She had a daughter to raise, and she needed the steady income and its accompanying benefits.

Pacific Grove was a bit more casual than the golf course dotted coastline which meandered to the south. This helped to buffer the conflicting lifestyles which intertwined along the beaches. The city was quirky. Artists and beekeepers lived here among the vacation homes of the super-rich. It almost seemed a disgrace that $30 million estates sat empty in Carmel most of the year, welcoming inhabitants only during world famous golf championships. In sharp contrast, Pacific Grove was home to predominantly two types of people. Those who lived in rundown midcentury apartments supporting the lifestyles of the wealthy, and upper middle class families paying huge mortgages for a tiny slice of ocean view. The homes were painted in an array of pastel color schemes and sat inches from each other on steep hillsides facing the bay. The view was spectacular and the night sky nearly always clear. The area was known for its laid back restaurants, a nostalgic movie theater, and an amazing library filled with books and computers. It was here, in the library which vaguely reminded one of a Spanish mission, where Sarah methodically became Elizabeth. One magazine article, story, and Google search at a time. The family, upbringing, even the California sendoff party in New York had all been carefully crafted over many years by a young girl wanting desperately to have a different life.

In the beginning, it was a project of sorts. Sarah had written a book report about England's royal family in the fourth grade. As a nine-year-old, she wondered why there were no royal families in America. That wondering led her to read about the blue bloods in her own country. The Rockefellers, Waltons, and Mars. They had extreme wealth. Then, there were the famous political families. The Roosevelts. The Kennedys, who Sarah discovered were considered American royalty. The Bushes. She longed to be from a prominent family. At a young age, she knew she didn't want fame for herself in the form of a movie star or musician. She cultivated her relationship with her character, and by the time she was a freshman in high school she no longer cared about fame at all, rather she had decided that power and influence were what she valued most. She thought about who was considered important. Not politicians. They were simply vehicles to be driven by the elite. Doctors. Maybe. Silicon Valley tycoons. Perhaps. Lawyers. Everybody was one, wanted to be one, or needed one. Her fictitious father would be from a long lineage of internationally renowned attorneys. Their headquarters would be situated in Manhattan, with offices in Washington D.C. The firm would be multi-generational with a reputation for being tough combatants in the court room.

Sarah's character, Elizabeth, would go to law school, but she would never practice. Her mother, Elaine, would be the socialite. She would be well educated, but her identity would be as a wife, mother, charity supporter, and always on the right arm of her father, whether or not she actually enjoyed the position. Elizabeth would have two older brothers; she would be the baby of her invented family. The oldest brother would be expected to follow in the footsteps of the father. They would have the same name. They would be the third and the fourth in the family line. The middle son wouldn't be expected to be a lawyer, or much of anything for that matter. Sarah wasn't sure what type of occupation he would have, but the expectations placed on him would center around keeping their mother company. He would be fun, have fun, and bring fun to others. Sarah wanted Elizabeth to be pretty, and smart, and agreeable. She wished Elizabeth the "perfect" life.

At 16, Sarah was hired by the Fishhouse, a restaurant with a history dating back before California had become a state. It was an unobtrusive place, sitting on a beachfront corner along a narrow two-lane road. Its large windows revealed the friendly atmosphere. It was more coffee shop than posh restaurant, but the prices equaled those of the cuisine served at the establishments of the more famous Carmel Village. The chef had been trained in France and loved the opportunity to try new dishes out on the customers. The smells coming from the kitchen, accompanied by the chef's boisterous humming, were all part of the atmosphere. A hefty, well-worn oak bar painted yellow sat in the middle of the restaurant. Eight backless barstools stood at attention, although they were a little beat up as that sort of thing tended to happen over the years. Each barstool had a brass rod between the legs serving as a foothold, and several residents had weekly reservations to sit in those coveted chairs for dinner. It would be a three-hour affair with talk about the news along with the community gossip.

The bartender had worked at the Fishhouse for more than a decade. He knew the drink orders and meal preferences of his regular patrons. Every now and again, he would ask his customers if they wanted to try something new, but the answer was almost always "no." It frustrated the chef at times, but he was always available to impress the tourists. On any given night, half of the folks at the bar were recognized, the other half were strangers. It took weeks to get a reservation, and walk-ins didn't bother to try. Take-out was also not an option. Ever.

Sarah worked on Friday and Saturday nights during the school year, clearing tables and cleaning the bathrooms. On busy weekends, she would help with the dishes. She found it relaxing to load the commercial washer with the white plates, carefully placing each one in an individual slot. She was given a pair of heavy duty gloves to protect her hands from the intense heat. It fascinated Sarah that so many dishes could be cleaned in just a few minutes. She would then carefully remove each plate, stacking them so that food could be plated without a break in the kitchen's rhythm. The owners of the Fishhouse loved Sarah, so they saw to it that she had full-time work during the incredibly busy summers. By the time she was 18 and had finished high school, Sarah had become one of their top earners. She knew every item on the menu, recited the specials without ever making a mistake, and was happy to offer meal suggestions. She had literally tasted all of the entrees one delicious morsel at a time, so she understood the flavors and what starters played best with each main.

Having saved nearly all her earnings, Sarah was able to pay the tuition for Monterey Peninsula College, where she studied business during the day and continued to work at the Fishhouse at night. While a lot of kids her age would have spent the money on a secondhand car, Sarah chose to take the bus from the apartment she shared with her mother to school, and then to the restaurant. A car also meant insurance and gas. Those costs alone would be equal to a year's fees at the junior college. To help Sarah out, the restaurant's bartender would drive her home at the end of the evening. He had a daughter of his own and knew how much it meant to Lynda that her child was safe. In a small town, locals looked after each other, especially those who made their living serving others. They were proud to be part of the hospitality industry and always worked hard to honor guests. Without them, there would be no jobs. Lynda worried that Sarah was too busy, too tired, and too grown-up at such a young age. Her daughter seemed to have no friends, and certainly no love interests. Still, Sarah appeared happy. And that's all that mattered.

It was a part-time professor at the junior college who suggested Sarah apply to the state university in her own backyard. Her academic achievements gained her a full scholarship to California State University at Monterey Bay, and at 24 she graduated with a bachelor's degree in business. All the while, she had been forming a plan in her mind. Who she wanted to become. What she wanted to represent. And how she was going to make her way in the world.

She didn't want to leave her mother behind, but she couldn't stay either. She wanted to finally assume the identity she had longed to adopt. Where she wouldn't be recognized as Sarah. But she also needed a place where money found a home in the form of lucrative businesses, wealthy international entrepreneurs, and visitors who enjoyed flashing their platinum cards at Chanel, Neiman Marcus, and Hermes. Relocating to Manhattan, the city where her story took place, was unobtainable. San Francisco, however, was within reach. Just two days after her graduation ceremony, Sarah filled two duffle bags with her belongings and boarded the Amtrak from the nearby farming community of Salinas into the City. Sarah J. was left behind, and Elizabeth Catherine Stevens was born.

CHAPTER
2

The enormous revolving door was curious, but rather ridiculous. And most definitely impractical. Designed by a not so famous artist, now dead, it was originally construed as a statement against an otherwise entirely flat skyscraper facade. It made no sense whatsoever, because the structure enveloping the door had its own identity and was completely apart from its ground floor opening. There was, of course, a story.

The Ellerton building had been designed by an architectural firm in Germany some 20 years prior. San Francisco natives were outraged that a company from the City, or at a minimum, the country had not been selected. It was a private holding, and as such, the owners and investors could do as they wished. However, to avoid protests which always ensued with these types of things, the partners took two measures. First, every element of the construction was contracted to a Bay Area company. Second, a competition was held to fashion the main entrance. The applicants had to live or work within San Francisco County. More than 20 engineers, designers, and craftspeople applied, hoping to be rewarded with five minutes of fame. Their renderings were displayed at City Hall, and the public voted for their favorite. Thus, the revolving door.

It was much simpler to enter the 45-story high rise from one of the more practical expansive brass-trimmed doors to either side. Made from the same glass as their rotating counterpart, the material was heavy and reflective. This was an office building. There were no bellmen in matching uniforms standing under awnings at attention and holding open the doors as was so often depicted in Hollywood movies. Instead, the doors were automatic. Hundreds of employees passed in and out each day. They all had busy lives. They didn't use the revolving door.

Elizabeth Catherine Stevens wanted to make an entrance. She wanted to stare at herself as she slowly passed through the revolving glass. It was the middle of July, and it was freezing. A fog hung over the city as it did most days, not allowing the sun to peak through. She was dressed in an iconic Burberry trench, a perfect shade of tan. Her brunette hair was carefully brushed and smoothed across her shoulders, gracing her spine. Her handbag, a statement Birkin, was purchased on a special holiday trip to Beverley Hills which Elizabeth had given herself as a reward when she had finally crossed the threshold of a seven-figure salary.

The trip had been an adventure. She secured private appointments at the most exclusive boutiques, purchasing jackets and dresses, jeans and perfumes, and so many exquisite pairs of shoes. After careful consideration, Elizabeth had chosen to stay at the Beverley Hills Hotel. It was no longer the most exclusive, and certainly not modern, but East Coast Elizabeth from old money found it alluring. Her suite featured a spacious living room where two down-filled sofas welcomed guests to lounge. The bedroom's California king was covered in the finest Egyptian cotton duvet, with no fewer than a dozen pillows aligned in three rows along the walnut headboard. The décor was green and pink and white, all very fresh and very Southern California. Elizabeth dined at Spago and Wolfgang Puck's Cut. She had room service brunches and allowed herself one dessert at the hotel's Fountain Coffee Room. She didn't usually indulge in dessert. But just this once.

As she placed her leather gloved hand on the door's handle to slowly turn the axis, Elizabeth lifted her eyes from behind her cat eye sunglasses for a brief moment. The large black rims concealed most of her face, but her perfectly crimson lips were in full view. It wasn't her pale skin or legs that turned heads as she passed through the revolving door. It was the pair of four-inch black patent heels which got her noticed.

The Ellerton Building wasn't the most famous in San Francisco despite its past controversies, but its mirrored exterior had found itself plastered on the center pages of Architectural Digest some years earlier. Critics called the building's entry "dreadful," "misguided," and "appalling" among other slights. The magazine had not shared any photographs of the egress, but aficionados in the industry were quick with their cutting words. It housed several law firms, three financial institutions, a couple of mortgage companies, and oddly enough, a recruiting organization. It might have seemed out of place among the more high profile corporations, however Mason Recruiting International, Inc. had a worldwide reputation for putting those already in power into even more formidable positions around the globe. Originally a small family company doing business in the Midwest, over the past two decades, Michael Mason, Jr. had taken his father's ideas to unimaginable heights. Truthfully, it hadn't hurt Michael that he had married into a wealthy Napa Valley wine family. His wife's father had invested heavily in his son-in-law just days following the market crash in 2008. That investment had paid off. It wasn't exciting work, but it more than covered the bills, and it allowed Michael to meet the demands of his own agency, as well as his wife's enterprise.

Michael and his wife had lost their parents by the close of 2010. Both had been groomed to learn and then take charge of the family businesses. This commonality had brought them together, in part, because they both understood what it meant to have historical pressure placed upon their shoulders, in addition to the knowledge that their enterprises were supporting so many others. Michael enjoyed his work, but he readily admitted to himself that he was looking for something meaningful. Weren't all men passing middle age in similar positions, he often wondered.

Huge gray tiles met Elizabeth's heels, echoing in rhythm as she stepped through the revolving door and walked across the lobby. A rectangular desk stretched endlessly in the center of the extensive main floor space. Behind it were no fewer than six people ready to greet anyone clearly not a part of the regular landscape. Elizabeth approached a slim young man standing behind the desk, his face looking down at a computer monitor. He could feel her presence and instantly looked up.

"Good morning. May I help you," he said as he had probably done hundreds of times. He, and the others, were clothed in white dress shirts, matching black suits, and black ties. It was so outmoded, but Elizabeth immediately loved it. An East Coast look, though here in the West. She smiled inside. At least, that's how she imagined it must be in Manhattan, and Boston, and Washington, D.C.

Removing her sunglasses with the precise element of drama, she replied, "Good morning. Yes, thank you. I am here to see Michael Mason." She opened her easily recognizable handbag and carefully removed her gloves, placing them inside her Birkin. Nearly simultaneously, she produced a thick, stiff business card, gingerly handing it over. Almost no one used cards anymore. A QR phone scan was in vogue. But it didn't say old money or East Coast in Elizabeth's world. No, Elizabeth Stevens would never be a black and white square. She would be ivory uncoated cardstock with crimson engraving to match her lips.

The young man glanced over the card. It read: Ms. Elizabeth Stevens, Law Firm of Stevens and Associates. No title. An email and phone number were present, but no address. He quickly picked up a phone. Within a few seconds, the receiver was returned to its cradle.

"Yes, Ms. Stevens, Mr. Mason is expecting you. Please proceed to the second bank of elevators. His office is on the 27th floor." He handed her a key card to access the elevators. It felt heavy in her hand. "And please return the key upon your exit."

Elizabeth nodded but said nothing. She turned, as she had been directed, toward the bank of elevators some 10 yards past the rectangular desk. Several people were gathered, heads down, scanning the latest Internet thread. There were actually two sets of elevators designated by floor series. Six doors in all. She could feel a couple of people look at her from behind. It wasn't unusual. In fact, she rather enjoyed the subtle attention.

The elevator doors finally opened, allowing the occupants to quickly escape. Elizabeth stepped inside the modern space along with several other people who were obviously permanent daytime career residents of the building. In her four-inch heels she wasn't too tall, but tall enough to demand a second glance. There were no buttons. Instead, occupants were required to scan key cards. It was useless high tech, thought Elizabeth. The ride was quick and quiet. When the doors slid across at the 27th floor, Elizabeth carefully stepped out. A very blonde, very attractive young woman stood directly in front of her, staring her up and down.

"Welcome to Mason Recruiting International, Ms. Stevens. May I take your coat?"

Elizabeth declined the offer. For a moment, she felt old. So silly. She was only 34. But the young thing in front of her was barely of legal drinking age. She was a girl, not a woman. It sometimes worried Elizabeth that the world or more specifically, grown men, just wanted an hour with a 21-year-old once a week. No dinner. Not even a glass of wine. Why waste time getting to know somebody when you could meet, have sex, and then do it all over again the following weekend? Despite admitting to being lonely. Gen Z could have an AI relationship, or none at all. They couldn't care less. It took too much effort. Better to work from home, play online video games with strangers, binge docuseries after docuseries, and scroll endlessly across whichever platform suited your interests. It left the bulk of a generation home alone on a Saturday night. Sad.

Some young people had come to realize that by giving an older someone a little attention, they could have everything from designer clothes to vacations to even their rent paid for by a desperate soul hoping to hold onto one last glimpse of youth, before they died. A text here and there. A hotel room for a few hours. Nothing long-term. No danger of a commitment. Ever.

This was Elizabeth's competition. Super young girls who valued possessions over connections. Elizabeth had always wanted both.

No, this isn't my competition, she thought to herself. There were still men out there, who wanted something more. Something deeper. They didn't want to feel completely used for their money. They wanted a nice evening out. Or in. They wanted to be heard and made to feel powerful and important. Even if they had to pay handsomely for it.

CHAPTER
3

Pretty young thing ushered Elizabeth through a set of double doors into Mr. Michael Mason's office. It was well-appointed, though Elizabeth had certainly seen far more elegant spaces. A decorator had probably had a hand in the furniture selection, but it wasn't anything memorable, unusual, or exceedingly expensive. It would have been a typical corner office, except for the fact that it had a breathtaking view of the Golden Gate Bridge. It was both spectacular and odd. A silent photograph, barring the moving traffic, thought Elizabeth.

Mr. Mason's desk sat in front of the windows. A power play. The bridge at his back while he faced outward. A standard oversized black leather chair sat behind the desk looking toward two smaller, and no doubt less comfortable, black chairs placed about three feet apart. If a client or an employee were sitting across from Mr. Mason, he meant business. A round table made from nondescript dark wood, with four equally spaced black leather chairs, was situated in the far left corner of the square room with a speaker phone directly on top. A gray leather sofa sat in the center of the space and was perfectly aligned with a square glass coffee table. Two gray leather club chairs were opposite the sofa and completed the room. Too much leather in one space, Elizabeth concluded. No bookcases. No giant monitor. No art on the walls. It was the view which made the room special.

"Mr. Mason is just finishing up in a meeting," young thing announced. "He will be with you shortly. May I bring you anything? A cup of coffee or a water?"

Elizabeth had learned long ago to decline all offers of food or beverage, unless she was specifically taking a meeting for lunch or dinner. She never agreed to coffee. So West Coast. East Coast encounters occurred over cocktails after hours, not cappuccinos before mid-day. Unlike a restaurant, in an office environment, something could easily spill and distract her from her work. Looking somewhat disappointed that she had completed her immediate duties, the blonde turned away, closing the doors to her boss's office behind her, and leaving Elizabeth to survey the room.

It had taken years for Elizabeth to perfect her skills as a consultant. She reviewed every detail from making the decision whether to remove her coat prior to receiving her client to carefully selecting which chair or sofa she should sit in while patiently waiting. Quietly. She was *always* kept waiting. She had never once entered a room where she was welcomed by the executive. Male, of course. This amused her, but at the same time, it had become a fixture of her conceptualized and finely executed presence. She nearly laughed out loud as she looked at her watch. She knew the wait would be approximately seven minutes. Not so long that she was bored, but long enough so that the man felt busy, important. Like he mattered.

Michael Mason was handsome. He was just shy of six feet tall. He had jet black hair, which was professionally colored every month. His wife, Laura, made sure of it. She didn't like the salt and pepper, I think I'm George Clooney, impression which men his age oftentimes tried to carry off. Besides, he didn't look a thing like Mr. Clooney. Michael worked out regularly in the gym, and he had the upper body to show for it. But his legs were a bit thin, and he didn't have the six-pack abs to match his toned shoulders. Still, in a pair of slacks and the right dress shirt, he was easy on the eyes. His were brown.

The left side office door opened, and Michael appeared. Elizabeth had decided to sit in one of the gray club chairs opposite the sofa facing toward the doors. She had placed her trench coat and handbag in the matching chair. Her legs were crossed, and the narrow heels of her pumps were on display, along with her legs. Michael walked over, expecting Elizabeth to stand. She didn't. Instead, he had no choice but to reach his hand out, taking hers and giving it a gentle shake. Elizabeth waited for the dialogue to begin. More pretending. But that was the job.

"I'm Michael. It's nice to meet you Ms. Stevens. You come highly recommended."

"Thank you," Elizabeth responded in a soothing voice.

"I understand from your in-house counsel that you would like some specialized legal advice." Elizabeth wasn't going to waste time with pleasantries. She knew that busy men wanted an audience when they entered a room, but they didn't want to expend unnecessary effort either.

"Yes. I know you've spoken with my staff. I have a great legal team here and in our London, Dubai, and Shanghai offices. But sometimes I want an outside opinion, particularly when I'm being asked to do something not within our normal scope."

Michael moved towards his desk, motioning for Elizabeth to shift from the more casual club chair to one opposite his, overlooking the Bay. She acquiesced and stood up. She walked toward the desk, then lowered herself into the chair to the right. Her attire was conservative, although not overly so. An ivory blouse with long sleeves. It was sheer, showing off her petite frame. The skirt was of the pencil style, hugging her hips without being obscene. The fabric was a light wool from Italy. It was finely woven and smooth to the touch. She wasn't wearing any jewelry, but she was wearing one of her favorite perfumes, purchased on her excursion to Beverley Hills.

Elizabeth didn't have so much as a pen in her possession as she sat down at Michael's desk. Her things were still sitting in the club chair. She hadn't made any sort of effort to reach for them. Elizabeth could see confusion on Michael's face. He was likely used to a flurry of activity. Laptops, tablets, or at a minimum, a yellow legal pad and pen at the ready of the underling waiting for direction. Elizabeth knew this unnerved him. Was this woman paying attention, he would ask himself. Elizabeth was aware that Michael would test her ability. He needed a show of power.

Slowly, Michael pulled open the top desk drawer and removed a somewhat thick stack of papers. They appeared orderly, though they were not placed inside a folder as was customary. This amused Elizabeth. Most people would have a computerized file on a memory stick to share with a colleague, along with a subsequent hard copy to be handed out. For an issue which demanded the attention of a second party, it was out of sorts to have a pile of papers sitting in a desk drawer. No matter how orderly the documents might have appeared. All of this could have been better accomplished via email. Though, many people were afraid to send anything considered confidential. And with good reason. Stealing data was a full time profession for some. Elizabeth watched as Michael began to look through the stack, until he finally pulled out several pages which had been held together by a rather large paperclip. Elizabeth hated paperclips. They could so easily become detached, misplaced, or commingled with other documents. The only office product she despised more was the rubber band.

"I've asked you here to take a look at this contract," Michael explained. "It's an international firm wanting to establish a relationship with us." This really didn't sound unusual to Elizabeth. Unless of course, Michael was being cryptic in his use of the word "relationship." It had become an overused vocabulary term. It wasn't necessarily a positive word. But it was vague. Vague was the enemy of precise or specific or even clear. She was certain that a company with offices worldwide was quite aware of foreign country legalities when it came to new ventures. What in the world was this "relationship" that Mr. Mason referred to, Elizabeth sighed to herself. She waited for him to get to the point.

Michael's desk was just large enough that she could not view the document from across its polished top. Clearly, he had made it a habit to intimidate the person or people across from him by standing over the desk to distribute materials. He liked authority, *that* Elizabeth did not question. In fact, she was entertained. Why did men already in high places need to feel larger? As was no doubt his practice, Michael stood up and then went to the extra trouble to walk around the edge of his desk, politely presenting Elizabeth with the contents in his hand. He wasn't handing over sealed documents belonging to the CIA, she thought. The theatrics started to bore Elizabeth. She was a lawyer in this scenario, but she was ready to take on the role that she had been hired to transact.

The thought had no sooner crossed her mind when the atmosphere suddenly changed. As Michael passed over the paper clipped stack, he gently placed his left hand on top of her right hand, which was resting comfortably on the arm of the chair. Elizabeth didn't flinch. Yes, they were all the same. He was careful. Waiting for her unspoken reply. It was a precarious business to flirt. A fine line. Cross it and find yourself behind bars or in front of a sea of cameras, with your reputation and more importantly your financial status, in ruins. The rules applied to both sexes. Michael bent his neck ever so slightly as if to review the document's wording. Instead, he leaned in and kissed Elizabeth's neck. She had brushed back her dark hair, leaving it exposed, as if anticipating his touch. She slowly rose from the chair, quietly walked across the room, and locked the office doors. She paused before turning to face him again. Michael was now seated on the sofa. It was an invitation she was being asked to accept.

Elizabeth remained standing within a foot of the doors, as if trying to decide her fate. She was in no hurry to walk toward Michael. She lingered for what felt like minutes, as he sat meeting her stare. Finally, she stepped toward him, intently. Michael opened his crossed legs summoning her to stand between them. She allowed him to remove first one shoe, and then the other. As he did, his hands moved along her legs, pushing up her skirt to reveal her black lace panties. Michael gently removed the silk fabric then kissed the soft mound of flesh which had been exposed. Elizabeth could see Michael's erection grow. She reached over and pressed her hand against his pants. He was fully hard. Michael did not rise to her but remained seated on the sofa. She waited for him to remove his belt. She unzipped his pants and slowly lowered herself onto him, her legs wrapped around his lower back. Elizabeth carefully moved her hips back and forth, teasing him with her motion. He unbuttoned her silk blouse uncovering an ivory lace corset. She had taunted him with her delicate lingerie hiding beneath her sheer blouse. His fingers released the tiny hooks as he touched his lips to her breasts. Elizabeth did not kiss Michael. Instead, the movement of her hips continued to intensify. He took her face in his hands, staring into her blue eyes until he could no longer control his physical response. She, of course, always controlled hers.

CHAPTER
4

Fuck. Danielle Philipson had overslept. This was rare. Hadn't she set her phone alarm? This could not be happening. Not today. Danielle pushed aside her bed's white down comforter and stepped onto the gray wood flooring in her bare feet. She was wearing a men's Hanes tee, which hung down to her knees on her five foot three inch frame, and nothing else. She bought the t-shirts in packages of five. It was so much less expensive than buying anything designed for a woman. Seriously she would say to herself, when she went to Target to make her semi-annual "lingerie" purchase, these same tees for women were triple the price. Sometimes, it was life's smallest details which resonated the most loudly with Danielle. The men's tees were white, comfortable, and washable, and they never went out of style. Pragmatic. The men's version suited her personality. Of course, she wasn't quite certain what that meant in the grand scheme of things, but she didn't give a fuck. Getting up late? That was an entirely different matter.

It was exactly three steps from the edge of the bed to the room's sliding glass door. Her place was tiny, and she loved every square inch of it. She pulled opened the pure white sheers, as she did every morning. Shit. It was raining. In August. Of course, it was. The sky was dark and uninviting. Giant drops of water were splashing from the condo's roofline and onto the balcony. The cushions on her patio chairs were soaked. It was 9:30 a.m. She hadn't slept this late since, well, she had no idea. Not even on a Sunday. She wasn't one to panic. But fuck! Peter was scheduled to appear in the Ninth Circuit Court at 11:00 a.m. It would be a miracle if she made it. The drive from Berkeley could take 45 minutes on a *good* day. But with the rain and the traffic. Shit. Shit. Shit.

There was no time for a shower. Instead, Danielle raced into the bathroom and splashed water on her face. She didn't fuss with make-up, but there was no way she was leaving the house without a little blush and pale pink eye shadow. This was a big day. A monumental day. The Ninth Circuit Court. She looked through her closet for her black skirt and matching blazer. She grabbed a silk blouse. The same style in five different colors. Practical, unlike her waterfront condo. She had purchased it using her entire inheritance from her grand-mother. Her parents were not happy about the decision, worrying that on a cop's salary, their daughter would struggle to pay the property taxes, association dues, and general upkeep. She was furious that her parents hadn't supported her decision. She wasn't some newly gradu-ated college co-ed. She was in her early thirties at the time, and now closer to 40. But her mind had been made up, and since she had been promoted to detective a couple of years ago, she finally had a sliver of breathing room financially. Well, barely a sliver.

Danielle jammed her feet into her one-inch block heels, grabbed her keys from an orange ceramic tray she had made for her grandmother in the third grade, and headed out into the rainy morning. Her bril-liant white Ford Explorer was parked across the street. No umbrella or rain jacket. There wasn't time to hunt for either of them. She was grateful that she didn't have a car expense on top of everything else. The Alameda County Sheriff's Office allowed their detectives to take vehicles home, because their responsibilities stretched for nearly an 800-mile radius across the Bay Area. It was one of the largest counties in California, so it only made sense to keep your vehicle close. Often-times, it served as a makeshift office. It would have also made sense to store a jacket, or at the very least, an umbrella, in the vehicle. Not that being locked inside a car would have done Danielle any good as she ran across the street from her front door. No, the umbrella and jacket should have been on a hook inside the condo's small entry. Danielle's SUV did contain teargas, a soft armor vest, a shot gun, ammunition, a pair of steel-toed boots, and other government issued items much more vital for the job. It was all stored in the back of her vehicle inside a digitally secured metal locker.

There were a series of three thoroughfares required to take Danielle to her intended destination. After using a frontage road, she needed to merge onto I-580 which became I-80. Technically, it was the same piece of interstate. But, with two names depending upon the exact location. Frankly, getting across the Bay Bridge was straightforward, though crowded and very annoying. These were the words that came to mind. Wet highways in bumper-to-bumper traffic were not for the weak. One needed to use every instinct available as a driver. This included the obvious, the horn. And the less obvious. Flashing head-lights, high beams, and the middle finger stuck outside the driver's side window. Fortunately, Danielle's SUV had the added benefit of being an undercover, nondescript sheriff's vehicle. Usually, her red lights were reserved only for emergencies. Danielle decided being late today definitely constituted an emergency. She took full advantage of her car, telling herself it was imperative she operate her blinking red lights all the way into downtown. She screeched to a halt and parked the SUV in the fire lane directly in front of the courthouse steps, throwing her sheriff's office plaque onto the dash. It was a get out of jail free card, no pun intended.

The James R. Browning United States Courthouse was a national landmark. But today, it was the site of an appeal that Danielle's brother was arguing. She couldn't imagine the honor, or the stress. Peter had been preparing for months and might only speak for a few minutes. He was arguing for the federal taxation of marijuana sales. It had been an ongoing dilemma since California had legalized it for recre-ational use in 2016. Marijuana was still considered by the feds to be a controlled substance like heroin. Legal businesses had to find creative means to pay their federal income taxes. The result was a bureaucratic nightmare which needed fixing.

Peter Philipson was four years younger than his sister, Danielle. Their mother had suffered two miscarriages between their births. Danielle was thrilled when she became a big sister. She pushed her baby brother in his stroller, fed him Cheerios, and sang to him. When he was old enough to attend kindergarten, Danielle took him by the hand and led Peter down the hallway to his classroom. She waved at him during lunch and sometimes he was allowed to sit with Danielle and her friends at recess. He missed his sister terribly when she moved from the elementary school to high school. Their birthdays fell in place such that Peter was a high school freshman the year his sister was a senior. Danielle ran track. Peter was the junior varsity speech and debate champion. He was also six feet tall at 14, which got him noticed. At first, Danielle thought it was cute that her friends made comments about how much her little brother had matured. But when senior prom came around and a couple of them seriously considered asking him to be their dates, she no longer found it funny. In the end, brother and sister went to the latest Lord of the Rings movie saga instead.

Despite his size, Peter had never been overly athletic. He had always been an intellectual. Unlike Danielle, who was bright but didn't concern herself with a B or two on her high school transcript, Peter went to the mat taking the most difficult courses and earning a nearly perfect SAT score. That and his impressive national debate record resulted in a flood of college scholarship offers. His top contenders were Stanford and Princeton. Peter chose Princeton for undergrad and Harvard for law school. But he never thought his impressive educational track held a candle to Danielle, the police officer. He admired, no, he worshipped his big sister.

Most of Peter's friends believed he would make his career in the Boston area. He surprised even his own parents when he returned to San Francisco and decided to take the California Bar. Although he was a tax litigator for an important firm, he primarily defended the rights of those who he felt were defenseless. Small business owners. US residents who were not citizens. People in the marijuana industry navigating endless and constantly changing statutes, regulations, and ordinances. His work was almost entirely pro bono, which served the law office well. With each win came state, national, and sometimes international attention, and the firm used his notoriety to its full advantage. It was inexpensive marketing and kept the partners in the forefront of the big guns. Congress.

As a law enforcement officer, Danielle felt at odds about the whole marijuana thing. She had observed too many overdoses, murders committed as a direct result of the drug trade, and the pain which drugs inflicted on families. But marijuana was legal in her state, and she upheld the laws which had been passed. Laws supporting the economics of the cannabis industry needed to catch up.

As Danielle shut off her ignition, she remembered what it had felt like to testify as a uniformed police officer. She had served as a witness in multiple local trials over her 15-year career, but she had never walked the halls of a federal courthouse. Technically, there were four courts for the Ninth Circuit Court of Appeals. It was an impressive complex and made Danielle feel proud to be a part of the judicial system. Her brother was allowed to have viewers present. When he learned he was going to argue an appeal, he immediately asked his older, and brave sister to attend.

The courthouse security line wasn't as hectic as Danielle had expected. She had a couple of minutes to spare. Quickly, she removed her firearm and badge and handed over her backpack. She never carried a purse or briefcase. A backpack was much more practical.

"Alameda County, huh," the security officer stated more than asked, as he looked over her ID.

"That's right," Danielle responded.

"Have a good day," the officer replied.

She picked up her things from the conveyer belt just as her phone began to vibrate. Danielle was late, wet, and aggravated. She immediately recognized the number. It was her boss. She stood in the busy main hallway just past the security checkpoint, her phone in her hand. Ironically, she could carry a weapon into court, but she was absolutely not permitted to have the phone. Technically, she could have it, but she wasn't allowed to use it. The security officer shot her a "shut it down" glance.

Danielle was up against a decision. Ignore her boss or take the call. She was tired of the job always coming first. But she couldn't help herself. It was a habit. She knew in her gut she needed to be in that courtroom. This could be a once-in-a-lifetime opportunity to hear her younger brother argue in front of the justices. She turned and headed back outside into the rainy morning, her phone to her ear. Peter would forgive her. Someday.

CHAPTER
5

Elizabeth fastening the pearl buttons aligned narrowly down the front of her blouse. She didn't need to freshen up. She was still perfectly put together, despite their 40-minute encounter. Michael handed her a sealed envelope. It would remain sealed. She was well aware of its contents. She had done this so many times. Rather than wait for Michael to escort her from the office, she calmly wrapped herself in her trench coat, picked up her handbag, and placed the envelope inside. It was thick and full of cash. A public daylight rendezvous was expensive.

Dinner and a hotel room were always preferred by Elizabeth. It was private. Quiet. She had a better opportunity to know the person she was sharing herself with. An office setting typically wasn't ideal; it brought a sense of anxiety. While that excited some, for Elizabeth it felt impersonal. She loved the day and being with someone, especially before noon. But calmly and unhurried, the opposite of what she had just endured. Crossing the lobby reception, encountering a crowded elevator, and of course, the pretty young thing. The morning was for awakening, and sweetness, and stolen moments. Soft whispers, or none at all. The morning felt safe and tender. Playful. A brief morning encounter remained all day, and sometimes kept Elizabeth thinking about a touch well into the night. But this entitled "office visit," which made Michael Mason feel important, was immature and absolutely not sweet or stolen. It was planned and fake and felt like a scene from a bad romance novel. It was so predictable. It was so sterile. But the money. It was impossible to refuse.

Elizabeth pulled open the left half of the double doors. The bright lights and office sounds felt like a wall. The blonde was nowhere to be found. Thankfully, thought Elizabeth. Her four-inch heels took her back to the bank of elevators. Just a few floors down and she would be safe again, with $15,000 and her mind free to think about her fantasized life. She wished Michael to be different. To be intimate. To flirt. To be kinder.

Not all men Elizabeth "dated" were married. However, Michael Mason had a wife from a famous Napa Valley family and three sons. Elizabeth always did her research. The funny thing was that she believed the couple were for the most part… well, maybe not happy, but adjusted. Michael had been a client for four years. Their encounters weren't always sexual. Occasionally, he would simply talk about the boys and their sports or grades. He would laugh about the winery parties where he would sometimes meet a movie star. He was fascinated with their fame. He didn't talk incessantly about his wife, Laura. But he did talk about how incredibly busy she was with her family's 400-acre vineyard and the accompanying industry. He almost seemed proud of her accomplishments. She had been slowly taking on more responsibility over the past couple of years, and since her father's passing, she was now in complete control.

Michael was lonely. Laura wasn't unkind, but she was in her early 60s, relishing her role as an executive in a male-dominated field. She was a couple of years older than her husband, but he didn't seem to care. Their eldest son was at UC Berkeley. He wasn't far from the Valley or the City, but he didn't come home much. Their second son had just graduated from high school. He had received admission to Georgetown and was counting the days to freshman welcome week. It was their youngest son, Aiden, who still had any need for his mother. He was a rising high school sophomore. He loved learning about the wine industry and had already declared that he wanted an active role in the family business. If it had been possible to head to college at 15, he would have leapt at the opportunity to study the agriculture and sommelier fields. It was just a matter of time, and his SAT scores.

Elizabeth was used to small talk, about Michael's family or business dealings or general loneliness, but sometimes he would also share his secrets. This was when she felt closest to him. He was not a great lover. He wasn't even good. He never approached Elizabeth to hold her from behind. He never kissed her gently or playfully. Elizabeth would try to lead the way, but Michael was either too selfish or didn't care to understand. He didn't know how to make Elizabeth feel desired. He never asked, "Too much?" He never took her hand to guide her to a chair, or a bed. He never tucked her hair behind her ears. Her never pleasured *her*. But he was wealthy. Very.

"Laura makes it look so easy," Michael would say. "But truthfully, her father left her drowning in debt. I don't know how much longer my company can front the expenses. It's a lot easier to run Mason Recruiting than it is a business where you have everyone from the FDA to the Bureau of Alcohol, Tobacco, and Firearms breathing down your neck." Elizabeth would listen attentively. That's what she was paid to do, and she didn't mind. Most of his stories were interesting. She felt as if she were drawn more deeply into the life of Elizabeth Catherine Stevens. She really *was* a lawyer helping wealthy Napa clients. For a few hours each month, her imagined life felt real. She would much rather listen to him than have sex with him, and she had learned how to shut herself away when he was on top of her or inside of her, emotionless. Detached.

Money always worried powerful men. The more they had, the more they worried. Or in his case, the more Laura's winery lost, the more Michael became concerned. If anyone in the industry got wind of the truth, there could be a play for their acreage, the buildings, the label… all of it.

"Sometimes, I wish someone would take over," Michael admitted one afternoon to Elizabeth. He was tired of maintaining a three-story home in the City and a ranch in the Valley. The family was rarely to-gether anymore. The middle and youngest sons had stayed with dad, so they could attend school in San Francisco. But that was rapidly coming to an end. Laura would spend Sunday through Thursday in Napa, then make the drive to the coast for the weekends. Unless, of course, there was an event too big for the staff to handle alone. Then she would remain in Napa to assist. To play hostess or whatever her guests needed her to be for them. She loved it. The weddings, the parties, the corporate awards ceremonies. As much as Laura said she wanted to be in San Francisco for the weekends, Michael knew that she relished the attention. The wine industry itself was grueling. But the winery business was fun, especially when you had procured a staff over many years that had become more like family.

Michael enjoyed Elizabeth's company, but what he honestly wanted was his family back together again. He hoped to retire in a couple of years, so that he and Laura could finally travel. He wanted his wife to love him, not to think of him solely as a companion; someone to pay the bills and to be her plus one when required. They didn't hate each other, but Michael knew they had both fallen out of love long ago. They simply co-existed, floating around the house in opposite rooms. They slept in separate beds and hadn't had sex in years. The situation was irreparable. They weren't unkind to each other, but Michael and Laura were no longer Michael and Laura.

Elizabeth had become a welcomed distraction for Michael. In turn, Michael had become part of a means to an end for her. Financial. And with money came stature. Elizabeth had four men she saw on a reg-ular basis. She had cultivated them slowly. She had lived in San Fran-cisco for 10 years. In the beginning, the men were of the usual sort. She would sit at a bar and practice her skills, taking home as much money in one evening as her mother, Lynda, brought home in a week. But this soon became dull, and there were only so many restaurants and hotel bars across the Bay. It was also somewhat embarrassing. It had never been her intention to become an escort. She wanted to be in significant relationships, knowing that "her men" were thinking about her at work, home, and even on their vacations. Not that they would be quick to contact her on a weekly basis. Oh no. The power element always loomed large. Each man had his own approach. Some only wanted to spend time together in the evening. Others wanted her dressed in a particular fashion. Still others wanted her to pretend to be a stranger. These men all had one thing in common, though. They all required the illusion of being in control. Disengaged. They were all far from it.

The first man to become a more permanent person in her life was Richard. Then came David. Colton was third, and lastly Michael. Of the four, she preferred Michael. He was 25 years her senior. Richard was 70 something. David and Colton were uninteresting. But in the end, their money helped her maintain a beautiful home on California Street. She was living her life as Elizabeth Catherine Stevens. She had a closet full of designer clothing, with shoes and handbags to match. Her home was draped in modern luxury, from the kitchen cabinets to the glassware. Yet, after each encounter, she would immediately retreat to her safe space, only to peel off her opulent clothing, and instead reach for a sports bra and a pair of leggings. She played dress up when she worked. She never went out in public as Elizabeth in any other circumstance. She ordered take out on most nights when she was alone. She didn't take a bubble bath but preferred a lukewarm shower. It reminded her of her real home, with her mother, in Pacific Grove.

Sarah, the waitress, had become a woman of means. She told herself she didn't feel empty. She was proud to be setting aside money for her mother. She considered philanthropy, and her East Coast character would have most certainly made an impact in that world. But she wasn't interested in pursuing that lie. There would be too many questions she couldn't answer. Her disingenuous life did not allow her to build sincere relationships. She had no friends. In this regard, Elizabeth was so very similar to Sarah. As a schoolgirl, Sarah only had acquaintances, and in college she had been too busy, between studying and working at the restaurant, to have a social life.

She was standoffish. The restaurant crew had been her only friends. They cared for her and watched over her, and that was all she needed. No drama. No disappointment. No being lied to or chosen second, or worse, not at all.

A sort of subdued loneliness suited Elizabeth. She was an introvert. A beautiful woman. And ironically, painfully shy at heart.

CHAPTER
6

Danielle removed the sheriff's plaque from her dashboard and pulled away from the courthouse. Her brother was going to be pissed. Worse, he was going to be hurt. She navigated the narrow streets of San Francisco, finding the onramp that would take her to the office. At least it had stopped raining. She hated the drive into Oakland, especially now that she was inside the City, but she hated being the third or fourth to learn about a case even more. In this instance, her boss had called her in for an incident concerning a large fire in neighboring Napa County. Early in her career as a uniformed officer, it would have been rare for two sheriff's offices to work together. Over time, it had become common. Many crimes involved multiple jurisdictions. Too many of those crimes went unsolved because egos got in the way, and the higher ups refused to work together. With the explosion of body cams, CCTV, and cell phone recordings, police officers were under intense scrutiny. It was mostly a good thing. Transparency was crucial, and justice was more oftentimes served.

The Alameda County Sheriff had multiple locations from Berkeley to Dublin to San Leandro. The organizational chart was something to behold. Under the direct supervision of the sheriff were an undersheriff and two assistant sheriffs. Officers had assignments ranging from the Oakland International Airport to the San Francisco Bay, where a marine patrol unit was permanently stationed. The local jail was situated in Santa Rita and operated by Alameda County law enforcement. It was one of the largest detention facilities in the United States. Larger, in fact, than many state-run prisons.

The Berkeley office was about a 10-minute drive from Danielle's front door. However, she had been commissioned to the Special Investigations unit as a detective which meant driving to the Dublin Police Services office some 30 miles away. The daily commute was a grind, but she wasn't about to give up her water view condo. Besides, she would never be able to afford it now. The value had gone through the roof since she had purchased it. If Danielle had been a spiteful person, she might have considered her equity a sort of "revenge" against her parents who had protested the purchase. But she knew they would never stop worrying about their children. Mom and dad had only raised concerns in the first place, because they cared. They didn't want their daughter to struggle to make her condo payment.

Easing into the middle lane on the Bay Bridge, Danielle crossed its lower deck to the steady rhythm of perfectly engineered groves in the concrete slabs beneath her tires. Hypnotic. The drive into the City was so painfully slow, yet the drive back was surprisingly fast. Changing lanes felt like an old school game of Need for Speed. It was just after 11:00 a.m. on a Wednesday, so traffic was light. Relatively speaking. Danielle was surprised that her boss had asked her to meet at the Oakland office, rather than out in Dublin. The phone conversation between the two had been brief, but Danielle knew it would all be thoroughly explained soon enough.

Everyone assumed that when Danielle said she was a detective, she handled murder investigations. It was the result of too many CSI episodes and Netflix documentaries. Not all crimes ended in murder. Yes, Danielle had seen more than her fair share of terrible things as a cop. As soon as she made detective, her brother had sent her a Sherlock Holmes deerstalker hat from Amazon. Even the lawyer in the family assumed she was going to homicide. Instead, when Danielle got the chance to join the team working major theft and cyber security, she took it. Both areas were intertwined in so many crimes. Most recently, the drug trade.

The sheriff's substation sat at a busy intersection in downtown Oakland. It was multiple stories, though nothing like a San Francisco skyscraper. To anyone passing by, it was a standard office complex, painted a muted shade of beige. Since this wasn't her usual place of work, Danielle wasn't quite sure where to head as she entered the building. Thinking she would need to ask the receptionist; she was surprised to find her boss standing to her left just inside the door. He had been waiting for her. Sergeant Ronald Hauser was a burly guy. He looked like a detective, thought Danielle. Whatever that meant. Maybe she *had* surrendered to the Netflix view of the world. She hoped not. Sergeant Hauser wore suits from Macy's and made sure his black leather dress shoes were polished to a shine. He carried his gun on his left hip. Danielle guessed he was six feet two and weighed a fit 250 pounds, minus the cliché gut. Ron had long ago lost all his hair, but bald looked good on him. He had 25 years of service, and could retire, but age and years in service no longer meant a mandatory cut off, and he loved the job. He had no intention of quitting anytime soon.

"There you are," Ronald greeted Danielle, who was barely inside the building's walls.

"Sir," she responded with unusual formality, a bit startled to see him standing in the lobby.

"We're this way," said her Sergeant as he motioned toward a brightly lit corridor.

Danielle followed her supervisor down a hallway and into a large conference room. Seated around an oval table were at least eight people. Two were uniformed Napa County sheriff's officers. An Alameda County sheriff's officer was also present. The others were all dressed in plain clothes. Danielle took the only empty seat at the table. Her boss walked to the front of the room where giant white boards had been screwed into the wall. How early 2000's, Danielle thought. Then again, the department had the latest technology in the form of computers, surveillance, and weapons, so she supposed the white boards could stay.

"Let me get right to it," Sergeant Hauser began. "We're all here, because the offices of the Palmer Family Vineyard burned to the ground overnight, and the owner called her two buddies for help."

About half the room had puzzled looks on their faces. The other half didn't appear to be paying attention.

"For those of you listening, the friends I'm referring to are both the San Francisco sheriff and the Napa Valley sheriff." He paused. "As you know, San Francisco law enforcement has been in the midst of a crisis since eight o'clock this morning, so they asked for support from Alameda."

He continued.

"I haven't been to the scene, but from what I understand, there's not a whole lot left to sift through."

The mood in the room suddenly shifted. Everyone was now giving the sergeant their full concentration.

"I get that this is overkill, but for those of you who don't know, the owner of the Palmer Family Vineyard Winery has a lot of pull." Translation, some rich family wants to move to the top of the list for service, thought Danielle to herself. She wasn't the only one in the room thinking it.

"Before you all start rolling your eyes and wondering how much money we are spending just sitting around this table, I want you to know that the sheriffs from our respective counties want us to work together on this one. Even if it's likely just a Keurig that spontaneously caught on fire." A couple of people in the room started looking at their cell phones.

"If it's a fire, why are we here," asked one of the suits. "Isn't that the fire department's job?" It was a smart-ass remark.

"How about you let me tell you how we're going to run this thing so maybe we can all go home tonight," the Sergeant shot back. What appeared to be a couple of college interns entered the room with stacks of folders in their hands.

"Thanks. I'll take those," Hauser stated. "Okay, these files are thin, but it's all we've got so far. I'll get all of this uploaded into our shared system by end of day."

He wasn't kidding. Other than a few photos of what was allegedly a once rather large office compound, there wasn't much to look through in the identical files being passed around the table. In fact, had the Sergeant not explained that the fire had burned down an office, Danielle wouldn't have been certain what she was looking at in the pictures. The only other pieces of information in the folders were a Napa Valley sheriff's office intake report, and a copy of a standard 9-1-1 form. All calls were recorded, so that paperwork was basically a formality.

"We are going to send one detective from each of our counties out there to the winery," said Ronald. The Napa Valley sheriff is making sure the scene is secure at the fire marshal's request. That's all I've got."

"Why the "f" did he call us all here, if ninety percent of this room is about to get up and leave," Danielle mumbled under her breath. "I just missed my brother's moment of glory." Yeah, she only had herself to blame, but having a scapegoat made her feel just a tiny bit better. Well, not really.

Danielle's unhappiness with the situation registered on her face. However, it was short-lived.

"Okay, Detective Danielle Philipson, you and Detective Jeff Sufford are going to the site, accompanied by Officer Mendoza here," declared her sergeant.

Officer Mendoza was from the Napa Valley Sheriff's Office. It only made sense that he would go to the site. It was his county. He should know the entire region like the back of his hand. Danielle stopped paying attention to her boss's words. It appeared she had been assigned to an arson investigation.

Within seconds, everyone was out of their chairs. Detective Sufford was at the farthest end of the table from where Danielle had been seated. He walked over, as she stood up, and stuck out his hand.

"Hi, I'm Jeff. I guess we're going to be working together," he said. "Well, at least today," he followed up. Danielle took his outstretched hand and gave it a firm shake.

"Hey there, Jeff. I'm Danielle. I guess we'll have to take two separate vehicles," she responded.

Crap. Too cold, Danielle wondered. She wasn't the best at opening lines. "Hi, nice to meet you. Looking forward to it.," she said in her head. But those hadn't been the words that came out of her mouth.

She could have been more pleasant. Oh well. Move on. Detective Sufford was from Napa Valley. He was heading toward home unless he didn't live within the county. Danielle, on the other hand, was moving farther and farther away from her jurisdiction. Taking only one car meant that they would have to drive back and forth from Oakland. It made no sense.

"Seems so," said Jeff rather matter-of-factly, countering Danielle's tone.

On the bright side, they wouldn't have to endure small talk to size each other up on the ride over. How long have you been a detective? Where did you work as a uniform? Are you from a law enforcement family? Or, to fill the void, law enforcement's radio transmissions. Or even worse, the actual FM radio. There was never any accounting for a person's taste in music. Danielle tended toward pop. Since there was little to no information regarding the fire, they wouldn't have talked about the case in the car anyway, other than maybe a little speculation. But most detectives didn't speculate. They relied on hard facts.

The pair walked out to the parking lot and peeled off toward the Palmer Family Vineyard in their respective vehicles. It was 2:00 p.m. The traffic leaving the Bay was building. The hour-long drive would take longer, and Danielle hadn't had anything to eat. She was pretty sure she wouldn't be having a glass of wine, either.

CHAPTER
7

It was 3:04 a.m. when Michael Mason's cell phone gave off a shrill ring. There were only five numbers that could get through his "do not disturb" setting. His three sons, the CFO of Mason Recruiting International, and his wife.

Through a half-asleep mental fog and nearly shut eyes, he could make out his wife's name on his screen, like a beacon in the darkness. This couldn't be good. His heart started to race as he unlocked the phone, but before he could clear his throat to answer, he heard his wife's nearly screaming voice, "Oh my God! The winery is on fire! The entire complex is burning down! Oh my God!" He had never heard her this upset. Not even when the school had called telling the couple that their middle child had fallen off the bleachers in the gym and was headed to the hospital in an ambulance. In that moment, Laura had been silent. There were no words. Just two parents, racing from their offices to their boy. Now, she was almost incoherent. In the middle of the night.

It took a second for Michael to comprehend what Laura was yelling at him.

"Wait, what? What's on fire?" Michael pulled a pillow from behind his head and lifted himself up in the bed at a sort of 45-degree angle, leaning against the headboard. The room was pitch black, except for the phone's glow, and even that was too much light on his very tired eyes. He wasn't going to reach over and turn on a lamp. He was too busy trying to decipher Laura's words.

"I just got a call from the vineyard manager. He said there was a loud explosion. That the night crew could see flames shooting up from the buildings. I'm driving over there right now. The guys have water on it, and the fire department is on their way. " Michael could hear Laura's labored breathing between her rushed sentences. She had stopped screaming, but the panic in her voice scared him. He still wasn't comprehending the full picture. Something about an explosion and the winery being on fire and her crew putting it out but calling the fire department. How bad could it be then, he asked himself. But Laura was still ranting.

Michael listened. But he hadn't responded.

"What don't you understand? There was an explosion. The winery offices are on fire. They are burning down." Laura was repeating herself, only now, Michael was fully awake and sitting straight up in bed.

Fucking hell, Michael said almost out loud. This can't be happening. What would possibly cause an explosion at the winery offices? They didn't keep any pesticides or other chemicals anywhere near that vicinity. Everything toxic or flammable was housed in a separate locked facility with limited access and nowhere near the main buildings, per government regulation. The offices had an elaborate fire sprinkler system as well as electronic security. Any sort of heat activity was supposed to be reported automatically to the fire department. The sprinklers should have alerted at the first hint of flames. This wasn't making any sense. But he was starting to realize that his wife's words were true. There had been an explosion. Part or all of the winery was in danger. This night was not going to end well. Fuck. He needed to calm down, which meant that he needed to calm his wife down first.

"I don't want you driving while you're this upset," Michael said. "Can someone from the winery come and get you?"

Laura's mood immediately shifted from terrorized to angry.

"I'm fine," she responded in a curt tone. "I know this isn't *your* family's business, but shouldn't you be just a little bit upset?"

Now, it was Michael's turn to respond in an equally terse voice.

"Seriously, Laura? I've poured a shitload of my company's assets into keeping PFV from going bankrupt. For Christ's sakes, are you really going to do this right now?"

Laura was now thoroughly disgusted. She wanted help, not a lecture. He had turned on her. As usual, it had become all about him. Everything was *always* about him. Michael telling her how to feel or act or pretending to be protective. She knew better. All she wanted was to be at her winery. Not in a fight with her husband. She was so upset. Through tears he couldn't see, she told Michael she would drive from their ranch, just a few miles down the road to the winery headquarters and call him back when she had something to tell him.

Michael turned on the reading lights above the bed. He didn't want to drive from San Francisco out to Napa in the middle of the night, but he knew it was the right thing to do. He had absolutely no choice in the matter. If he didn't show up, he would be the asshole, leaving his wife alone. Abandoned. Regardless, he needed to assess what they would be facing. He hoped that the night crew foreperson had overreacted. That this was just a small fire, and the sprinkler system had taken care of it. But Michael had learned many years ago that hope was bullshit. Hope was what you manufactured when you lacked control.

A fire could spell absolute disaster for any business, but offices could always be rebuilt. If the vineyards themselves were on fire, there would be no recovery for years. Award winning wines came from perfect combinations of grapes grown in soils which were analyzed for their natural, chemical, and moisture content. Every hour of sunlight, drop of water, and insect species making its home among the vines played a role in creating their product. It was a difficult process. Even smoke could damage the fragile crops and result in an undrinkable product for an entire decade. Grapes were not simply churned into wine. It took years under the best of conditions.

Michael's instinct was to call Elizabeth. Of course, he would never wake her in the middle of the night. It would be immature and weak. And for what reason? To tell her that his wife's winery was on fire and that they had been angry with each other on the phone? He wasn't about to attest to his poor behavior. He didn't want to seem small or petty. No, for Elizabeth he was always in control. Even when he talked about his family, or trade secrets, he saw himself as being the perfect man in Elizabeth's presence. Never demanding or unsure. It would make zero sense to call her right now. He had never done anything of the sort. He wasn't going to start now.

He would end the relationship before he would ever admit to Elizabeth that he had feelings for her, or missed her when he wasn't with her, or that he thought about her and what it might be like if they were a couple. He knew it would never happen, but still, he thought about it. He also, at times, treated her poorly. Michael didn't want to acknowledge that he felt close to Elizabeth. He played a sort of push-pull game with her and with himself. Spending time with her and then going silent. He wanted to keep her wondering, but in truth, he was the one who couldn't let go. And she was always what he needed, with no drama or expectation. She was perfect. He was so far from it with his insecurities and wishing he could be more.

Forcing himself up and out of the king-sized bed, Michael walked across the room into the oversized closet, turning on the light. Even though Laura was rarely in the house, most of the clothes were hers. Every item had been compartmentalized from her panties to his neckties. Funny, he couldn't remember the last time he wore a tie to the office. He only put one on for her, and rarely. He pulled open a drawer and found a navy sweatshirt. He then reached over for a pair of faded jeans carefully hanging on a rod. Jeans didn't belong hanging carefully anywhere, he thought. Jeans should be folded on a shelf, or better, thrown haphazardly over a chair. Or, lying on the floor. Just once. Not nice and neat and aligned. That was her world. And it was now coming apart. But it was his world, too.

Michael had so much capital parked in her company. Hell, it wasn't even parked. It had been sunk into a dying operation. And now, his money was literally going up in smoke. He hated that phrase. Just thinking it made him feel old. It was something a person of advanced age would say. Like a warning to the younger generation. Christ, who had he become? God forbid, his own father. Michael's father had been a good man, but he never understood the need for growth and innovation. At least I have a forward thinking business acumen, Michael said to himself as he got dressed. He slipped into his dark gray cowboy boots, then headed downstairs. The boots were in sharp contrast to the brown loafers which he wore to the office. He hated the damned boots. They were a reminder of his divided life.

The wood floors throughout the house gave off their familiar creak as Michael navigated the stairs down to the kitchen. He grabbed his keys off the marble counter and walked out to the garage. He hadn't bothered to check on his sleeping son. Aiden wasn't a child anymore. Besides, he still had a few days of summer break to enjoy, and that meant he wouldn't be getting out of bed before noon. Michael hit the garage door opener on the back wall, loaded himself into his Santorini black Range Rover, and slowly pulled out of the gated drive. He looked like shit and he felt even worse. What the fuck had happened in Napa? He needed to think straight. Now.

CHAPTER
8

Three fire trucks, an ambulance, the entire Palmer Family Vineyard night crew, and his wife greeted Michael as he pulled up to the main parking area. The sky was still dark, but the moon's glimmery sheen lended itself to the scene, bringing it frightfully alive. Lines of beige hose ran everywhere, in an oddly orderly manner, their light color in sharp contrast to the blackened ground. Several firefighters had begun the laborious process of folding up the hoses, stacking them in their rightful places onto the huge fluorescent green fire engines. What was left of the 10,000-square-foot office premises was still smoldering, but the fire was out.

Michael put his Rover in park and shut off the engine. He took a deep breath before opening the driver's side door. He knew the second he stepped from the safety of his vehicle, the quiet would disappear and a flurry of words would confront his ears.

Laura ran toward Michael immediately. She didn't hug him, but he didn't reach for her either. Instead, she began to describe, in great detail, the very obvious fact that there had been a catastrophic fire. Michael wasn't listening. He was too busy staring at the charred remains of what had been a beautiful set of buildings. Ash was raining down on the gathering, just as it had during too many California wildfire summers. The smell was a pungent mix of barbecue and wood burning fireplace. He was startled to see an ambulance, so when Laura came up for a breath, Michael reacted with, "Was anybody hurt?" He quickly learned that it was fire department protocol to send an ambulance for a fire of that size. Nobody had been injured.

Two Napa Valley sheriff's officers were busy looking very official. One was putting stakes into the ground while the second wrapped yellow tape around the posts to keep people out. Not that any miscellaneous people were roaming around. It was nearly 6:00 a.m. and the sun was beginning to rise. Two of the three fire engines were pulling out. Their job complete. Michael hadn't noticed it at first, but a fire marshal vehicle was also parked in the distance. He guessed it had been hiding behind one of the now disappeared trucks.

Thank God there were no news crew trucks. The PFV Winery had a long history here, and a reporter listening to a scanner might have jumped at the opportunity to show up unannounced. The winery was not visible from the road, so it was likely nobody else was aware. Michael was honestly surprised not to see any cameras, and very grateful. He doubted this would be the case for much longer. There was no way a fire this size, and a winery this famous, wouldn't make the newspaper and social media posts. Especially with so many staff and emergency services people involved.

As the sheriff's officers finished cordoning off the area, a man wearing a jacket with "fire marshal" emblazoned across his back came strolling over to Laura. He had a black binder in his hand.

"Okay, Mrs. Mason, we've done everything we can for now," he said. "We've taken pictures, and the 9-1-1 call made by your nightshift foreman was recorded. I'm going to contact the Napa Valley sheriff myself to give him an update, but I need to send one of my investigators out here in the next couple of hours to carefully go over the scene in full daylight."

The scene? Laura cringed. This was her family's blood, sweat, and tears. It had been reduced to a few chunks of wood and giant piles of debris. The only thing keeping her sane was the fact that nobody had been hurt. If it hadn't been for a booming explosion alerting the night shift, the fire probably would have swept across to the nearby tasting room, the wine cellar storage, and maybe out to the vineyards themselves. She walked away from the fire marshal and her husband, found a stand of shrubbery, and threw up. She didn't care if anyone noticed. She didn't care that Michael hadn't come to her side to comfort her in this mess. She was physically and mentally exhausted.

Michael didn't know what to say. Clearly, an investigation would get underway. He had always been the type to listen, and then assess. There wasn't any point in asking the fire official a thousand questions about what he thought might have happened. That's what an investigation would determine. Michael wanted to demonstrate his concern mingled with some compassion. He finally walked over to his wife and gave her a hug. She accepted it momentarily, but it was not a long or comforting embrace. On the inside, Michael was a fucking mess. He could feel his heart pumping, and he hated it. His mind was spinning with the imminent financial disaster on his hands. An investigation would include the winery's insurance. Michael knew that the bill had been paid, but he also knew that he had significantly lowered the coverage to save tens of thousands of dollars. Fire insurance costs had literally burned up many businesses as the result of the state's disastrous fire seasons. Existing businesses had seen their rates triple or quadruple, and that's if they were able to get insurance at all. Two or three insurance companies now had a monopoly across the state, as dozens of agencies fled California.

Then there would be the cost of new construction. It could bankrupt him. Well, actually her. It was *her* business, but he would never recoup the money he had spent to keep Laura's legacy alive.

Michael knew there was no way insurance was going to reimburse the winery for the full value of the property. He'd be lucky if they paid out 50 percent. And that was assuming that PFV wasn't found at fault. He prayed that this wasn't the result of negligence on their part. He needed the cause of the fire to have an explanation which left the winery cleared of any wrongdoing. And, if that was the case, what the hell *had* happened? Michael was desperate to know the why.

CHAPTER
9

Detective Danielle Philipson and Detective Jeff Sufford arrived at the Palmer Family Vineyard visitor's area within minutes of each other. Sheriff's Officer Eric Mendoza was positioned down the middle of two blacktop paved parking spaces. He was sitting inside his running cruiser, talking on his cell phone. Danielle got out of her SUV and opened the passenger's side door to retrieve her backpack. Jeff was already out of his car. They gave each other a nod then walked over to the black and white together, signaling to the officer that they were ready when he was. Officer Mendoza held up his hand from inside the comfort of the air conditioned vehicle, motioning that he needed another minute to finish up his call and pointing in the direction of the office complex. It never ceased to amaze Danielle how much warmer the Napa Valley was in comparison to the Bay. It was actually hot. Jeff was no longer wearing the jacket he had sported at the meeting. Danielle wished that she had left her blazer in her SUV. It was too late for that now. Even the one-inch heels were not terribly appropriate for a winery, but they had been perfect for the Ninth Circuit Court hours earlier. The guilt was already weighing on her mind, especially now that she had been sent to a fire scene. She was mad at herself.

Danielle and Jeff took Mendoza's gesture as the "okay" to head off on their own. They turned and began walking toward a sign pointing them in the direction of the winery's tasting room. Mendoza finished his call and caught up with the pair.

The main winery office complex was about 150 yards from the visitor parking area to the left. To the right, the wine tasting room was still standing, with no apparent damage. The wine cellars and barrel rooms were beyond the tasting room and stood like giant shadows over the much smaller tasting facility. A series of concrete walkways meandered between each building. All three appeared to be constructed from a dark red brick, and all three were equally covered in some sort of white flowering ivy. Large metal signs posted near each identical glass door entrance identified the function of the buildings. This allowed tours to be led easily from one building to the next, while keeping people away from the business complex. The entire area had been deliberately landscaped with flowers and grasses native to the Napa Valley. It was pleasant and well thought out. Danielle guessed that it was also quite functional.

Thousands of visitors passed through the winery each year. Once upon a time, tasting had been a free activity across the Valley, and all guests were welcomed. That had changed. So had the entire region. Gallo, Mondavi, Sterling, and Beringer dominated. Gallo's immense holdings made it the largest wine producer in the entire country. The small shops and unique restaurants in the region's original town still stood, but trendy chains and shopping malls had encroached.

Luxury hotels and spas where people from Silicon Valley came to rest and unwind didn't apologize for their thousand dollar an hour massage treatments. Anyone wanting to sample wine without a reservation and the accompanying $25 tasting fee would not be served. It had become standard practice in the industry. Wine by the bottle, or the case, could also be purchased directly onsite.

While many wineries had small restaurants or markets where cheeses and breads and pastries could be bought, PFV prided itself on staying true to the grape. "This is a winery," Laura could remember her father saying from the time she was a small child. "Not a three-ring circus!" And so, following his death, Laura kept the business pure. They did not have a restaurant. No picnic baskets filled with treats for purchase. Wine tasters were provided with crackers to cleanse their palates, but that was the extent of it, unless of course, an after-hours event was being held. Weddings and parties did bring in some additional revenue.

Despite knowing that they were deeply in debt, and with pointed suggestions from her husband that they sell the lesser quality grapes to a lesser known brand down the road, Laura refused to budge. As had become a common practice between the two. In complete frustration and when he knew he would not be able to stop the bleeding, Michael had gone so far as to stupidly say, "Jesus, can't we do something to encourage people to buy a few extra bottles?" It was going to take a lot more than the sale of a few charcuterie boards or truckloads of grapes to resolve their financial crisis. Michael knew they needed an infusion of cash. Laura, however, was convinced that with one stellar growing season the books would be in the black.

The real money came from distribution and retail sales. Costco was the largest wine retailer in the United States. If the Palmer Family Vineyard could get their bottles into *that* market, they would be golden. However, it was not an easy process, and Laura was extremely suspect. She hated the idea that her grandfather's vintage would be sold alongside big screen TVs and giant jars of peanut butter. However, even Laura admitted that Costco would be a cash cow, and a guarantee that their wine would be sold at a profit. It would eliminate a considerable amount of stress and help their brand come into the homes of people who had never heard of PFV. Michael, and Laura's own CFO, were finally getting Laura to come around to the idea. A meeting had been set with the purchasing agents, and a draft contract had been sent over for review.

There was a sense of charm with a mix of old world for good measure when one stepped onto the PFV Winery grounds. In fact, the original fields had been planted in the late 1950s by Laura Palmer-Mason's father and grandfather. Hardly old world, the men had felt that it was important to create an image of luxury, despite the fact that they were operating on a month-to-month basis and needed their wives' income to pay the household bills. Back then, they had just 30 acres and two buildings. Her father and grandfather had purchased used metal desks at auction for $15 a piece. They placed them facing each other in a corner of their larger building, which served as a makeshift office among chemicals, a label making machine, dark green wine bottles, and a manual corker. They worked diligently to make certain the vineyard was as pretty as it was healthy. And they had the foresight to plant roses and wildflowers and grasses which would become part of the permanent landscape. Father and son produced 150 bottles their first year. They were proud.

It was Laura's father who suggested they enter a wine competition their second year in production. Although the idea of using two-year-old grapes would be laughable for any wine, a tiny corner of the vineyard had been originally planted in the very early 1900s. The first vines no longer existed, but they had been grafted again and again. So, technically PFV produced wine from grapes that were between 25 and 50-years-old. Laura's grandfather wasn't excited about the idea of putting his wine on display for so-called connoisseurs to judge but eventually gave in. That decision resulted in two, first place finishes above prominent French brands. The little winery was featured in several national and international magazines. Over time, their popularity grew and so did their bottom line, until the family owned 400 acres and sold its wine in 14 countries.

Modernization and an indulged generation had taken hold over the past seven or eight years. Young drinkers loved the amusing labels and hashtags associated with dozens of trendy wineries which had popped up across California, Oregon, Washington, New York, and Texas. Gen Zs and Millennials were not interested in long-standing and expensive brands such as PFV. Alcoholic beverages in aluminum cans had a sizable market share across the country and made up nearly 20 percent of all beverage purchases. Wine had no place in a beer drinker's refrigerator, either. Five dreadful growing seasons, new computerized equipment, and contemporary marketing practices had taken their toll. The winery now found itself in millions of dollars of debt. It was a secret which Laura and Michael hadn't shared with even their closest confidants. Laura allowed Michael to look over the financials. She was aware of his concerns, but she did not truly understand the mounting pressure he was under. Michael, on the other hand, was hyper aware that things needed to turn around soon or the business would be lost in a matter of months. Mason Recruiting International was hemorrhaging cash, and it could no longer afford the mounting costs of "life support."

CHAPTER
10

Danielle, her new detective friend, Jeff, and their sheriff chaperone stopped for a minute to look at the serene landscape to their right. The brick buildings and white flowers stood in utter stillness, unaware of the damage their counterparts had endured. The business complex area sat slightly around a bend, so it didn't immediately come into view. When it did, it was shocking. The monochromatic remnants caught Danielle off guard. A couple of Napa Valley sheriff's officers were standing just outside a strict grid of yellow tape. Officer Mendoza approached them, shaking their hands. He then turned and allowed the two detectives to introduce themselves. Although Jeff Sufford was a member of the Napa Valley Sheriff's Office, he didn't know either man. Danielle greeted the officers without extending her hand.

The ground had become a muddy mess, the result of having been assaulted by thousands of gallons of water hours earlier. Ash was no longer falling in the late afternoon sun, but the smell of smoke continued to loom. Two California state fire marshal investigators were shifting through debris with gloved hands. Three technicians had been allowed inside the yellow tape. The first was taking photographs. The other two were collecting items from the investigators and putting them into paper bags. Dozens of these brown, old school grocery store looking bags were lined up near the area where the sheriff's officers were standing. Each was labeled with a numbering and location system. These officials had clearly been at the site for a while. Watching over the entire operation appeared to be the Napa Valley fire marshal himself, judging by the words printed on the back of his jacket. And, his dress shoes.

The fire marshal looked over and saw the detectives. He stood up from his crouched position and walked towards them. Danielle felt more like a snoop than someone who was supposed to help. This wasn't Alameda County territory. At the moment however, the fire marshal didn't know who she or Jeff were or what they wanted.

"I'm Tom Navarro, the state fire marshal. And you are…" he questioned; his hands still gloved. Jeff spoke first.

"Good to meet you, Tom. I'm Detective Jeff Sufford from the Napa Valley Sheriff's Office and this is Detective Danielle Philipson from the Alameda County Sheriff's Office."

Before Jeff had the words out of his mouth, Danielle knew she was being labeled an intruder. It was bad enough that a couple of detectives had been sent out to apparently supervise the fire marshal's work. It was so much worse that she wasn't from Napa County.

"Listen, we're just here as a formality," Jeff continued. I guess the owners of the winery have some pull, so our offices agreed to send a couple of us out to get the lay of the land." Jeff knew he had said enough.

"I see," said Navarro.

He clearly didn't see at all. His back was up at the thought that he was being observed. "Well, what we've got here is a lot of ash, and not a lot of answers," he said. "It's going to take some time to sift through all this back at the lab. There are no obvious signs of an explosive device. There is no obvious smell of an accelerant, either."

The two detectives just looked at each other. This was going nowhere, and it didn't look like there would be any further information, at least not this afternoon. Danielle was hungry and tired. It was after 4:00 p.m. She really didn't want to go toe-to-toe with the fire marshal, and she didn't want to watch Detective Jeff take him on either. But

Danielle had learned as a cop that if you made someone feel important, you could usually get somewhere.

"You must have some suspicions based on all of these bags," said Danielle. "This is something that only an experienced investigator would do. I mean, you aren't just taking a few samples. Looks like you are going through every inch of the place, or what's left of it anyway."

The fire official just looked at her for a second, clearly trying to decide how to respond.

Danielle had hooked him. Fire Marshal Navarro uncrossed his arms which had been folded in front of him. Danielle guessed that he was in his late 50s. Not tall, but not short. Gray hair. Dark eyes. Not slim but not overweight. She knew it wasn't his job to be on-site to oversee the work of his investigators. No, he probably did that from the comfort of his office most days. Then again, she and Jeff were standing there alongside him. The Palmer Family Vineyard sure had clout.

"Well, I've been doing this for almost 30 years. I've learned that if you think there might be something to a piece of charred paper or a frayed wire, then bag it," he explained in a commanding-like tone. "I think we rely too much on technology. Yeah, it can help when you're looking at a scene, but sometimes you just need to go with your gut."

Danielle made her move.

"And what is your gut telling you, Tom," she questioned. Navarro took a deep breath.

"I've got a lot on my mind. And yeah, it's no secret that this is a prominent winery owned by a prominent family. Just not sure why the heavy guns," he finished.

Jeff responded this time.

"We don't really know either, especially the need for the Alameda sheriff's presence."

Fine, thought Danielle. Throw me and my entire department under the bus. She honestly didn't care. Frankly, it was a good question. She was tired of the chit chat. She wanted to go home. She thought maybe she could give her boss a call and get some real answers if it didn't get too late.

"I'm not sure what we have here," said Navarro "I don't think this was an accident. The complex had automatic sprinklers. They should have gone off. The other thing is that the night foreman said he heard a loud explosion." Tom Navarro was on a roll. "I think my investigators may have collected a couple of pieces of the fire sprinkler system control box. We'll try to determine if it was intentionally disconnected, but I'm not holding out much hope."

That was at least something for the two detectives to go on.

"I need to have the technicians get this stuff over to the lab and tell my staff to go home. They've been out here for hours." He put his right hand in his pocket, pulled out a couple of business cards, handed them to Jeff and Danielle, then turned and walked off toward the crew which were now standing around talking to each other.

"I don't know," Jeff said to Danielle as Navarro walked off. "I don't think he's going to find anything here. He's just showing off. I can't stand that crap."

Danielle agreed. Evidence? There wasn't going to be any physical evidence. Whoever or whatever had started the blaze was not going to be found by looking through brown bags filled with ash and tiny pieces of wire, carpeting, floor tiles, coffee mugs, or whatever else Tom Navarro had deemed "important." She suspected the fire marshal, and his entire team, already knew it. Then again, he did have a job to do.

"I'm starving. There's a great diner up the road that makes the best burger you've ever tasted," said Jeff. "Want to join me before you head home?"

It was a kind gesture, and since they were going to be working together, it would be smart to get to know her new temporary partner, Danielle thought to herself. But she was exhausted, and she wanted a bath. Besides, she decided that this "temporary" relationship probably wouldn't last the week. The fire marshal was in charge. The two sheriff's offices had now put on a show for PFV Winery. What was left?

"You know, thank you so much, but I need to get home to my cat," Danielle said. They walked together back out to the parking lot. It was quiet, except for some birds singing to each other. Please don't ask me about my cat, thought Danielle as she turned and headed toward her vehicle. She didn't have one.

CHAPTER
11

Michael Mason didn't waste time. He drove back into the City, toward home. If the smell of charred building remains hadn't permeated his clothes, he would have gone straight to the office. Instead, he desperately needed a shower. He also needed some sleep, but it was after 7:00 a.m. He threw his keys on the kitchen counter, searched the lacquered white cabinets for a coffee cup, and set it under his Miele. The aroma hit his nose instantaneously. Pure heaven. He has spent the past four hours reacting to his wife's 3:00 a.m. phone call and thinking about the subsequent catastrophe which was going to come rolling downhill until it landed in a big pile of crap at his feet. He needed to dig into the insurance to determine what value he had placed on the office complex and its contents. He knew it wouldn't be sufficient to rebuild, but maybe it would be enough to start reconstruction until a more permanent solution could be found.

Grabbing the cup with his left hand, Michael headed up the stairs, into the primary bedroom, and then into the bathroom. Within moments, a steamy shower was waiting. The house was large, but in San Francisco, large took on an entirely different meaning than it did in comparison to the enormous estates found in Oakland's Crocker Highland. The Mason home was drastically vertical, three stories in all, plus the ground floor garage. He loved the house. The boys had one floor all to themselves, each with their own bedrooms. An open space had been designed originally with desks for studying but had quickly become first, a playroom, and now a video game escape. It was rarely occupied these days. It was a space that served as a reminder of the years when the boys were younger, more connected to each other, and enjoyed hanging out with mom and dad on a Friday or Saturday night. Those years were slipping away, and with it, Michael's family. He missed the laughter of his sons, and sometimes the fighting, which echoed through the house. It wasn't all that long ago. And yet, it seemed a distant memory.

The primary bedroom and adjoining bathroom occupied the top floor, along with a lovely office for his wife, which she almost never used. The main floor housed the kitchen, great room, laundry room, his office, and a guest bathroom. They didn't have guest quarters, largely because most of their friends preferred the ranch in Napa Valley to the City. It was tranquil there, with plenty of space for guests to spread out.

Michael felt safe in the house. Despite the fact that his children had begun departing its interior one by one, it didn't feel empty, probably because the rooms were nestled together and not oversized. It was modern, but not too modern. The furniture was inviting, but it wasn't overdone. It was expensive but not pretentious.

Less than an hour after having arrived home, Michael had shaved, showered, made certain Aiden was breathing, and was back in his Range Rover heading to the office. The attendant in the underground parking garage took his keys with a familiar, "Good morning. Have a great day." Michael's corporate headquarters had been in this building for years. He knew all the attendants. They were friendly, but it was an unspoken rule that chit chat was to be kept to a minimum. If you stopped to talk for more than 30 seconds, there would be a line of cars filled with drivers waiting to make an entry or exit. The valets were incredibly professional and knowledgeable. They all had extensive experience working on cars and would offer to assist vehicle owners with mechanical problems or provide recommendations for service when they couldn't help. The attendants also knew a good deal about the City, who ran it, and how to navigate the business of politics. Not actual politics, but the unspoken type, as the most influential people in the region were not elected officials but those who supported them. Michael's wife fit that description.

The elevator doors slid open on the 27th floor. It was still early, before 9:00 a.m., so Michael wasn't forced to confront any staff. He could see lights on in a couple of offices, but generally speaking and given the fact that a large portion of their business was international, he never expected to see people at their desks before 10:00 a.m. He liked it that way. He enjoyed staring at the view through his office windows in silence before business took hold.

However, today was not like any other. It had officially begun at 3:00 a.m., and he had no idea when it would end. He picked up the phone on his desk and dialed the familiar number to his CFO, Dennis Smith-Hodges. Michael knew that Dennis didn't usually come into the office before 11:00 a.m., and seldom left before everyone else had gone. Dennis was not a young man, but he had married a young woman who insisted they hyphenate their last names. He didn't care one way or another, and so he became known around the office as Mr. Shhhhh. The "S" was obviously for Smith. The elongated "h," as in Hodges, was just fun. A compliment. People liked him. He crunched the numbers, complained about overspending, and reprimanded people for their quarterlies, but he wasn't fierce or condescending. Michael didn't want a hot head overseeing assets. He wanted someone low key, trustworthy, and able to keep their mouth shut.

Dennis picked up on the third ring.

"Jesus, what's wrong," he asked, not bothering with a standard greeting. "You never call before ten. What, is your office on fire," he continued with a note of both sarcasm and laughter in his voice.

Michael was taken aback. He knew Dennis was joking, but it hit too close to home. It was chilling.

"Not my office. Her office," Michael stated flatly.

Dennis wasn't following. He didn't like talking in code one bit.

"What are you talking about," he replied in a somewhat annoyed tone.

"The winery. The office complex at the winery burned to the ground last night. There were cops and a fire marshal, and God knows who else combing through the place. And because my wife enjoys her prestige, detectives from two counties are going to be assigned later today to start digging around."

Michael knew it would take a moment for his words to sink in.

"Are you telling me there is nothing left of the winery," Dennis questioned.

"Not the entire winery, thank Christ. Just the offices. The tasting room and barrel storage, and hell, even the grapes are all still standing. But you know I underinsured everything, and now I'm facing a whole lot of shit," Michael blurted out.

Dennis gathered his thoughts, as the air between the two men went silent.

"Are you THERE," Michael asked hotly. "This is not a joke. The next thing will be the news media. Can't wait to be a hashtag."

Dennis cleared his throat.

"Okay, first, was anybody hurt?"

Michael was mentally on his knees with gratitude that his response was, "No."

Then the CFO asked, "Do the cops or the fire marshal suspect a crime?"

Now, Michael cleared his throat.

"I don't know. It's too soon to say. I mean, this all just happened. The foreman called 9-1-1 and the calvary came running. I left Napa before seven, so I have no idea what's going on out there now. Except, Laura called me on my way back into the City to inform me that she'd contacted the sheriffs of both Napa and San Francisco counties," said Michael. "And Dennis, I mean she literally spoke to the sheriffs."

This was a lot of information for Dennis to digest. He was used to dealing with financial matters, and even white-collar misgivings, but not a potential felony involving one of the most well-known families in the entire valley. Of course, a fire didn't necessarily mean a crime had been committed. In fact, Dennis was a bit upset with himself that he had gone immediately to the darkest possibility. What was unusual, however, was the heightened level of investigative detail that seemed to have been set in motion practically within minutes of the fire being discovered. A fire marshal? Okay, that probably made sense at such a big event. But cops? Well, if Laura had called her sheriff friends in the middle of the night, Dennis guessed they would want to make the affluent winery owner happy. What didn't make sense to Dennis was the fact that no matter how upset Laura must have been, there was no need to call not one, but two county sheriffs. She was definitely abusing her pull.

On top of law enforcement involvement, there was the additional problem that his boss had chosen to reduce the insurance coverage on his wife's winery, without her knowledge. Laura had signed whatever paperwork he and Michael had put in front of her. She trusted her husband, and she trusted anyone whom Michael trusted. Dennis wasn't a lawyer, but there was probably something illegal or fraudulent, or at the very minimum, ethically corrupt about what he and Michael had done, and all in the name of trying to save the winery from bankruptcy. Justification had its way of being slippery at times.

Dennis knew that Michael wanted answers. He needed to ascertain what answers to seek out first. He went into spreadsheet mode, thinking to himself how to best organize what his boss would want to know and in what succession. It wasn't any different than preparing a pre-quarterly report before the actuals were published.

"Okay. Let me call you back in thirty minutes," said Dennis. "I'm going to make some phone calls and then decide where we should direct our attention. It's still early. Don't start borrowing trouble."

Michael already felt better. He knew his CFO was discreet and would strategize over various potential outcomes. Dennis would be the one to figuratively "borrow trouble" so that he could help Michael head it off.

"You focus on your wife. Play the dutiful husband. Take her calls and do what she asks. Maybe ask her why she's made these phone calls to two county sheriff's," said Dennis. "And Michael, if she asks you to come out to the ranch, just do it."

Michael didn't want to go back out to Napa Valley and definitely not to the ranch. He wanted to run straight into Elizabeth's arms. She would calm him down. She would make the world disappear for a few hours. She would give him the opportunity to feel strong and important, and he always exhibited his very best self when they were together. He never wanted her to see the messy side, the insecure parts of himself. It was one thing to talk about being lonely, but he never wanted to reveal his weaknesses. Of course, what Michael didn't know was that Elizabeth saw and understood his weaknesses from the very first night they had met. She had been capitalizing on his flaws ever since.

CHAPTER
12

Thirty minutes felt like an eternity, but as promised, Dennis was back on the phone to Michael quickly. He had a lot of information. Some of it not necessarily bad.

"What do you have for me," Michael asked his CFO.

Dennis got straight to the point.

"Okay, first thing. I don't think you are going to get much media attention," he began.

"Really," Michael shot back with an air of "you are so wrong" in his voice.

"Yeah, I hear your sarcasm, but here's the thing. "There is an ongoing preschool hostage situation in San Francisco that began about an hour ago. It's all over the national and local news. I'd tell you to turn on the TV in your office, but you don't have a TV."

Michael began to scroll through his phone. There it was. Dozens of headlines and videos had already been posted. Sadly, it had become a common occurrence to hear about shootings, and bomb threats, and kids and teachers never feeling totally secure. It was happening across the country, not just in big cities. It was sickening to think that a school hostage situation was a "good" thing. But Michael was honest enough to admit to himself that he was breathing a small, pathetic sigh of relief. The fire wasn't going to be tomorrow's headline.

Dennis continued.

"I spoke with a friend at the Napa Valley Sheriff's Office. Apparently, there's going to be a meeting of officers, detectives, public affairs and the like at the Alameda County Sheriff's Office in Oakland this afternoon to discuss your fire. Looks like Alameda's Detective Ronald Hauser is acting as coordinator, because the San Francisco Sheriff's Department and SFPD are obviously dealing with something more serious, and they asked for the assistance."

Interesting, thought Michael. Sure, he supposed. He and Laura were San Francisco County residents. If San Francisco law enforcement was tied up, someone in charge had probably asked Napa Valley what type of help they needed. Then again, who knew what his wife had said on the phone in order to get action. A call from Mrs. Laura Palmer-Mason got instant attention. It was something unwanted by Michael. Playing *that* card. The, I've got money and connections in this region card. Laura knew that, at their core, all sheriffs were politicians. It was something she had learned as a little girl by watching her father interact with the who's who at grand openings, festivals, and all manner of local events. Sheriffs had to get re-elected. They needed money, and they always went out of their way to keep their friends in high places happy. Friends in high places had friends in even higher places. They hosted fundraisers and made certain that good works got media attention. The more wealth, the more likely people were to trot out their favorite "electeds" and checkbooks at luncheons and cocktail parties.

"Now, before you start wondering why an Alameda detective is co-ordinating rather than someone from Napa County, it's a policy all the sheriff's departments agreed to a couple of years ago," explained Dennis. "They want joint action among agencies, especially in instances like yours. You own a business in one county, you live in another. This is a fire, so the Napa Valley Fire Marshal's office will ultimately be in charge. But to demonstrate there isn't any nepotism, Alameda makes sense regardless of the hostage thing and …"

Before Dennis could finish his sentence, Michael interrupted. He was starting to get the picture.

"Okay, we live in the City. The winery and the ranch are in the Valley. San Francisco law enforcement is receiving unwanted national attention, so they've called in a favor to Alameda. They're also serving as a neutral third party. But this is probably going to be a fire investigation, with a side of police work. Sound about right?"

"I think so," Dennis responded. "I mean, who knows what the fire marshal will find. As you said, they're already out there. You're not going to have any news media at the winery for now, but I guarantee that after this meeting of officers and whatnot in Oakland, you will have two different counties sniffing around."

Dennis wasn't going to sugar coat the fact that law enforcement had been prematurely called by Michael's wife. Under normal circumstances, it would be the fire marshal's decision whether or not to request law enforcement. Other than to secure a potential crime scene maybe. It went without saying to be careful what you wished for, particularly when your wish was to get attention. Immediate attention. That had been Laura's goal when she started making phone calls in the middle of the night. Dennis wondered if it would be a decision she would come to regret. However, it couldn't be rolled back. She was always in such a hurry to get noticed. React first, think about it later. It was an unusual personality type for someone who ran a well-known winery.

Fine wines took years, and sometimes decades to produce. You couldn't rush the methods if you wanted award winning products. Mrs. Laura Palmer-Mason was a dichotomy of sorts. When she wanted something, she wanted it yesterday. However, she treated the grapes like fragile pieces of china, on the verge of breaking with a single touch. And there was some truth to it. One bad rainstorm or frost or too much sun and the entire crop could be ruined. It had happened to PFV, and there in part was the reason behind the financial disarray. As a business owner, Laura's knee jerk reactions at times seemed puzzling to Dennis. Sooner or later, it was going to get her in trouble, and it seemed the sooner had arrived.

Michael was worried about investigators on his wife's property, but he also had the added problem of the insurance, or more accurately, the lack of insurance.

"The final matter to discuss, for the moment anyways, is the insurance," said Dennis, as if he was reading Michael's mind. In fairness, that had been the focus of Michael's early morning phone call to his CFO.

"So, you have just over two million in coverage on the office complex. It's not bad, but it's not going to be enough to cover a new build. Of course, that's not a crime. It will more likely appear that you and Laura didn't realize the cost of a total loss in today's dollars given the fact that the buildings were more than twenty years old."

Dennis paused. He could practically hear Michael thinking. Dennis was absolutely certain that the insurance piece was sending his boss over the edge. It was going to send Laura into absolute overdrive when she discovered that her husband and his CFO had, for all intents and purposes, lied.

Michael thought about this last bit. The idea that he and Laura would have such a skewed understanding of the value of their holdings seemed implausible. The actual worth of the office complex was probably closer to four million. Earthquake standards and IT infrastructure and Christ, the art. He hadn't insured the paintings by Wayne Thiebaud or Ralph Goings either. Both had passed, making their pieces even more valuable. Really? Michael questioned his CFO silently. He had a mega-million-dollar international business, a CFO with a stellar reputation, brilliant staff, and a wife with a Stanford MBA. Nobody ever called Michael dumb. Ever. The idea that he and his wife would be blissfully unaware of the current value of their property? It was an incredible stretch. Especially since there had been continuous upgrades made over the years to keep on top of everything from changing office technology needs to the damned décor. Still, Michael knew this was the story he was going to have to sell to his wife, the fire marshal, the sheriff, and the insurance company, because Dennis was selling this bullshit to him.

The insurance company wasn't going to care. It wasn't their problem where PFV would get the additional cash to rebuild. Their payout would be the stuff that agents joked about at the Monday morning office meeting. How could these people be so stupid? Even better, the Palmer Family Vineyard would either have to pay up for a new policy or face the possibility of becoming uninsurable. A new policy would be excruciatingly expensive. There had been a fire. A claim had been filed, and that fact in all practicality would be a death sentence. Insurance was something you needed but were never supposed to use. It was amazing, though, how money talked one's way out of difficult situations. Pay up suckers. Christ, Michael said to himself yet again. He had to stop this internal dialogue. He had allowed himself a pity party for three hours. It was time to cut the crap and get to work.

The conversation between the two men calmed Michael down. No news media was huge. The interagency sheriff and fire thing still seemed odd despite the explanation, but he trusted Dennis enough to understand that it was a bad idea to start borrowing trouble. Michael had decided he wasn't going to say one word to Laura about calling her sheriff buddies. Quite frankly, he needed her to feel she had taken control and was getting a substantial level of support. She actually *was* in control. But she had no idea about the backstory. The insurance was the piece that Michael would absolutely need to tackle. He had always been in the driver's seat when it came to the insurance. He couldn't recall the exact details, but he had taken it over when Laura's business manager had been out on leave. Several years later, and he had become the defacto insurance liaison between the insurance company and the winery.

Laura hadn't called again, so that was also a good sign. If there were any sort of problem, other than the blatantly obvious fact that the winery buildings had burned to the ground, she would have been on the phone to him. Michael guessed that Laura was feeling better. She had made her phone calls and knew that law enforcement would now provide their perspective in addition to the fire marshal's full investigation. He also knew that he needed to shut down the business side of things for a short period of time and be ready to be more attentive to his wife. This was her family's winery. She would feel responsible for the fire, no matter what the cause.

Michael pushed his leather chair back from his desk, then swiveled around and faced the office windows. He allowed himself to look out at the bridge, sitting in stillness with his thoughts. If it was negligence, their insurance would most likely be cancelled. If it was a crime, well, that would be too much to wrap his head around. Who? Why? He had to force himself to think only about the day in front of him. It was already painfully long, and it was just before 11:00 a.m. Narrow your focus, he thought to himself. As he did, Michael came to the realization that the only positive outcome of any investigation would be one that went unresolved. He hoped there would never be any real answers about the fire in the Valley at 3:00 a.m., where the darkness met the light.

CHAPTER
13

The bar at the Ritz-Carlton was tragically loud. Elizabeth was disappointed. It seemed people wanted to hear themselves. Not think, but rather talk. She had so many pleasant memories of this space, when she had first come to San Francisco to practice her new life of East Coast pretense. Those images had long since faded. Fortunately, her looks had not. Of course, she was not yet in her mid-30s, but in a sea of Gen Z's, she felt distracted at the very least. It was an internal battle she faced regularly now. Telling herself that she was young, when confronted with the flawless skin and easy good looks of girls like Michael's blonde assistant. Then coming home and recognizing that the fine lines were beginning to show, and the grays needed to be colored more often. This East Coast narrative had made its presence felt.

Elizabeth only bothered with the Ritz because Richard, her very first seduction, enjoyed it. He had an old soul. Then again, he was old. He was nearly 80, and although drearily uninteresting, he didn't ask anything of Elizabeth, except her company. Years ago, he had insisted he make the down payment on a home for her. Elizabeth didn't resist. She learned early on that elderly men with money wanted to use it. Truthfully, money was the only commodity that men like Richard still possessed. It gave them power as they were becoming powerless in the ever-speeding world. She thanked him for his generosity by attending events and sitting with him through endless four course meals. He rewarded her further by paying a large portion of her mortgage.

Old school men, who projected affluence, enjoyed conservative women. Elizabeth would never wear something revealing when she was with Richard. He preferred a dark knee-length dress, pearl earrings, and a scarf. He appreciated her for agreeing to pull her thick brunette mane into a tight bun at the nape of her neck. Of course, she always wore heels. She felt more like 70 dressed in this manner and believed it defeated the entire purpose of her role as his mistress. But this play-acting was her chosen profession, and she knew how to keep her clients entertained.

Richard wasn't set to arrive for another half hour. The Ritz was definitely a place where people rounding the corner on 40 purposefully spent their time, hoping to meet boomers, and their wallets. Elizabeth eyed two vacant stools at the end of the bar top. Normally, she would sit at a table, but she felt eerily lonely tonight. She wasn't certain why these feelings had possessed her this evening. Her day had been pleasant. Waking in the August San Francisco fog. Taking her three-mile jog to her favorite coffee spot. Returning home and placing a call to her mother. There had been no interruptions. No client calls. She never wrung her hands worrying about filling her schedule. She likened any woman who waited around for a boyfriend or potential significant other as careless and weak. Only childish women waited. Worrying about whether someone found her attractive or interesting. Hanging on every text message or lack thereof. Carefully crafting every word to ensure she was what the other person wanted. It was so silly. It was the type of behavior that the young blonde in Michael's office probably participated in on a regular basis, despite thinking of herself as being strong.

Elizabeth slipped onto the seat of the ivory leather stool at the far end of the bar, leaving an empty chair between herself and a well-dressed woman who was nursing what appeared to be a gin and tonic.

The bartender approached Elizabeth, placing a cocktail napkin down on the empty marble space in front of her.

Rather than a standard greeting, he grinned at Elizabeth and asked, "Guest or resident?" He made Elizabeth smile through her red lips.

"I'm not certain," she replied easily. She never gave away anything which wasn't necessary.

"Alright, Ms. I'm Not Certain, do you know what you'd like to drink," he responded without missing a beat.

"Yes, of *that* I am certain. May I please have a cosmopolitan?"

"Absolutely," responded the bartender. "How very New York of you."

This time, Elizabeth smiled on the inside. It was what she wanted. To be so engulfed in her identity as Elizabeth Stevens that she had indeed become a wealthy East Coast lawyer with two brothers, a socialite mother, and a father who was punishing and loving all in the same breath. She had perfected her character. She had left behind any feelings of being exhausted in her carrying out her illusion a long time ago.

The only exceptions were speaking to her mother or spending time in Pacific Grove. Her mother knew only that her daughter was working as a legal assistant and had a roommate, Grace, to split the rent. Sarah spoke to her mom on the phone a couple of times each week. Lynda was still working for the Inn at Spanish Bay and would share her stories of the rich and famous. In turn, Sarah would make up tales about the lawyers at her fictional firm. She told her mother that she was casually dating someone she had met at a beachside bar. He was an accountant. This pleased Lynda very much. She wanted to think of her daughter as being content, living her life in a darling apartment, and spending her free time with friends along the coast. Sarah protected her mother from the truth in this way. She was kind and agreeable. Her mother deserved it. No one should have to raise a child alone at 19. In these moments, Elizabeth sometimes longed to be Sarah again. Uncomplicated. Living exactly as she pretended, with a roommate and a steady job.

Richard was 10 minutes early. He spotted Elizabeth immediately. His olive-green trench coat over his arm, he walked over to the bar and joined his paramour, taking the empty seat beside her. He placed his trench over the back of the chair, then leaned in and kissed Elizabeth lightly on the cheek. To an outsider, the exchange might have just as easily been noticed as a grandfather meeting his granddaughter. They had a nearly 50-year age difference. The bartender set Elizabeth's cosmopolitan in front of her, then turned to Richard to take his drink order in the customary manner. Richard asked for a Wild Turkey on the rocks.

After sitting at the bar and talking about nothing of any consequence for nearly two hours, the couple walked out of the hotel together and said goodnight. Elizabeth was numb. She suspected that Richard scoured the New York Times and Wall Street Journal before their encounters to impress her with his knowledge of the latest goings on in finance, world events, and even sports. She casually smiled through it all, thinking about her warm bed with extra soft sheets waiting for her at home. She was grateful for his tenderness, but with her mortgage completely paid off, she knew this relationship would soon end. Elizabeth suspected Richard felt that she was pulling away, but he was desperately trying to hold on to whatever they had left. My how similar the young and inexperienced were to the elderly and accomplished. Both held on so tightly. She missed Michael.

CHAPTER
14

Detective Danielle Philipson faced a decision. She was back in her Berkeley condominium searching through her refrigerator for the third time. Food hadn't suddenly or magically appeared. She could either eat leftover lasagna or an entire bag of sour cream and onion potato chips. She should have taken her new and probably short-lived partner, Jeff Sufford, up on his offer to get a burger. As further proof of her mistake, she now had a make-believe cat. She was getting too old for this shit.

Grabbing the plastic container from the top shelf of the refrigerator, Danielle opened the microwave door and warmed up the lasagna. She wasn't a college student. Hell, she was nearing 40. She should at least attempt to be healthy. For the most part she was, except in instances when her day would completely turn sideways from its original intention. She had left a voicemail for her brother. He was not returning the call. She didn't dare text. He would need a few days to cool off. She was equally disappointed in herself. Would it have killed her to have ignored her sergeant's call for one lousy hour? It was the Ninth Circuit Court! An incredibly rare opportunity for even the most prestigious lawyers. And, for what? This winery fire thing? *This* was important work? No, this was the result of entitled people throwing their money and prestige around, and on a day when preschool children had been taken hostage. Thank God *that* had ended well with no one hurt and a child's father in custody. Except these things never ended well. Children and teachers and parents would be scarred forever.

Danielle removed the hot container from the microwave and scooped the lasagna onto a white plate. The container would have been fine, but she could envision her beloved grandmother rolling her eyes and letting out a heavy sigh of dismay at the thought of her granddaughter eating straight from a container. I know grandma, Danielle said to herself. A plate is a must. She poured herself a tall glass of iced tea, then sat down to eat. She had purposefully placed her bistro-sized glass table near the main sliding door so that she could sit and look out onto the water.

The condo itself was a one-bedroom, not large. But it boasted high ceilings and a balcony which had just enough room for two patio chairs which held thick white cushions. A square cocktail table painted a flat bright white sat between them. Danielle never used the patio space for dining. Instead, it was her early morning coffee spot, and occasionally a confessional when a good friend came around for a glass of wine. She loved her white window sheers in both the living space and the bedroom. They floated. The entire place felt as if she were living inside a cloud. Everything was washed in white. The sofa, the two chairs accompanying the bistro table. Her bedding, towels, dishes, living room area rug. Even the toaster. So much white would have been a giant mistake with Snuggles roaming the place while shedding his long gray fur. Danielle had settled on a name for her make-believe cat while warming her dinner.

This job made Danielle rigid, and yet she loved it. In her days as a uniformed officer, she felt she was doing her civic duty to respond to emergency calls. You had to have ballsy nerves, she learned quickly, especially in a field dominated by men. There were more women now, but still under 20 percent of uniforms nationwide. Something needed to be done about that statistic. Women made great officers. Strong when necessary, but also sensitive and able to listen, especially at the scene of a domestic. They were also good at the gun range, and in court.

It was so cliché, but Danielle had dated cops, because they were the only people who really understood. Investigate the unimaginable and then go out to the waterfront on a casual date for drinks. She had been engaged, forever ago. He was a good guy. Not a cop. With a day job. A great paying job in IT which allowed him to work remotely, travel almost never, and be available in the middle of the afternoon as well as 2:00 a.m. He had understood her hours. He had understood beers with the team after a long day. But he didn't understand what motivated Danielle to get out of bed and do it again day after day. They met on a dating app. He was the first guy who hadn't ghosted her after just one coffee or dinner. He had found her darling in her own unique way, and he told her so again and again. Their jobs were dramatically different, but they shared similar interests. They worked out together several nights a week. They watched Monday Night Football and all the Warriors games. They enjoyed time in Bodega Bay and Marin. It was a chance to escape to the beach within an hour's drive of the City.

Danielle had introduced him to her parents six months into the relationship. They adored him. Her mother made it very clear that she hoped the couple had a future together. She stopped short of telling her daughter not to screw it up, but she certainly implied it on a fairly regular basis. The pair never lived together. They wanted their own space. And that was part of the problem. They weren't in their twenties. They had become accustomed to living alone. And there were fights. He had suggested she change careers a couple of times. He worried about her every single day. It tore him up inside, until he finally ended it. He might have felt differently if she had been a detective at the time. The daily grind was different. More observation. Less danger. She was rarely part of an active situation. However, he was long gone. Her parents heartbroken. She was too.

Danielle lingered over her lasagna for precisely seven minutes, then looked over at her laptop. She wanted to see if any additional information had been posted to the department's G drive. She doubted it, but she couldn't help herself. Pushing aside her plate, Danielle flipped the computer cover open. Within seconds she was online, password entered, and looking through files. She opened the folder marked, "PFV Winery." As she suspected, nothing new. The electronic file shared the identical contents which the entire team had been handed earlier that afternoon in the thin brown folders. Twenty minutes and 127 email deletions later, Danielle closed her laptop, placed her dish in the sink and headed for her bedroom.

She peeled off her clothes, then washed her face and brushed her teeth. She hadn't been to the gym in three days, so she set her alarm for 5:00 a.m. She would go for a jog in the morning, Danielle found the switch on her bedroom wall and turned out the lights. The moon's glow streamed into the room through the sheers. It didn't bother her in the least. She wasn't a blackout shades kind of person. She enjoyed the vibrant evenings on the water. She rolled over and pulled her duvet up across her back. Snuggles made herself invisibly comfortable on the empty pillow next to Danielle's head.

CHAPTER
15

Three weeks passed before there was any news from the Napa Valley fire marshal's office. Laura was furious. Fuming. Michael, on the other hand, was thrilled. He would have jumped up and down had nobody been looking. But someone was always looking.

There had been no choice except to call the insurance company. To have ignored what anyone would automatically do after a fire would have been immediately suspicious. Michael had done the right thing. Following his calls with his CFO on the morning of the blaze, Michael picked up the phone and anxiously dialed State Farm. The company held the distinction of having the largest footprint in California and wrote over seven billion dollars in policies annually. Michael knew the facts because he had pitched them as a client some years back. They had politely declined. Normally, Michael would have never given them any of his money but securing insurance for large-scale businesses in California over the years had grown arduous. So much so that he had transferred the policies for Mason Recruiting International, as well as his personal policies, from another company out of necessity.

The initial insurance agent on the line "elevated" Michael's call instantly. Michael felt his heart rate rise as he waited. Ten minutes. Fifteen. Twenty-three minutes before a woman's voice greeted him.

He was irritated. Mostly at himself for his own entitled attitude. As he waited impatiently, he had run through a conversation telling the phone representative that he was not an insignificant client and expressing his complete outrage at this disservice. Okay, maybe Mason Recruiting and PFV weren't Amazon or Facebook, but twenty-three minutes? Then he reconsidered. Had he finally become his privileged wife?

"Good morning, Mr. Mason. This is Kim from priority customer support. How are you today?"

Now, Michael was ready to throw up as Laura had done hours earlier. Was this a joke? Dead air.

"I suppose it's not a very good day," the woman reacted having realized that her opening had been insensitive.

Jesus, thought Michael. Didn't people at this "elevated" level receive training? He didn't respond.

"I have your policy pulled up. You are calling to report a fire at the PFV Winery, is that correct?" Michael was not amused. He wanted to hang up, but she had him by the balls, and she knew it. This was going to be a painful process. He had to go along and play the game.

"Yes," he responded. He wasn't going to give her an inch.

"So, this event occurred at approximately three o'clock this morning?"

"It did."

"I see here that the offices are documented as ten thousand square feet. Is that correct?"

"It is," Michael said flatly, for fucks sake he wanted to add.

"Alright, can you please give me an estimation as to how much damage occurred as a percentage? In other words, twenty percent of the building? Fifty percent?"

"One hundred percent." He was too tired both physically and emotionally to be answering these questions.

"I see," she said so calmly that Michael wanted to scream.

She added, "Well, I am so sorry for your loss." She sounded as though she were sharing condolences upon the death of a great uncle. Michael said nothing.

"Was the fire marshal called?"

Ha, thought Michael. Fire marshal? Try two county sheriffs. At 3:00 a.m. He decided to play it close to the vest. Truthfully, he was a bit taken aback that she would ask about a fire marshal. Then again, she *was* an insurance agent handling a fire claim.

"The fire marshal introduced himself," Michael responded. "But I don't have any additional information. He wasn't about to add that he had the guy's business card.

"That's fine," said the insurance representative. "I will follow-up."

Michael waited for her to ask about law enforcement. Surprisingly, she didn't.

"I'm looking at your policy now. Your payments are up to date. I will get an initial claim started, but I have some bad news."

Fuck.

"I don't like to guess, but because the fire marshal was sent to the winery, there will almost certainly be a findings report prepared by their department. A ten thousand square-foot building is considered a large asset. A fire of this size will be recording by us as a significant event." Her voice seemed to carry off. She wasn't finished.

"Until the fire marshal releases a report, our hands are tied. We will not be able to move forward with your claim. Do you understand, Mr. Mason?"

He did. This was great news. Michael had been given the gift of time to digest it all. To hold off his wife's questions. To work on his story about the lack of insurance coverage. To maybe spend some time with Elizabeth.

"I understand," Michael replied, then added, "I appreciate your honesty and your professionalism." It seemed like the appropriate response.

There had been no mention of the cause, coverage, or reconstruction costs by either side. The insurance representative and Michael were acutely aware that they were tip toeing through the situation. The company didn't want to lose a profitable account. Actually, accounts. Plural. He was certain the agent knew Mason Recruiting had its policies parked in her office. Michael absolutely didn't want his wife to know that she was woefully underinsured, and he certainly didn't want to know what their renewal coverage was going to cost them, that was if they survived this ordeal.

CHAPTER
16

The fire marshal's report was finally released on the 31st of August. What appeared to be a benign memorandum was marked with the words "INTERNAL REVIEW" across the top. Michael's eyes scanned the two-page document. Inconclusive. Undetermined. Uncertain. It was nothing but a laundry list of disclaimers. Now what, Michael wondered, until he read the final paragraph. "The Napa Valley Fire Marshal has determined it necessary to recommend that this inquiry be brought to the full attention of the Napa and Alameda County sheriffs for further review by law enforcement." The paragraph went on to say that Detectives Danielle Philipson and Jeff Sufford would be opening their own investigation. "Fuck," Michael said under his breath as he read the final lines of the memorandum. Three weeks to learn what the fire marshal probably knew the morning following the fire. He wasn't going to find anything, so he was leaning on law enforcement to take control.

Michael picked up the phone and called his CFO.

"I don't know what to think," Michael said into the phone. "Laura is so upset. The insurance company won't move forward. This is on her. She's the one who called the sheriffs." Michael didn't seem to be coming up for air.

"Now we're going to have the f-ing cops up our ass." He was on a roll. "Oh, and she's brought in portable offices for her staff, but it's not ideal. I don't think she's wrapped her mind around the fact that construction will take at least eighteen months, regardless of an investigation. And she had no idea about the insurance business. Thank God, I guess."

On the other end of the line, Dennis listened. He had been heading out the door to the office when he received Michael's call. There was nothing more he could do, which felt odd as a numbers guy, because there was *always* something that could be done. He understood that this new investigation would be much more obtrusive than the inquiry made by the fire marshal. Detectives would question everyone. The fire marshal had focused his attention on, well, the fire.

"I think you and Laura need to make these detectives your new best friends," Dennis answered.

He knew it wasn't the response that Michael wanted. No, Michael needed to be reassured that this was all for show. To provide Laura comfort that no stone had been left unturned. But Dennis wasn't so certain. It wasn't likely that the fire marshal would simply drop it. No, the marshal suspected something, but had no evidence. So, he was handing the hard work over to the cops.

Dennis hoped Laura, and even Michael would relax and take the news as routine. However, he knew better. Sure, one detective might be put on display to dot the I's and cross the T's. But two detectives from two counties would be invasive. These detectives were not going to be disagreeable, but they were not being positioned to make PFV feel at ease. Instead, it was going to have the opposite effect. Laura would be nervous. She would feel as though she were a suspect, all the while the detectives would be observing as they put the winery, its owner, and the entire staff under their own version of a microscope.

"You must have received something other than the two-page letter," Dennis stated, redirecting the conversation.

"Yeah, there's a forty page attachment. I haven't looked at it yet," Michael admitted. "Not sure what I would be looking for anyway. It looks like a lot of photos and lab results."Dennis asked Michael to forward him the materials.

"I think we should have someone review everything. We aren't scientists. How do we know if the lab work was done correctly?"

Dennis figured the work was most likely accurate, but he wanted to give Michael something he could chew on and digest. In other words, hope.

"I would suggest Lawrence Livermore," said Dennis, "but I think we need to find someone who isn't associated with our firm. We need someone who can keep this quiet."

Michael considered Dennis's suggestion. It was a good one. Mason Recruiting International had several large scientific based organizations as clients. He needed someone scholarly and discreet. Maybe someone who was recently retired. He had the names of professionals who had been employed through his company, but he certainly didn't have a complete rundown on every employee for every firm who used his Mason Recruiting's services. Plus, in most cases, Mason Recruiting sought out high-level executives for its clientele. CEOs, CFOs, managing partners, and others with seven figure descriptions. Not scientists. He didn't feel comfortable calling around to executives. He would need help.

Dennis could sense Michael beginning to panic on the other end of the line.

"You know what? Let's not be dramatic," Dennis responded. There's no reason why we can't contact a lab and have them put this report into language we can understand. It's perfectly reasonable that PFV Winery would want to grasp all of this in layman's terms."

Maybe Dennis was right. Be friendly to these two detectives. Get a condensed version of the lab report. Michael guessed that the detectives would look through the fire marshal's report, get a second opinion from another lab, interview winery staff, and then make their own determination. But what were they expecting to find? What did the fire marshal have on his mind when "inconclusive" had been registered? Clearly, the fire marshal had some sort of instinct, but about what? Either that, or he was trying to save face. Had there been a rash of fires at businesses across the Valley? Did the fire marshal have a hunch that it was arson? Mason Recruiting hadn't become successful through hunches and assumptions. The firm had been built on contacts and connections. Dollars were dollars. He helped companies find professionals who fit specific needs based on resumes and reputations.

It was rare for Michael to spend time at the winery, unless it was to attend an event at Laura's request. He would need to finesse this with his wife. She would be the vehicle through which information flowed. It would have to be accomplished casually. Spending additional time at the ranch wouldn't be possible. He had two sons in college now, but he still had a child who needed his attention. On the other hand, Aiden loved the vineyards. This opportunity had possibilities.

"You know what," Michael asked Dennis rhetorically. "I think someone on the winery staff should get involved. Let them get a dumbed-downed version of the report. It makes sense. Laura needs to comprehend what's in these pages."

Michael knew Laura well. He could certainly steer her in that direction. She was already fired up. She would want to dissect every detail. Hell, she probably knew who to call to get a straightforward version of the lab results.

CHAPTER
17

Danielle was wide awake and very annoyed. It was only 4:20 a.m. She should still be asleep. She was also annoyed for having acquired a fake cat and turning down dinner all in one sentence. She almost never got an offer to go to dinner, even if it was just a burger. That was the best kind of dinner. Casual, with great food and no pretense. Then there was the fact that it had been nearly 24 hours since she had disappointed her brother. She reached across her pillow to the night-stand and grabbed her cell phone off its charger. No voicemail from her little bro. No text either. It was going to be the silent treatment for at least a week, she figured. She retreated into her crisp white sheets and matching duvet. It was a luxury to relax in bed on a workday. Sleep was also a luxury, she thought to herself, and she had lost 40 minutes of it.

Danielle scrolled through her texts a second time. Her boss, Ronald Hauser, had left a message at 1:27 a.m. He wanted her in Dublin today. Just as she had expected, the fire was still smoldering, but it was back to business as usual. "So much for my new partner, Detective Jeff," Danielle said aloud as she pushed herself out of bed, walked to the room's sliding glass door, and parted the white sheers to reveal a blackish blue sky. She was happy that she wouldn't be wasting time on a rich woman and her winery. But secretly, she had hoped for a second chance to have that burger. She was a bit surprised that her boss would text at such a late, or some would say, early hour. Who had he been working with overnight?

The Alameda County Sheriff's Special Investigations Division was not large. Danielle, and fellow detectives Angela Ortiz and Ben Tuffton, worked under Sergeant Ron Hauser. Together the team was responsible for assisting both the Violent Crimes and Property Crimes Units with evidence gathering, surveillance, operational planning, and ultimately arresting suspects. Over the past couple of years narcotics and sex crimes had skyrocketed. As a result, Danielle had come on board to assist when she made detective, joining Ortiz and Tuffton. She had learned a lot about crime beneath the surface. As a cop, she had gone out to scenes, calmed situations down, and written reports. But ultimately, if necessary, she handed it all over to a detective and moved on. Only in cases where she was called into court as a witness had she ever taken a deep dive into the details. Her routine was to go to the next accident, or smash and grab, or assault. Sometimes, she took someone into booking. Oftentimes not.

The fire wasn't a violent crime, but it might possibly be a property crime. Danielle guessed this was the reason she had been asked to attend the prior morning's meeting. The Alameda County Sheriff's Office didn't have its own fire investigative unit. It worked to provide regional training and exercise programs which included fire agencies, though. In California, everyone guarded their respective territory. Fire departments were their own entities. In fact, they were considered special districts at the local level. Then there were the state agencies and the feds. Lots of layers, thought Danielle. Too many.

The three detectives were well suited to their jobs. They enjoyed the tedious details of operational planning. They didn't mind spending hours surveilling subjects, though it had been several months since they had found themselves parked down the street from a crack house, or any house for that matter. The team had just wrapped up a huge case involving the smuggling of methamphetamine from Honduras, through Mexico, and into the East Bay. More than 20 Honduran and

Mexican nationals had been arrested, along with 10 Americans. It was now up to the DA to prosecute, and it was highly probable that all three detectives would have to testify if the cases didn't settle out of court. Unlike sensationalized TV shows which wrapped up neatly in an hour, these things could take up to two years to wind themselves through the system. Each suspect was entitled to an attorney, which would cause a headache for the DA's office. Still, over 97 percent of cases never went to trial. Plea deals were almost always reached unless the DA really wanted to drag a particular case out in front of the media.

"Buckle up," Sergeant Hauser had said to his three detectives when the arrests were made public. Hauser believed that at least some of the scumbags were going to want to have a jury trial, and the DA would be more than accommodating.

Since the team was small, it wasn't unusual for the detectives to be given individual assignments. This often meant working alone as liaisons to the larger Violent Crimes and Property Crimes units. The recent drug case had been an exception. The three detectives had pooled their efforts for months. So it had felt a bit odd to Danielle to find herself in a room full of strangers the previous day in Oakland talking about a fire in a county outside her jurisdiction. It was the nature of the job, she guessed, and she appreciated the fact that no two days were ever the same. Her friends who worked in banking and real estate and even info-technology seemed to grind it out for big paychecks. For Danielle, law enforcement had never been a grind, and her salary covered her expenses. Well, with some help from her grandmother's inheritance.

Danielle pulled her SUV into the Alameda County Sheriff's Dublin office at 7:56 a.m. She was still annoyed. Maybe she *should* get a cat. She swiped her key card letting herself into the building's back entrance. She could hear a couple of people talking but couldn't make out the conversation. The Special Investigations office was to the left of the main corridor. Gone were the days of metal desks and coffee makers. Each team member had their own space, separated by gray partitions. The detectives had both desktop computers linked to the county's large mainframe, as well as laptops so that they could work out in the field, and at home.

Because Alameda was one of California's largest counties, law enforcement received a significant share of the state's budget. Over $400 million went into their coffers annually. Technology was always up-to-date and equipment, including their vehicles, was replaced regularly. The Dublin offices were bright and clean and for the most part, modern. More than 1,700 people were employed by the sheriff's office. That included 1,000 sworn officers. The coroner was also under the sheriff's command. And of course, Emergency Services Dispatch was an institution in and of itself.

Danielle pulled her laptop from her backpack. She yanked twice on the bottom desk drawer, finally kicking it, before it gave way. It was her morning ritual. She knew maintenance could fix the sticking drawer, but for some reason, she hadn't called them. She didn't like to ask for help for what she considered to be unimportant things. In this instance, it was a pain in the ass, and yet she just couldn't bring herself to get it repaired. Danielle reached to the bottom and grabbed a protein bar. She had, what she considered to be, a terrible habit of eating from whatever food truck showed up in the back parking lot at noon. Some of it was good. Some of it, not so much. She knew it would be better to bring her lunch, but other than the desk drawer filled with PowerBars, Hersey kisses, and Splenda packets, she relied on the mom-and-pop meals on wheels. Danielle logged into her desktop computer just as Detectives Ortiz and Tuffton passed through the doorway into the division's office.

"Hey," said Angela. "I thought you were going to be out in Napa sipping on a glass of chardonnay and sampling a cheese plate."

Ben couldn't help himself. He added, "What's the matter, was the vintage you were served yesterday not to your expectations?"

The two detectives laughed as they walked over to their desks.

"Very funny and so early in the morning," Danielle shot back, half kidding. She knew it was all said from a place of respect and love. "No, the boss texted in the middle of the night telling me to come into the office today," she explained. "So, here I am ready to give one hundred and ten percent to the residents of Alameda County."

All three detectives still had a mountain of paperwork to complete following their big drug arrests. There were several meetings scheduled over the next few weeks with the DA's office. All exhibits had to be carefully detailed. Complete logs of all surveillance needed to be meticulously entered into an electronic database system. Every piece of paper, photograph, receipt, and video clip had to be identified so that it could ultimately be cross-referenced. The three detectives, and their supervisor, knew it was monotonous work, but it was as important as the arrests themselves.

It was mid-morning by the time Sergeant Hauser came down the hall and stopped at Danielle's desk.

"Good morning Detective Philipson," he addressed Danielle. "Sorry I couldn't get away from my meeting to come and explain why you're back here today." Danielle listened. "So, the fire marshal is going to handle the winery fire. They aren't requesting law enforcement assistance at this time. Not from us, and not from the Napa Valley Sheriff's Office either, if that makes you feel any better."

Frankly, it did. Danielle didn't want to think she wasn't wanted. Neither she nor Detective Jeff Sufford appeared to be very popular with the fire marshal.

"As it stands now, you can go back to working with these two to put away the drug pushers," said Hauser as he turned to walk into his office a few feet from the open room shared by the detectives.

Danielle was disappointed, but she had learned a long time ago to hold a poker face. She looked at the stack of folders confronting her in a pile on her desk, grabbed the first one, and got to work.

CHAPTER
18

Summer was coming to an end. Nearly five weeks had passed since Michael had spoken to Elizabeth. He missed her. There had been too much cluttering his mind, and his time, following the fire. His wife, Laura, along with the Palmer Family Vineyard manager, chief financial officer, cellar master, accountant, support staff and marketing reps were occupying large portable offices on the very same ground where the winery offices once stood. The fire marshal had not yet released his report. The insurance company had been contacted but seemed uninterested for the moment, although Michael knew better. Law enforcement had disappeared as suddenly as they had arrived. There had been no story about the fire in the news media. The employees had been reassured that they would not lose their jobs. There was nothing more to do, except work and wait. And of course, worry.

Laura had only returned to their San Francisco home for an overnight visit one time since the fire. It made Michael miserable inside to think that he used the term "visit" to describe her presence. He told himself that he understood. He was empty, and he knew he would never be consequential to her again. It was difficult on his ego. Even though he hadn't loved her romantically in years, he couldn't stand the thought that she didn't need him. They had lived separate lives for so long that they had become strangers. They used work as an excuse. It was a transactional relationship. Roommates now. Each doing as they wished. He had Elizabeth, but he had no idea if Laura had someone else. Honestly, he didn't care. He wanted Laura to see him as the great provider and supporter. But she hadn't for years, despite the fact that his company's funding was the only reason the winery hadn't gone under. It cut to the quick.

Michael recognized that his oldest children were most likely out of the house for good. He told them about the fire, but neither were concerned. Of course, he had downplayed the event when he broke the news to them. They were busy "studying," or more accurately, having the time of their lives which came with the freedom of being away. Michael longed for that freedom. It was exhausting to know that hundreds of others depended upon him for their livelihoods as part of the Mason Recruiting team. It was a daily burden to carry the weight of admitting to himself that his wife's business was woefully underinsured. It was also tiring to be trotted out at winery gatherings, political fundraisers, and other time wasting events carefully choreographed by his wife. Maintaining a home in the City and a ranch in the Valley was also growing old. Yes, he understood that his problems were blessings, but he and Laura had both worked hard to acquire their holdings and their status. And God knew, that's what mattered most.

It broke Michael's heart that Aiden, their youngest, missed his mother so much. He was a sharp kid. He understood that his father was also suffering. Aiden pretended to accept why his mother had chosen the winery over her son and husband. The fire. That was the rationalization. Deep inside both Aiden and Michael knew that Laura had always put her career above everything else. Michael watched over the years as Aiden compensated by showing his interest in his mother's family business. He spent time wandering the vineyards. He asked questions of the cellar master. He spent pieces of his summers out at the ranch. Aiden seemed to enjoy it all. He probably knew that if he studied, eventually he would continue his mother's legacy. A recruiting business, even at its most glamorous as an international Fortune

100 company, was uninteresting. The PFV Winery felt as though it were the only tie that bound Aiden to his mother. He accepted it.

The relationship between father and son was a bright spot for Michael. At one point, he had been jealous of the commitment Aiden seemed to share with Laura. However, over time Michael came to recognize that Aiden needed the winery. He wanted to earn his mother's love. Michael had his son's love and adoration. Aiden cherished his father for being his dad. Not as a business entrepreneur, or wealthy status driven person, but rather for the million little things. The soccer games. The rides to school, which occurred more often than not. The packed school lunches. Knowing that his father quietly opened the bedroom door to check on his son before going to bed himself.

Each Mason family member did their best to fulfill their individual needs. For the boys, it was school. For Laura, work. For Michael, it was complicated. He needed his job. He needed the boys. But he also needed Elizabeth.

* * * * *

It was an unusually warm evening when Michael's name flashed across Elizabeth's phone screen. He had finally picked up the phone and dialed her number. She had missed him, but she would never tell *him* that. She felt sick inside that they might never have another encounter. It wasn't the money anymore. Or the attention. Definitely not the sex. She cared about him. She wanted to know that he cared about her for more than an hour, an afternoon, or a weekend. Elizabeth wanted to know that she was on Michael's mind. That he thought about her, and wondered how she was spending her time, and if she were happy, and how he could make her happy. She was endlessly lost in a relationship which she no longer controlled. He had all the power. She had given it to him. She pretended that she had competence, strength, and of course, sexiness as only Elizabeth might. She wanted him. All to herself. She couldn't relax anymore. She thought about Michael constantly. Wondering where he was, what he was doing with his time, and who he might be sharing himself with on a Saturday morning or on a Sunday evening. She wanted him to think about her, not Laura or even the boys. Elizabeth knew that Michael's marriage to Laura was only on paper. Still, she couldn't stand the possibility that the two spent any time together as a couple. He had made it clear that it wasn't the case, but where had he been hiding for these past weeks?

It was as though Elizabeth were slipping into her authentic self. She was, after all, Sarah. The girl from Pacific Grove with big dreams. Sarah had been left behind nearly 10 years ago. Elizabeth was a woman. But Sarah had been a mere child. She was the girl who would never quite be enough. Sarah would never escape her difficult upbringing, her job at the restaurant, or her inability to rise above it all. She would never be fully competent, instead apologizing as her default to make others feel comfortable, just as her mother would do when assisting guests at Spanish Bay. Sarah knew that she would never be wealthy like all those tourists and vacation homeowners in Carmel. Instead, she could strive for middle class, get married, have a child, and work full-time alongside her husband to afford daycare, an annual vacation, and two car payments.

Identically as frightening was Elizabeth's counterfeit East Coast life. She would never escape her wealthy family, soulless pretense, and sheer boredom. She would always be her father's darling while accepting his cruelty. She would remain jealous of the relationship that her mother and middle brother shared. She would never have the influence of her older brother, the Fourth, despite knowing that she was brighter and more capable. Elizabeth would return from her West Coast adventures to settle for an affluent someone. He would be handsome and witty, standing out among their friends, and quite pleased with himself that he had acquired her. She would follow her mother's path, volunteering for all the most visible charities, joining clubs, and remaining particular about her looks. She would use her law school education to have a seat at the table, but she would never be taken seriously.

As she contemplated answering Michael's call, she was appalled with herself. She hated both roles and how they might play out. Elizabeth no longer preferred either woman. She only wanted one thing. Him.

Elizabeth answered on the fourth ring. She was surprised that Michael would call before 7:00 p.m. She cleared her throat before answering, wanting to sound self-assured and not at all bothered by the fact that Michael had left her wondering. Longing.

"Well, hello," she answered. She had nearly added the word "stranger," but already that sounded desperate. God, she hated this game, and yet, she was so very good at it.

"Hi, it's me," Michael replied.

Funny, he didn't sound like himself, Elizabeth thought. Then again, maybe she was starting to forget what he sounded like on the other end of the line.

"Will you have dinner with me in Sausalito tonight? I'll send a car."

Elizabeth wanted to scream, "Yes. Yes. Yes. I miss you." Instead, she calmly replied, "Of course. What time were you thinking?"

Michael agreed to send a car at 7:30 p.m. He asked her to dress casually. He knew she would comply.

The car arrived at her California Street home at exactly 7:20 p.m. Elizabeth made the driver wait. The optics were those of understated elegance. Sheer white blouse, faded jeans, sneakers, a backpack, and a baseball cap. It was a $10,000 ensemble disguised as something thrown together. Michael would know. That was what he paid for when he shared his time with her.

The drive across the bay took 40 minutes. For the first time, Elizabeth would keep Michael waiting. He had chosen an easygoing place on the water, the Topmast. The driver dropped her directly in front of the restaurant's entrance. Elizabeth waited for him to open the sedan's door. The ride had been uneventful. Elizabeth was lost in her own thoughts about the meeting. His last minute plans. His driver. His location. She said nothing to the chauffeur for the entire drive. She nodded that she was grateful for his silence as she exited the vehicle and walked the dozen or so steps to the restaurant's entrance before disappearing inside.

The sun was setting on the Topmast's dark interior. Soft jazz music was piped in across the dining room. Small votive candles danced light across the tables which were covered in standard white linen. She could see Michael from the hostess stand. He was sitting at a table for two in the far-left corner overlooking the water. She took a deep breath then slowly approached the table, placing her hand on his right shoulder to signal she had arrived. He turned and motioned to the chair opposite his. He didn't stand or even place his hand on hers. It was all so very cold. Elizabeth imagined that this would be their final encounter. How she wished she was sitting across from elderly Richard. The man who had bought and paid for her home. The man who had nothing but money left to give. She would be in control. She would be the bearer of bad news. Instead, she found herself in Richard's position. Just waiting. Being summoned only to be burned.

Michael had a glass of red wine in front of him. There were two water glasses and a small vase filled with tiny blue flowers also adorning the table. There was no bucket of ice chilling a bottle of champagne as he had so often ordered over the years. This was not a celebration. It was a funeral.

Elizabeth pulled her chair out and sat down. She thought about removing the baseball cap but decided to wear it. The hat's visor felt like a shield. This entire scene was beyond casual in her eyes. Elizabeth Stevens would have expected Michael to rise and greet her, pulling out her chair as he had done so many times. But not tonight. Her poker face was almost certain to have a tell if Michael's behavior continued in this manner.

"Relax," he said to her in an almost intimidating tone.

She was furious. With herself for so obviously wearing her feelings on her face. But also, for allowing him to behave like a spoiled frat boy. She didn't deserve this, no matter what price he was willing to pay. This was not a made-up office scene or a naughty hotel rendezvous. This was her life, and he was playing games.

"I have something I need to tell you," he began. "But first, I want to apologize for being so incredibly distracted these past few weeks. I know we have no commitment to each other, but I have been completely absent, and for that, I *am* sorry."

Elizabeth sat so still she could hear her own heartbeat in her ears. She wanted to soak up every word. This was not what she had expected. Certainly, a kind word about how much he had enjoyed her company, or maybe some sort of excuse as to why he was concluding their relationship. But she hadn't expected an apology coming after such a cool reception from the moment she had entered the restaurant and approached him.

She decided it was best not to respond. Instead, she leaned into him from across the table. Her unspoken language told Michael that she wished him to continue. She would be patient and wait until he was ready. She would smile and twist the ends of her dark hair in her fingers, as if the gesture had been unconscious. Nothing she did was ever unscripted.

"There was a fire at the winery," Michael said, ready to disclose his news.

CHAPTER
19

The Napa Valley Sheriff's Office was infused with men. The sheriff, undersheriff, three captains and five lieutenants were all men. Their Operations Division housed most of its sworn personnel. This included patrol officers and detectives. Technically, Detective Sufford was listed on the roster under the sheriff's Investigative Bureau. This meant that his cases could include a broad array of criminal activity, ranging from child abuse to sexual assault to murder. Fortunately, the number of homicides in Napa County hovered around three annually. In fact, Detective Sufford had yet to work one.

In a region of seemingly endless vineyards, rolling hills, and majestic oaks, there was a fact which the sheriff's department didn't want shared with visitors, or most especially its residents. Statistically speaking, Napa Valley's residents were at a relatively high risk of becoming crime victims. Mainly property crimes; theft and destruction. These were the crimes that Detective Jeff Sufford was regularly assigned. It was a dirty little secret that homes were broken into at an alarming rate. Not violent crimes by any means, but the victims would become emotional, oftentimes shedding tears. The majority of the thefts occurred when the occupants were not at home, between the hours of 10:00 a.m. and 3:00 p.m. Detective Sufford spent a great deal of time taking statements and acting as a counselor while people told stories about the loss of irreplaceable antiques or their grandmother's heirloom jewelry. The victims felt vulnerable. Violated. It was draining at times to listen to their stories. It was also mundane and repetitive work. So, when Jeff got the call to represent Napa County at the law enforcement meeting in Oakland, he wasn't disappointed.

His enthusiasm to be involved in a possible arson was suddenly shut down. In less than 24 hours, the assignment had been withdrawn. No interviewing potential suspects. No looking over lab reports and reviewing evidence. No burger with Detective Danielle Philipson.

Maybe he could take one last look at the scene, Jeff thought to himself. The winery *was* in the Napa Valley Sheriff's jurisdiction. It was just a 20-minute drive from the office. Would anyone notice if he disappeared for an hour, the detective asked himself. He retrieved his keys that he'd thrown across his desk in frustration, after having been dropped from the investigation.

It was broad daylight and nobody so much as offered a nod toward Jeff as he passed several officers in the parking lot, where every make of law enforcement vehicle was housed. Jeff preferred a sedan to an SUV, particularly since most of his duties involved taking victim statements. He felt the car was more subtle than an oversized SUV.

Detective Sufford soon found himself pulling up to the gate at the Palmer Family Vineyard. An official looking guard was posted, and the gate was closed. A sign read, "Closed to the Public for Special Event." Okay, Jeff thought to himself. It hadn't occurred to him that the gate would be locked, but it made sense. Once the public saw the damage, word would get out, he guessed. Still, the winery wouldn't be able to use this ruse for more than a few days.

Jeff rolled his driver's side window down. The guard walked the few feet toward the car.

"May I help you," asked the man dressed in a long-sleeve dark green shirt, and sporting a PFV logo on his left breast pocket.

"Yes," said Jeff matter-of-factly. "I'm Detective Jeff Sufford with the Napa Valley Sheriff's Office. I'm just doing a bit of follow-up. I won't be here long."

Jeff flashed his ID and badge. The guard responded by stepping back, pushing an automatic opener, and allowing Jeff to pass through the expansive iron gate. Funny, thought Jeff. He hadn't noticed the gate the previous day. Then again, it had obviously been open and he had been distracted by the fire.

The paved road leading to the visitor's area was about a third of a mile from the main entrance. Detective Sufford positioned himself into a compact parking space and shut off his engine. He looked to his left and saw a couple of trucks parked in the employee lot. It was eerily quiet. It had been just over 30 hours since the fire had occurred. The detective was almost certain that nobody was working at the winery today, except for field and plant operations which couldn't wait. The first order of business would be to clear the area, so that visitors could be welcomed back as soon as possible, Jeff suspected.

Detective Sufford got out of his car, shut the door, then simply stood still. The scene was in sharp contrast to the previous day when multiple fire marshal trucks, Napa County Sheriff's cars, and a slew of PFV Winery employee vehicles covered the area. The smell from the embers continued to loom. There had been so much activity that it hadn't occurred to Jeff, or apparently to Detective Danielle Philipson, to survey the entire property. Jeff understood that it was about 400 acres, so it wasn't something he was going to do in his sedan in just a few minutes. However, he wondered to himself if having a complete picture of the area might be beneficial. He also wondered whether someone from the fire marshal's office had made the trek, or if they might be investigating in the next couple of days. Jeff supposed that a drone might be the answer. Still, he always thought it best to have boots on-the-ground to fully understand the landscape. The longer he stared at the burned out complex, the more he wanted to be assigned to this case. And, he wanted Detective Philipson to partner with him.

As any good detective does, Jeff began thinking about the circumstances leading up to this point. It had been Laura Palmer-Mason, the winery's owner, who had gone so far as to make personal phone calls to the Napa Valley and San Francisco sheriffs in the middle of the night. She had enough pull to get San Francisco to reassign the fire to Alameda County, as a result of the chaos surrounding the hostage crisis in the City that morning. She had apparently rushed to the winery ahead of the fire department. She was the third generation to run the family enterprise, and she was all in. So, it made sense to Jeff that the best way to tour the entire property might be to contact Mrs. Mason directly. Jeff suspected that she would not only be ready with whatever vehicle and accompanying winery personnel he might request, but she would appreciate being given the VIP treatment by law enforcement, which she clearly expected.

The detective returned to his car and made the short drive back to his office. First, he would need to determine if the fire marshal had toured the property, either with personnel or using some sort of technology: a drone, satellite imaging, or maybe a CAL Fire helicopter. If not, were they planning to survey the entire region in the next few days, if at all? Detective Sufford was a practical person. There was no need for an elaborate story to get the information. He still had the business card which Fire Marshal Tom Navarro had handed him the previous day. Detective Danielle Philipson had been given an identical card. Jeff picked up his office line and dialed the number. He knew the caller ID would read "Napa Valley Sheriff's Office." The phone rang four times before Navarro's voicemail picked up. Jeff left a brief message asking Navarro to return the call. The detective purposefully did not give a reason. Based on the limited time spent with the fire marshal the previous afternoon, Jeff decided that Tom Navarro would be more than curious, with his, "I've got a lot of experience, and I know what I'm doing out here," attitude which he had revealed to Jeff and Danielle the prior afternoon.

It wasn't five minutes before Jeff's line rang.

"Detective Sufford," Jeff answered in an official tone. He recognized the caller's voice immediately.

"Good morning, Detective Sufford. This is Tom Navarro returning your call. What may I do for you," Navarro asked.

Wow, this guy was an open book, thought Jeff, a bit surprised that Navarro hadn't held off on making the return call for at least a couple of hours. He would fold in minutes in any sort of interrogation. Jeff then admitted to himself that, yeah, he had an ego, too.

"Ah, good morning Tom," Jeff replied. "Thanks so much for returning my call. Hey, I know you are probably up to your elbows in paperwork and evidence over there, and I understand you've decided against a request for law enforcement support." Jeff waited. He wanted to make certain Tom's ego was playing catch up.

"Yeah," said Navarro. "As you saw yesterday, my investigators bagged a ton of evidence. It's going to be weeks before we get lab results back, and there's no reason to tie you or your partner up with this thing," Navarro responded.

Jeff wasn't about to correct Navarro. Technically, Danielle wasn't his partner. They had simply been sent on behalf of interagency cooperation, and at the request of the wealthy Laura Palmer-Mason. Well technically, Danielle had been sent at the request of the San Francisco Sheriff's Office. Not that it mattered right now.

"That's what Detective Philipson and I thought when we were out there yesterday. I think we were more of a distraction than any sort of help," Jeff said smiling to himself. He knew Tom Navarro needed a great big pat on the back.

"Well, we appreciate you all coming out there like that, but yeah, we've got it covered. So, what can I do for you?"

Jeff wanted his question about the property answered, but he needed to do it in a roundabout manner.

"Tom, do you think there's any need to look over the entire property or is that just a rookie idea and a total waste of time," Jeff asked almost holding his breath.

He didn't want to give Navarro any ideas to go looking outside his own yellow tape. Instead, Jeff wanted his question to sound as though an amateur was throwing darts at something and had no idea what a fire investigation involved.

"Yeah, I can see that maybe from your perspective in law enforcement you might want to look at literally every single thing. But from the fire perspective, you've really got to concentrate on the main scene and then a specific radius beyond the ignition, growth, and full development of the fire, and of course, the resulting ash and debris."

Tom Navarro was the one on fire now. He definitely wanted to impress the detective on the other end of the line with his technical terminology.

"Ah, I see," said Jeff. "Frankly, you're speaking a foreign language to me right now, Tom."

Jeff could hear Navarro chuckle on the other end of the line. The fire marshal was pleased with himself and the answer he had provided to the detective.

"Well, thanks so much. I'll let you get back to it," Jeff said sounding sincere.

"Of course," Navarro responded. "Have a good day."

The phone clicked and went silent. Detective Jeff Sufford had his answer. This guy wasn't going to have his staff look for anything more than a couple hundred feet from the destroyed complex.

Jeff's next operational step was to get his boss, and more importantly, Danielle's sergeant, to agree that the two detectives needed to go out and have a good look around, since the fire marshal wasn't going to do it. Alameda County Sergeant Ron Hauser had taken the lead on the hours-old investigation from the law enforcement side of things. Maybe Jeff ought to contact Danielle before speaking to his direct supervisor. If the request came from Hauser, he knew his boss would comply.

One of the unspoken rules that detectives carried with them was to admit that a crime scene was never straightforward. Evidence could be found hundreds of miles away, in dumpsters, on the side of a road, in someone's attic, on a computer, or just about anywhere. It was shortsighted to assume evidence came in the form of a neat little package. Jeff could take one of two tracks. Call Danielle and explain why the two detectives needed to get her boss to agree to his scheme. Or go with his initial plan to call Laura Mason and get her stirred up. Jeff opted with the latter option.

CHAPTER
20

Elizabeth waited patiently for Michael to continue while a cascade of thoughts passed through her mind. What is he talking about? When? What did this have to do with their relationship? She sat, poised, and waiting while he carefully chose his next words and sipped an expensive burgundy from his glass. Before Michael could say anything else, a waiter approached the couple and asked Elizabeth if she wanted something to drink. A white wine.

Michael then chronicled the events of the past few weeks. The fire. Involvement by multiple law enforcement agencies from two distinct jurisdictions. The thankfulness that nobody had been hurt. The fact that Laura had made personal calls to two sheriffs, much to his dismay. The reality that his youngest son, Aiden, felt clearly abandoned by his own mother. That nothing came before the family winery. The fire marshal's inconclusive findings. The words tumbled from his mouth like a raging waterfall. He could no longer hide his fears and concerns from Elizabeth. What Michael didn't understand, was that after sharing four years of intimacy, she was well aware of his weaknesses. He didn't hide them very well.

In unburdening himself with the truth, Michael shared that he had knowingly underinsured the winery. He justified his actions to Elizabeth, as he had justified them to himself and his CFO. The decision had been a matter of necessity. He had absolved himself with the lie that reducing the insurance coverage had been somehow made from a place of love to save hundreds of thousands of dollars and his wife's business. Elizabeth didn't care. About any of it. She only cared about the toll it was taking on Michael, and the distraction it had caused. Michael would never fully focus his attention on her, as long as he had other things occupying his mind. The fire wasn't something small. Clearly, it was consuming Michael's consciousness.

Michael seemed to almost tremble as he finished sharing his narrative with Elizabeth. He was emotionally and physically exhausted. Elizabeth felt Michael's uneasiness. It was her role to comfort him, not to be abandoned by him. She had completely misread the purpose of their rendezvous. She was relieved. She wanted Michael for herself. Maybe now, she would finally have him. Of course, she knew it would be complicated. Divorce was one thing. A fire investigation into his wife's business was another. The fire could ultimately cost him his reputation. She told herself she didn't care, but if she was being honest, she wanted Michael for who he was as a provider, thinker, and entrepreneur. It frightened her to think that he could become someone else. Ironically, it was what she had done intentionally all those years ago when she was practically still a child. Creating Elizabeth from ash.

The couple ordered dinner then proceeded to push their food around on their plates, barely taking a bite. After three glasses of wine, they were no longer sober. Nor were they drunk. Michael put his credit card down on the table, signaling that they were ready to leave. After exchanging niceties with the waiter, the pair got up from their chairs, walked out the front door of the restaurant, and placed themselves into the backseat of the town car which had dropped Elizabeth some two hours earlier.

The driver said nothing as he navigated the two-lane road through Sausalito in the dark. It became apparent to Elizabeth, through her slightly unsteady state, that the driver was headed for the Hotel at the Cliffs. It was perched high above the water, providing an expansive view of the Richardson Bay houseboat community along the shore. The houseboats dated back to the late 1800s when wealthy San Franciscans began buying up old fishing shacks and converting them into floating homes. Today, tourists came to admire the architecture of the structures which were largely occupied by full-time residents.

As the car climbed to the shelf of the cliffs, the hotel's façade came fully into view. Elizabeth could see hundreds of twinkling white lights strung across the roof, trusses, rafters, porches, and balconies. The charming inn glowed in the darkness like a beacon over the tiny town. It was impossible to eye the Golden Gate Bridge from the hotel's vantage point, but it wasn't necessary. The view had a magic of its own.

The driver pulled directly in front of a two-story cottage. He ushered his passengers from the car and helped Elizabeth inside. Michael quietly shut the door as he crossed the threshold. The view was breathtaking. Elizabeth needed to regain her composure and present herself as the sophisticated woman which Michael found so attractive. She was having difficulty between the effects of the wine infused with her true feelings. She was afraid, yet exhilarated. A bottle of champagne was chilling on the balcony between two chairs which overlooked a spectacular waterscape. It was perfect in every detail, except, of course, for the fact that Michael was a married man with no intention of ever leaving his wife. On top of that, he was now facing a potentially serious legal entanglement. She cringed. Wealthy, East Coast Elizabeth from a nearly royal Manhattan family should not have found herself in this predicament. But in this moment, she didn't care. Within seconds, Elizabeth was in Michael's arms with his lips on her neck.

CHAPTER
21

Laura Palmer-Mason was a person of action. When she wanted something, she wanted it now. She wasn't overly demanding. Well, *she* didn't think so. Others, if asked, would have disagreed. Laura believed that if she wanted something done purposefully and correctly, she needed to do it herself. This overbearing tendency had cost her nearly everything. Her family. Friendships. Her sanity at times. She pretended not to see it. And her professional demands bled over into her personal life. She would invite her Stanford University sorority sisters to the ranch for long weekends, providing them with lavish meals, spa treatments, and even horseback riding lessons. While her friends played and drank and went into town and shopped, Laura would remain at the winery for hours, proofreading contracts or fussing over private party details.

She treated her husband and children as if they were an obligation, a stopover on the way to an exotic destination. She could feel the panic build on weekends as she made the hour-long drive from the ranch across the Golden Gate and back to their home in San Francisco. It wasn't as if the house or her family were liabilities, where some sort of domestic duty beckoned. She had a chef who visited the local markets, purchasing the freshest ingredients for the meals he would prepare. A housekeeper made certain everything was tidy.

Her children, especially her youngest son, Aiden, were always happy to see her walk through the door. Michael, her husband, was never demanding. He would leave her alone to take a long, hot bath or just sit in the living room with a good book. Of course, that was largely a fantasy. She hadn't read anything for pleasure in years. Instead, she would spend her time looking over budgets or marketing concepts.

Occasionally, she had attended some of the many sporting events which her three sons enjoyed. She was relieved when their oldest was accepted to UC Berkeley. It was a short drive to the university, but he had become so involved in his new life over the past three years that he no longer bargained, or even asked, for her attention. With their middle son now across the country at Georgetown, she knew she would soon have to make the obligatory trip to the nation's capital for parent's weekend. Otherwise, she wouldn't see him until Christmas break.

It was Aiden who adored her, and she took full advantage. She would bring him to the winery on weekends when he wasn't involved in school activities, and he spent time with her at the ranch during the summers. It helped to maintain the illusion that they were close. But Laura knew she was never fully engaged. Instead, Aiden would trail behind the vineyard managers and workers, learning about grape standards, the equipment, and wine making processes. On rare evenings, they would watch a movie together with a giant bowl of popcorn between mother and son. Still, she would use the time to look through emails and send text messages, all the while pretending she was watching the movie plot unfold.

She didn't feel as though she had failed her three boys, but rather she had given Michael the opportunity to be the father they needed. A parent who was always available to them. The boys didn't require nurture and love from her to become men. They needed their father to be a role model, teaching lessons in responsibility, international business dealings, and a strong work ethic. It never occurred to Laura that she too could be a mentor in all three realms. However, she was a terrible example of how to find balance and peace in work. Laura

all would be back to business as usual after a long weekend. While the majority of the workers hadn't seen past the parking lot, the winery board was led over to the site by Laura, personally. The reaction had been expected. Tears from a couple, but mainly silence. It was a small team. They loved each other. If they were hurting, they knew Laura was barely breathing.

For such a modest group, it had always seemed a bit conspicuous that the winery office buildings had a rather substantial presence. It had been deliberately designed that way to symbolize how far PFV had come since their founding, when Laura's grandfather and father had shared a tiny warehouse space. Each executive occupied beautiful, individual offices. An extensive kitchen and separate dining room were also located within the walls. Laura had a corner office. Similar to her husband, Michael, she had sweeping window views, though not overlooking anything as dramatic as the Golden Gate Bridge. Three conference rooms had also been constructed. The largest could hold 25 people comfortably and was used for industry meetings. Two smaller conference spaces provided intimacy and were valuable when meeting with more than a couple of people. It didn't take a genius to understand that rebuilding would be a huge undertaking. Never mind the tremendous cost, both financially and emotionally as projects of this nature tended to drag on endlessly with more problems than solutions.

The Board of Directors maintained their silence following the impromptu parking lot gathering with the employees. Laura turned and headed toward the tasting room. She pulled open the glass door and stood aside allowing each executive to pass. It was an odd space for a meeting, and felt strange, knowing that they were directly across from their now burned down offices. Laura wanted the team together to discuss how they would present a united front. It was next to impossible to think about business when the smell of charred building hung in the air. But business was business, no matter how trite the saying.

The vineyard manager stayed only briefly. He had called his own staff together. They would need to head out to look over the grapes and the soil immediately. Nobody had expected him to stay. A polite but heated discussion then ensued, as each member of the executive staff began thinking about their own responsibilities. They would need temporary space right away, for two reasons. First, the wine industry didn't take time off. There was constant supervision necessary, not only for the grapes, but for the processes. Second, getting back up and running immediately would be an indication to the employees, vendors, and even visitors that the winery was in order and well situated despite the loss. The Board decided to bring portable offices onto the grounds so that office employees could visibly see a sort of "business as usual" scene. The executive team would also be able to continue their work in a co-functioning location. Laura did not like the work-from-home approach, which had become more than a trend. She wanted her employees to work together, face-to-face. Done. Operations would be back underway the following Monday. Visitors. That would be tricky.

Over the next hours, the Board agreed to simply close the main entry gates, station a guard, and post private event signage. The website would be updated to say the same. It was the cellar manager who suggested they confront the visitor situation head on. A new build would take months, and the entire team knew that there would be no construction for weeks at best. But it might be possible to give the appearance of construction. It could begin almost immediately with a load of lumber, a blackout fence, and giant signs reading, "Pardon Our Dust." For good measure a couple of construction company signs could also be posted advertising a contractor and a supplier or two. As long as they were arranging for portable offices, they might as well bring in a small construction trailer. It was brilliant. Laura was impressed. Then when things didn't move along, rumblings about permits and updating the electrical could be shared. It wasn't as though visitors would care, but it made for a complete picture.

The group was so entrenched in their meeting that no one noticed Detective Jeff Sufford's arrival or departure from the visitor's parking area. The detective had only been on the grounds a short while, thinking about the fire marshal's quick dismissal of law enforcement, devising a plan to fully search the 400-acre region, and how to ensure Detective Danielle Philipson would be assigned to join him.

The board meeting ended abruptly, as they almost always did. Once a direction was given and agreed upon, there wasn't room for small talk. Keeping busy and playing an active role in moving the winery forward would be crucial to normalize a punishing situation. Work was familiar. Laura needed to have a closed-door conversation with her CFO, but she didn't want to give even the slightest hint that she would keep information from the entire membership. She had already arranged to meet her chief back at the ranch for lunch. Laura left first. Her CFO stayed around for a few minutes so that no one would be the wiser.

The Mason family ranch was owned jointly by Michael and Laura. It had been Michael's suggestion some dozen years earlier, when it became apparent that her commute between the Valley and the City was taking its toll. On Laura. The children. Work. Their marriage. The ranch property was just over two acres. It was picturesque. The white fencing enclosing the entire property stood in sharp contrast to the surrounding golden green landscape. Cattle ranchers allowed their cows to roam, relying on thick iron crossings to keep herds where they belonged. Many wineries did not mark their property lines. It was enough to stake hundreds of rows of vine. The white fencing sig-naled to everyone that the property belonged to the Masons.

Laura had fallen in love with the place before she and Michael had ever stepped inside the main house. The landscape suited her taste. The home was a single story made of board and batten, with river rock accents. Every inch of the exterior was painted white. A porch wrapped completely around the raised foundation. The entry door was glass, offering a full view to a great room with gorgeous hardwood flooring. The same stone on the façade was used to construct a large fireplace. The bright kitchen was white wood paneled and opened directly onto the family room. The entire place was in sharp contrast to their tall and narrow San Francisco home.

A backyard deck housed an outdoor kitchen. Beyond was a horse stable. There were six stalls, three on each side, with a wide concrete walkway down the center of the barn. Every detail had been considered, from the ventilation to the storage to the hay racks. The stalls were large, offering their inhabitants plenty of space. Like the main house, everything was painted white. There were no animals on the ranch, but shortly after it had been purchased, the Masons brought a horse for each of their sons. Only Aiden learned to ride.

Laura sat at the large kitchen island waiting for her CFO to arrive. She had met Rachel Williams at Stanford. Laura was a senior when Rachel pledged her sorority, Kappa Kappa Gamma. It wasn't the most popular sorority on campus, but the girls formed close ties and were proud of their volunteer work within the community. Laura had served as Rachel's big sister. She helped her through the many rituals which had to be completed prior to initiation. Rachel was thrilled when she was accepted. Normally, their relationship would have fallen off once Laura had graduated. However, she continued her education at the university, entering the MBA program, so she and Rachel remained close. Some 30 years later, and with a lot of history between them, the two women remained best friends. Laura had thought about making Rachel a named partner, but Michael and more than one attorney advised against it. Rachel was handsomely compensated, and truthfully, thankful she had not been made a partner. She didn't want the headache that came with someone else's family business.

Laura could see Rachel's silver SUV pull into the circular drive. She got up from the kitchen island and met her CFO at the door.

"Thanks for driving over," Laura said to Rachel as she entered the house. " I had lunch prepared for us. It's out on the deck."

Rachel proceeded to follow Laura out to the backyard. She had been to the ranch countless times. Sometimes for business and sometimes for pleasure. Laura liked to invite the Board to the ranch for casual dinners away from the winery. They would hold quarterly meetings at the ranch, as well. The two women sat at the round patio table that held an array of salads, breads, and fresh fruits. They helped themselves to servings of each, though neither felt much like eating. Laura poured two glasses of water, then placed her cloth napkin in her lap. Rachel did the same.

"Listen. We need to talk about the insurance," Laura began. "I know it was disrespectful to assign that task to Michael without running it by you. That was my mistake. But now, we need to move forward and assess what our coverage looks like and how soon we can file a claim."

Laura could see that Rachel was stunned. Once she made a decision, Laura never looked back. No second guessing. No regrets. She had declared Michael in charge when it came to certain things, including the insurance. Laura knew that Rachel wouldn't want to look into it. Frankly, Laura wasn't sure she wanted Rachel to be involved, but what choice did she have? She had to get to the bottom of things without tipping off Michael.

"Of course," Rachel answered. "I just need a couple of basic pieces of information, like the name of the insurance company and maybe the policy numbers. Can you get that from Michael?"

Laura had signed a stack of insurance documents in the not too distant past, but she had no idea where Michael kept the information. His office? Their home? Paper copies? On a computer file? Laura quickly realized she would need to do some investigating of her own.

"I will get that for you in the next couple of days," Laura promised Rachel. The two women tried to stay focused on winery functions. Staff were working to secure comfortable and practical portable offices. The vineyard manager was out with his team assessing any vegetation damage. The night manager had assigned himself the job of finding a contractor to set up fencing and staging the beginnings of construction.

The one obvious thing the women didn't discuss was the fire investigation. The fire marshal had warned Laura that it would take longer than she might expect for the lab to complete an official analysis and come back with any findings. He didn't want to give a specific timeline, because he didn't want Laura Palmer-Mason breathing down his neck. He was well aware that she would never tolerate the usual six to eight week process. He would move heaven and earth to accommodate an accelerated timeline.

The two women finished their lunch quickly. She needed Rachel to get back on track with her daily workload to keep wine production flowing. On top of that, Rachel now had the added burden of taking on the insurance work. Laura had tasked herself with the bare minimum regarding the winery's policy. It had been careless of her not to know the name of the company. She was grateful that Rachel hadn't blinked when she disclosed that fact. Laura would have no choice but to leave the ranch and visit her house in the City immediately. She needed to gather the insurance information for her CFO as soon as possible. She would tell Michael that she was exhausted and wanted to come home. He'd buy that.

CHAPTER
22

Detective Jeff Sufford sat calmly at his desk, staring blankly at his two computer monitors as the sheriff's department logo bounced back and forth across both screens. He needed the private cell for Laura Mason. He didn't want to do a computer search from his own terminal. It wasn't as though he were doing anything wrong, but every action was recorded. He wanted to sell his idea as though it had come from the winery owner herself. As he looked around deciding who to ask to do the look up for him, he decided that he might have some luck by going to the file on the shared drive which could be accessed by both the Napa Valley and Alameda County sheriff's offices. He logged into his computer, found the shared folder quickly and opened it. Jeff had already reviewed the contents the prior evening and knew it merely replicated the scant brown folders which had been handed out at the meeting in Oakland. Still, it couldn't hurt to put his eyes on the documents again.

The original folder had contained only three files. This morning, that number had doubled. Jeff could see what time each file had been uploaded. He began with the newest of the three, hopeful that he would find something useful. His hope immediately turned to disappointment. It was the 9-1-1 audio recording Strike one. The second file seemed more promising. It had been uploaded by Fire Marshal

Tom Navarro. Jeff wasn't familiar with forms and documents from the fire marshal's office, so it took him a moment to comprehend what he was looking at on his computer screen. It appeared to be a mapped out version of the winery office footprint. It was a diagram of the fire site, complete with measurements and photographs taken in a grid-like pattern, identifying every inch of the ground that had been behind the yellow tape. The pattern took the shape of twelve-inch by twelve-inch tiles. It was interesting, but it didn't help Jeff. Strike two.

The third file contained more than 100 photos, all in vivid color. Navarro's team had done a thorough job documenting the scene. Jeff decided nothing here was going to help. He pushed his chair back from his desk and looked around the empty office. Strike three. He took a deep breath and for some reason decided to look at the fire scene diagram again. It was methodical and impressive work. Jeff had no idea what he was looking for, but he found the grid patterns interesting. That's when he saw it. At the bottom of one of the pages, scribbled in what was probably the fire marshal's handwriting was a note: Laura, 415-500-0900. The documents had all been scanned. For some reason, Tom had used an official document as a scratch pad. Jeff wrote the number on a lime green post-it note, closed the files, and logged out of the shared drive. He ran the telephone conversation that he was about to have with Laura Mason through his head, as he often did before contacting a victim or a potential suspect. It was just past 1:00 p.m. when he picked up the phone and dialed.

* * * * *

The Napa Valley Sheriff's Office caller ID scrolled across the vehicle's display screen. Laura Mason was nearly halfway between the ranch and her home in San Francisco, with the winery's insurance on her mind. She knew Michael wouldn't be home for hours, giving her the opportunity to poke around her own house unencumbered. The call both startled and pleased Laura. She picked up on the second ring.

"Hello. Who am I speaking to," Laura instantly questioned, fully aware that there was a law enforcement official on the other end of the line.

"Good afternoon, Mrs. Mason. My name is Jeff Sufford. I am a detective with the Napa Valley Sheriff's Office. I'm sorry for the loss you have experienced at your family business."

Laura's tone softened. "Oh. Yes officer. What may I do for you?"

"I'm not certain if you are aware, but yesterday afternoon I was out at your property, along with Alameda County Sheriff's Detective Danielle Philipson. We were asked to provide any assistance necessary to the fire marshal," Jeff paused. He wanted to hear the mood in Mrs. Mason's voice.

Laura answered, "Yes, I knew that detectives made a visit. I'm sorry I didn't meet you in person. You must have arrived after I had already left the property. What can I do for you?"

This was the moment of truth, thought Jeff. Laura Mason was clearly in her car. She wasn't going to talk much longer. He needed to get to the point.

"Well, as you may be aware, the fire marshal has decided to move forward without law enforcement. However, I believe that we may bring some unique insight to the incident. Specifically, I would like to work with Detective Philipson to do a thorough search across your entire 400-acre winery, rather than focusing solely on the radius near the office buildings."

Laura remained silent. Jeff had about 30 more seconds to sell the idea, and himself.

"I know you have a well-established relationship with the law enforcement communities in Napa Valley and in San Francisco. It would be a disservice to you not to have a full assessment of your property," Jeff finished, deciding he had said enough.

Laura was only too eager to continue the conversation. "Well, I appreciate your concern detective. Do you know if the fire marshal is planning such a review?"

"Well, Mrs. Mason. I spoke with Fire Marshal Tom Navarro a while ago. They are very busy as you might imagine working with the lab to examine dozens of pieces of evidence," said Jeff.

"I see," said Laura. "I think you have an excellent point detective. Can you text me the name and number of the person I need to speak with to get this larger search underway?"

Yes, thought Jeff to himself. He was fairly certain Mrs. Mason would contact Danielle's sergeant, Ron Hauser, and the ball would get rolling immediately. If not, Laura would make sure heads would roll.

"Absolutely, Mrs. Mason. I will send you his contact information right away," Jeff replied, trying to keep his voice from giving away his enthusiasm.

"Thank you," said Laura. "And detective, you can call me Laura."

The phone went silent. On one end of the line, Detective Jeff Sufford sat at his desk, pleased with himself. On the other end, Laura felt anxious and impatient. If someone was out to get her, she wanted to know sooner rather than later. If the fire marshal wasn't going to search every square foot of her property, law enforcement would, and her relationship with the sheriffs ran deep. They owed her more than a couple of detectives for an afternoon.

Laura pulled into the driveway of her San Francisco home. She made the call to Alameda County Sergeant Ron Hauser before turning off the ignition. She wanted someone out roaming her property as soon as possible. She could provide a vehicle, staff, or whatever officers would need to best understand and navigate the acreage and its many dirt roads.

The phone call to Ron Hauser had taken less than five minutes. Laura Palmer-Mason would get what she wanted. Attention.

CHAPTER
23

Sergeant Ron Hauser shook his head. "Jesus Christ," he mumbled under his breath. This morning he had been told by Fire Marshal Tom Navarro that the services of the Alameda County Sheriff's Office would not be needed. Now, he was being confronted by Mrs. Laura Palmer-Mason demanding that he get his detectives involved. Ron Hauser didn't like taking orders from anyone. This was God damned ridiculous! A younger Ron Hauser would have used a string of four-letter words after a phone call like the one he had just received from Mrs. Mason. He then would have slammed down the phone's receiver, ultimately winding up in his supervisor's office. Twenty-five years in law enforcement had taught him that outbursts got you nowhere. It was better to blow off a little steam at the gun range or after hours at a neighborhood bar.

Technically, Hauser didn't need approval from anyone to send officers out to look around. He had been assigned as the law enforcement lead to the fire just two days prior. But that was before the fire marshal had declared he didn't require any additional assistance. Hauser knew it was a bit of stretch to run a couple of officers out to the Palmer Family Vineyard since Alameda County had done this as a favor to the San Francisco Sheriff's Office in the first place, and the winery was situated in Napa Valley. In the name of interagency coordination, hc decided he'd better call his counterpart at the Napa Valley Sheriff's Office.

Laura Mason had been all too eager on the phone to volunteer her staff, vehicles, or anything else his officers might need. Hauser wouldn't accept the use of her private cars, but a couple of staff leading officers around the property was probably a good idea. He was surprised that Mrs. Mason wanted the entire region assessed. It didn't seem like something that would occur to a civilian. It sounded more like something that would occur to law enforcement. Even then, large searches didn't usually get budget approval unless someone had gone missing. On the other hand, Laura Palmer-Mason was not your typical citizen. She probably had multiple county sheriffs listed as favorites on her phone. She had money, influence, and power.

Sergeant Houser made the call to the Napa Valley Sheriff's Office. They were very quick to agree to the winery expedition, no questions asked. Probably because Mrs. Palmer-Mason and her fancy friends had contributed to their boss's campaign. Twice. Ron Hauser wasn't surprised by his counterpart's response. He could, however, note the displeasure in his tone with the fact that Mrs. Mason had contacted Hauser first and not the Napa Valley sheriff, since the winery was in their jurisdiction. Nevertheless, words like "absolutely" and "whatever she needs" came from his colleague's mouth.

Sheriffs didn't turn down requests from their biggest donors. Of course, nobody in law enforcement would admit to it openly. In addition to being a donor, Laura Mason owned one of the largest wineries in the entire region. That meant tax revenue for the county. Turn down Mrs. Laura Palmer-Mason and be on the receiving end of the fallout at some point. Since Detective Jeff Sufford had already been involved, they would re-assign him to the winery fire. Houser agreed he would do the same, designating Detective Danielle Philipson as the Alameda County Sheriff's Office liaison.

Danielle would be the first to get the news. The second Sergeant Ron Hauser was off the phone, he was out of his chair, standing in his office doorway motioning for her to join him. It was already the middle of the afternoon, so he wanted Danielle to start coordinating with Detective Sufford and the winery for the 400-acre site visit.

"Looks like you're going to go on a wine tour," Hauser told her as he sat down in his desk chair. Danielle remained standing and looked at her sergeant with a questioning glance.

"Mrs. Mason wants a complete going over of her entire property. All four hundred acres," said Hauser. "I'm re-assigning you to the winery fire. You'll continue working with Detective Jeff Sufford."

Danielle felt butterflies in her stomach, which seemed somewhat embarrassing at her age, she thought. She was excited, but she was also a little confused.

"What gives," questioned Danielle.

"Well, the fire marshal may not want us poking around, but Mrs. Palmer-Mason does, and we are still operating on behalf of the request from the SF Sheriff. So, you're it."

"Just to be clear," said Danielle. "You want me to work with Detective Sufford to run around 400 acres belonging to the PFV winery?"

"You got it. Better get to work."

Danielle walked back to her desk. On one hand, she was glad to be working with Jeff Sufford. On the other, what in the world could they expect to find by driving across 400 acres of land in the Valley? No one had been reported missing. They weren't looking for a dead body. It had been a fire for Christ's sake. An expensive fire, but there hadn't even been a single injury. As a cop, she would confront only the immediate facts of an incident. Robbery. Car accident. Domestic abuse. Sure, as a detective over the past couple of years, she had come to realize that where a cop's job ended, a detective's job began. There were always more than two sides to every story. Sometimes there were six or eight. The details leading up to a crime were oftentimes more important in getting to the truth than looking at the actual crime scene. Still, the fire was only days old. Was there even a crime? The fire marshal probably wouldn't have any results back from the lab for several weeks. It would be up to him to determine whether or not it had been arson or an accident. Sometimes, there was not enough evidence to get to a specific determination. Shit just happened.

* * * * *

Some 60 miles away, Jeff Sufford was learning from his supervisor that his actions had made an impact. He and Detective Danielle Philipson would be exploring the PFV Winery acreage together. Jeff had counted on Laura Mason to come down sternly on the sergeant, and she had not disappointed.

Jeff decided he would give Danielle a call. Now that his scheme to re-involve himself and Detective Philipson was on track, he realized that it was going to be a big project. He wanted to be as meticulous as the fire marshal had been with his grid layout of the burn site. It would be next to impossible to perform that type of exacting work over 400 acres. From an operational standpoint, however, a method needed to be developed before he and Danielle took to the winery's roads, fields, outbuildings, and whatever else sat within the property border. The entire point of the exercise was to determine if there had been any sort of foul play. Mr. Fire Marshal was all too eager to tell anyone who would listen that the buck stopped with him. But things got overlooked when egos got in the way. Waiting on lab results was exhausting. In the end, there were only two possible outcomes. Find something. Find nothing. Either way, Laura Mason would be placated, and that would in turn put a smile on the Napa Valley Sheriff's face.

Jeff was good at reading people. Mrs. Mason was sure to be someone who valued her privacy and her control. It was unlikely that she would allow two random detectives to have free rein over her extensive property. She would undoubtedly send a couple of her most loyal employees with the detectives to keep an eye on things and to report back to her. Certainly, winery staff would be necessary to navigate the land, but they would also be able to fill their boss in on the performance and behavior of the detectives.

The law enforcement pair would ride together, most likely in Danielle's SUV since his sedan wasn't made for any sort of off-roading. They would need to be able to talk without interruption but also with the knowledge that the Palmer Family Vineyard staff were taking mental notes. As it was, Jeff knew that Laura would expect her own team to report back to her, as she would absolutely want every single detail. He wanted to relay his thoughts to Detective Philipson to be conscious of the fact that Mrs. Mason would send well-liked and well-versed staff on the field visit. The best they could do to circumnavigate Laura's curiosity would be to give her regular updates, especially since there was no way he and Danielle would roam 400 acres in one afternoon. If they did the job too quickly, it would appear as though the detectives were "phoning it in." Oh no, that would not suit Mrs. Mason. Truthfully, Jeff wasn't in a huge hurry. However, he was aware that the two sheriff's departments were not going to let this investigation drag on very long. Unless of course, they found something that would impact the fire analysis.

Jeff was about to pick up his cell to call Danielle when it rang. "Alameda County Sheriff's Office" came across the screen. It was either Detective Philipson or her supervisor, Sergeant Hauser, on the other end. He hoped it was the former.

"Good afternoon, Detective Jeff Sufford," the detective answered.

"Good afternoon," said Danielle. "This is Detective Danielle Philipson with the Alameda County Sheriff's Office. I understand we are going to be working together again."

Wow, she thought to herself. That sounded awfully official. Almost too official. Cold. She had already turned down an offer to grab a burger, and she had lied to the guy about having a cat. Was she also starting to sound like a bitter woman?

"Hi there," said Jeff, a little taken aback. It wasn't like it had been two years since they had spoken. It had been literally two days. What was with the tone? He decided it didn't matter. Jeff was a laid back person, both in his professional life and personal life. He wasn't going to shoot back with an equally official, "I'm not even sure who you are," voice. Of course, he knew who she was and why she was calling.

"I just got the news," Detective Sufford responded. "Did you hear that Laura Mason wants us to review the entire four hundred acre property? That's going to take a while."

"I did," said Danielle. "I'm a little surprised. Figured she was high maintenance, but to expect us to look over every friggin' square inch of her property seems like a colossal waste of time."

"Yeah. It's a big ask, but I guess she's used to getting what she wants," said Jeff.

It suddenly occurred to him that if Danielle and Laura had a private conversation, his manipulation of events might be exposed. Jeff highly doubted that Mrs. Mason would say a word. She would want to appear as though it were her suggestion. That she had come to law enforcement of her own accord.

"Listen," Jeff continued, "I think we should get together to discuss operational strategy before we head back to the winery. It's a big area. We don't even know what we're looking for at this point."

"Agreed," said Danielle. "Hey, by any chance have you looked at the most recent documents that were uploaded to the shared drive? The fire marshal did a pretty amazing job mapping out a grid of the fire scene. Maybe we can take that approach, on a larger scale? Start with some satellite imaging or take a drone with us?"

Yes, thought Jeff. She's thorough, and she thinks like me.

"I did," Jeff told Danielle. "I think that sounds reasonable. Do you want to come out here to my office in the morning?" he asked Danielle.

It was a stupid question. It was the obvious choice. The winery was in Napa County. As happy as she was to be working on this investigation, and with friendly Detective Sufford, it would be an hour-long drive each way. Still, she was getting paid. And he was being kind. He was asking her, not simply telling her, or making any assumptions.

"Sounds good. What time do you want me in the office and is there anything you need from me between now and tomorrow morning," she asked.

"I can't really think of anything just yet," said Jeff. "I'll talk to someone here in our department about the use of a drone. How does nine thirty tomorrow morning sound?"

"Perfect," said Danielle. "I'll see you in the morning. And, I'll look over the files uploaded by the fire marshal one more time."

"See you in the morning," Jeff said, putting in the last word before the detectives ended their call.

Detective Jeff Sufford had some business to do before the afternoon ended. He wanted to start with the drone. He got up from his desk and walked down the hall to the other side of the building. The Napa Valley Sheriff's Department had seven trained pilots to operate the agency's drones. While the Alameda County Sheriff's Department was larger, Napa Valley was on the leading edge of drone usage in the Bay Area for everything from search and rescue to pursuits of suspects to using the technology to clear buildings. The Sheriff's Department often provided drone assistance to other agencies for critical incidents, as well. The program had a large budget, but it more than paid for itself, by reducing the need for personnel on certain operations, and helping keep officers safe in highly risky situations. It also gave law enforcement a starting point when searching large areas. The technology allowed resources to be placed more strategically and reduced the use of expensive resources like helicopters or small fixed-wing aircraft.

Drone operations occupied a large space in the building's east wing. They worked round-the-clock, with two to three pilots available on any given shift. Of course, they were also assigned overnight on-call duties. Jeff knew a couple of the officers, but not everyone. He hoped he would see a familiar face as he rounded the corner. He glanced back and forth across the space, recognizing two of the three individuals in the room.

"Officer Chapman," said Jeff, approaching the pilot he knew best. All three pilots looked up from their computers. "How are you this afternoon?"

"Good," said Pilot Amy Chapman. "What do you want, Jeff. Let's have it. I'm only on shift for another thirty minutes." The entire room was listening to Pilot Chapman as she gave the detective a hard time.

"Well, since you asked…" Jeff began.

He then explained the situation to the pilot, complete with the un-assigned, re-assigned details, his thoughts on the fire marshal and Laura Mason, the interagency work with Detective Danielle Philipson, and the highly specific diagrams that he'd found in the uploaded files mapping out the fire scene.

When Jeff had finished, Amy Chapman looked directly at him and said, "So basically, a rich woman with a lot of pull wants some attention and your ego is getting the best of you to make sure your work is better than the fire marshal's. That about sum it up, Jeff?"

The other two pilots in the room couldn't help but laugh. The whole thing did seem a bit stupid, cost prohibitive, and probably a complete and total waste of resources. But it wasn't for them to judge.

"Yes, you definitely have the complete picture as I know it right now," said Jeff flatly.

He was beginning to internalize the reality that he was to blame for this crazy situation, and he was using Mrs. Mason as a crutch for his bruised ego since being taken off the case so suddenly. Finished before he began. He wanted payback and he was getting it, but now he was involving other officers and agencies. Still, as laid back as he was in general, he wanted to hunt this one down to its conclusion.

"Okay," said Amy. "I don't think we have any detailed aerial of that area. It's more likely that we have computerized satellite images. But with the trees, it will be difficult to see much. Just to be on the safe side though, give me the physical address of the winery and I'll do a computer search on the surrounding four hundred acres. Assuming I'm right, we can take a drone, or maybe two, out and map the area. I can do it in the next couple of days You don't have to be involved."

This was absolutely not the response that Jeff had imagined. He wanted to work with the pilot in tandem with Detective Danielle

Philipson. He didn't want technology to simply do the work, while he went back to his desk and drank coffee.

But Jeff was also a realist. If technology could do the job, he wouldn't be able to argue. Still, he and Danielle should meet to discuss the best approach, utilizing the drones and what now appeared to be a lessening need to drive, walk, or otherwise be involved physically.

"That sounds about right," said Jeff after he'd had a moment to fully absorb what was likely to become the process to accomplish the business at hand. "Hey, and I appreciate you for working with me."

Jeff turned to walk back to his office. He would meet with Danielle in the morning, discuss plans, coordinate with the pilot and the winery, and set a schedule. It was already Thursday, so he doubted the work would happen before the following week. As Jeff made some notes, he thought about the entire situation which had unfolded over the past 48 hours. This was not a run of the mill robbery case that had become so familiar to him in his daily routine. For a moment he felt ashamed for thinking that way about his work. It was all important.

CHAPTER
24

Elizabeth awakened from a sound sleep as Michael carefully lifted himself from the bed. She had no idea what time it was, as she lay between the silk sheets. It had been a heavenly evening. She wanted it to be like this always. Just the two of them. She was in love with her client. She knew Michael cared for her very much. He had shared more over the past several hours than he had in the past several years. She understood men. They said little most of the time. They hated drama. And only in very rare instances did they feel it was acceptable to be publicly emotional. Even when alone, or in darkness, most men had difficulty understanding, and especially accepting, what caused happiness or pain. They were quiet souls. Saying very little. Only wanting acceptance. Unless of course, they were angry. In that emotion, they were all the same. Explosive.

Elizabeth opened her eyes, turned her head, and watched Michael as he put on his jeans. He glanced back and caught her looking at him.

"I'm sorry. Did I wake you," he asked.

"No," she said softly. She had wanted to say something flirty like, "Just admiring the view." Or, "Come back to bed." But she didn't dare.

"Listen, it's almost one o'clock in the morning. I need to get home. The room is yours. Sleep here tonight. Enjoy breakfast. When you're ready to leave, the driver will be waiting."

today. She did, however, use a little perfume and took some extra time with her hair. Detective Jeff Sufford was easy on the eyes, and Danielle assumed he wasn't married. It wasn't the lack of a ring. Lots of officers didn't wear rings. But he *had* invited her out for that burger. She hoped it wasn't simply because he was a polite guy, who had a wife and kids at home. Not that she assumed anything might start up between them, other than a professional relationship. She kept reminding herself of that as she unplugged her laptop from its charger, placed the computer in her backpack, and headed outside to her vehicle.

She had nursed two cups of coffee on her balcony and straightened up around her place. Still, she had time to kill. It was only 7:45 a.m. She knew there was a car wash a couple of miles from her home that opened at 8:00 a.m. She could take the SUV there and get it thoroughly washed, inside and out, just in case she and Detective Sufford shared a brief ride out to the winery. She doubted he would want to take his sedan if there was any chance they might end up on gravel or dirt roads. It didn't make sense to get a wash if they would be meandering through dirt. However, she wanted to make a good impression. Cops, in general, were neat and organized. They prided themselves on it. They had special relationships with their vehicles. After all, a vehicle served as an office, a storage facility, and even a shield under certain circumstances. Officers tended to treat their vehicles well.

Forty-five minutes later, Danielle was on the freeway headed towards the Napa Valley Sheriff's Office. She thought about stopping and picking up donuts, but that might make her appear too eager. She didn't really like donuts. She was a chocolate croissant kind of person. Instead, she made the drive with the radio off and her mind imagining what this search might turn up.

Although she had been born and raised in California's nearby Bay Area region, Danielle had never really taken an interest in the Napa or Sonoma Valleys. She was the daughter of a cop and a schoolteacher. She had two younger brothers. One, who had become a successful lawyer. He was still giving her the silent treatment after having abandoned him at the Ninth Circuit Court of Appeals in San Francisco.

The other was an engineer. It was her father's daughter who had followed in his footsteps. As a kid, her parents had taken their family to baseball and football games. They loved spending time at the many beaches within a couple of hours' drive from their home. The Phillipsons had lived a nice, middle-class life, making sure all three children went to college. Napa Valley wasn't the sort of place you took children or even teenagers. As an adult, Danielle enjoyed a glass of wine now and then, but it wasn't part of her culture. She was more excited to go to the shooting range.

* * * * *

Detective Jeff Sufford lived among the vineyards, so to speak. The image of the wine country was always the same. Endless miles of vine-laced fencing, quaint shops, outdoor terrace restaurants. Movies had been filmed in the area. Many articles had been written about what was once a sleepy town. The rich and famous visited. Regularly. It was a white tablecloth kind of life, where reds and whites poured freely at expensive parties and family gatherings. The region was considered among the wealthiest in the country.

On the flip side, however, were the working class who supported the affluent lifestyles. Migrants worked the fields. Immigrants worked in the hospitality industry. Nearly 40 percent of the population of the wine region was Hispanic. Most winery owners, hotel and restaurant entrepreneurs, and other service industry proprietors were sensitive to the disparity between visitors and residents. Business CEOs worked as a coalition to provide a living wage to their employees. Loyalties were formed and the community was close knit.

Detective Jeff Sufford had been a Napa Valley transplant. He was from a military family, and the youngest of four. He had lived in Germany and England, before his father retired from his final assignment at Travis Air Force Base, situated halfway between Napa and California's capital city, Sacramento. Jeff attended Vanden High School his junior and senior years. His three older brothers had already left home. Two had joined the Air Force, while the brother closest to Jeff's age had earned a football scholarship to UCLA. Jeff didn't want to go into the military, and he wasn't an outstanding athlete.

Law enforcement had long interested him. After high school, he attended Cal Poly at San Luis Obispo, majoring in criminal justice. From there, he applied to the California Highway Patrol. The process was grueling, with only a six percent acceptance rate. Jeff was among the successful applicants. He was with the CHP for 10 years in Bakersfield, but after a nasty divorce, he decided he needed a change of scenery. He didn't have any kids to keep him in one place, so he applied for a post as a detective with both the San Francisco and Napa Valley Sheriff's Offices. Napa Valley offered him a position first, so Jeff grabbed it. He liked being close to his parents who lived in Fairfield. It was just a 30-minute drive without traffic. He would often visit on Sunday afternoons to catch whatever game was on TV and to have a medium rare steak alongside a loaded baked potato; assuming he didn't have to work. Jeff had a good group of friends at the CHP and within the sheriff's department. He hardly put any energy into the two dating apps he subscribed to. He worked a lot of hours, and he didn't mind his own company.

Detective Philipson pulled into the Napa Sheriff's Office parking lot at 9:24 a.m. Perfect, Danielle said to herself. Early, but not too early. She reached for her backpack, opened the driver's side door, and stepped out. The vehicle looked great. It wasn't going to stay that way for long if she and Detective Sufford went out for a joy ride, but for now, the white paint gleamed in the sunshine.

There were three officers working the front lobby. Danielle approached the desk sergeant, identified herself, and then shared that she had a meeting with Detective Jeff Sufford. She was offered a seat in the lobby and told that someone would be with her shortly.

Jeff was down the hall at his desk. He had reserved a small conference room where he and Danielle could work. Pilot Amy Chapman would be joining them at 10:00 a.m. He had decided against making copies of everything on the shared computer drive. Nothing new had been posted since the fire marshal's diagrams and photographs had appeared. Jeff assumed Danielle would have studied the documents again. If the team wanted another look, they could open the files and project them on a large monitor mounted on the back conference room wall.

Jeff didn't expect Danielle for another few minutes. He was about to get himself a cup of coffee from the break room when his phone rang. Detective Danielle Philipson was waiting for him in the lobby. Let her wait, or go find her? Jeff decided he wasn't going to make her wait. He was laidback, but he valued punctuality. He walked down the hall and found Danielle sitting in one of the lobby chairs, scrolling through her phone. He cleared his throat and greeted her kindly.

"Good morning. Thanks so much for coming out to the office." Danielle stood up out of her chair and shook Jeff's hand. "I've got a conference room reserved for us down the hall," Jeff explained. He walked slightly ahead as Danielle followed.

It wasn't a large room, but it was well equipped. Computer monitors, comfortable seating, and plenty of charging stations. Danielle set her backpack on the table, unloaded her laptop, and waited for Jeff to start the conversation.

"I think we can skip the field trip," Jeff began. "Here's the thing. We have a fairly extensive drone program with several experienced pilots. I've been told that this technology can help eliminate a lot of the leg work."

"I see," said Danielle. "Well, that will make this a lot easier and probably a lot more accurate if we are looking to pull together something like what the fire marshal's office did for the burn site."

"Exactly," said Jeff. "I've asked one of our pilots to join us in a few minutes. But I think we need to strategize about how to handle this operationally. We will have to go out to the scene. We can't just fly a drone from the office parking lot."

"Right," Danielle responded. "And we are probably going to have to let PFV know what we're up to, especially if they are expecting to spend days with us combing their land."

"Yeah," Jeff nodded. "I've given the background to our pilot, and she said she would do a little reconnaissance of her own before our meeting."

"That's great. She'll probably have some ideas about where to start and how to develop our own pattern for the area," said Danielle. "Honestly, I think this makes a lot more sense than to drive around aimlessly. There would be no way to diagram it all properly."

Pilot Amy Chapman walked into the conference room with a stack of files in her hands. Jeff introduced her to Danielle and the three started in on a conversation. As Pilot Chapman had guessed, there were no detailed views of the area. Satellite images were great, but not when enormous oak trees served as a canopy. She discussed various portions of the property where drones could be flown to capture a bird's eye view. The drones were also capable of flying into and out of buildings while recording their flight path. To accomplish such a task, winery staff would need to cooperate to allow access to the buildings through open doors and windows. The pilot felt that three days would be ample to survey the entire 400 acres. She shared seven map points to use as potential staging areas.

At the conclusion of the discussion, Jeff and Danielle agreed to contact Laura Mason. They would give her the details of their plan and ask for supporting staff to escort them to the seven points around the property. Pilot Chapman wanted to begin the following Monday. She requested three full days to complete the assignment, but Jeff suspected she really only needed a day and a half. It was in her best interest to under promise and over deliver.

CHAPTER
26

The weekend had come and gone. There had been no offer to grab a burger by Detective Jeff Sufford. The drone work was scheduled to get underway today. Danielle threw on a pair of black jeans and a white tee. She had volunteered her vehicle. Jeff agreed. Pilot Amy Chapman would be taking a special unit designed to carry drones. It had a large array of radio and video equipment on board, along with mechanical parts and tools in case of a crash or malfunction.

Palmer Family Vineyard owner, Laura Mason, was only too happy to assist. She had shared the drone staging locations with a couple of members of her staff who would accompany the detectives around the property. Portable offices had already been brought onto the winery grounds. Construction fencing was going up to give the illusion that work was getting underway. The full complement of staff had returned following a long weekend with pay.

Just as Pilot Chapman had suspected, the drone work was quick. She finished the job in less than two days, driving from site to site with the two detectives and two winery staff in tow. Officer Chapman snickered. What a boondoggle, she and her counterparts lamented. The rich *always* got their way. Mrs. Mason had been fortunate that things had been relatively quiet where drone usage was concerned.

With the physical drone activity complete, an analysis of the footage would begin back at the office. The two detectives watched as several Napa Valley Sheriff's pilots and IT personnel worked to download the information from the mechanical drones, formulating crystal clear imaging of the winery property. The drones had also been used to capture delineations of buildings. A still photographer took additional photos, because some of the buildings on the property were no more than tiny shacks, which had long ago been abandoned. Still, they served as a reminder of the labor that Laura's grandfather and father had put into their beloved winery long ago. Additionally, Jeff Sufford wanted his grid pattern to be as complete as the fire marshal's had been.

It was fascinating for the two detectives to watch the semblance of data unfold. What was not so fascinating was the result. Absolutely zero. No stored fuel out of place. No vehicle tracks in unexpected locations. No missing equipment. For an agricultural operation, the place was pristine.

The detectives reported back to their supervisors and to Mrs. Mason. Jeff had to admit that Fire Marshal Tom Navarro, for better or worse, had probably been correct not to survey the entire area. Laura was disappointed. Michael Mason was relieved. It was already a complicated situation. He didn't need the cops finding canisters of gasoline or sticks of dynamite, or whatever else he might have imagined that would indicate a potential arson on his wife's land. Nothing to give detectives any reason to investigate further. It was now a wait-and-see game for the lab results.

Danielle was back in her office working the drug trafficking case. Jeff was at his desk filing detailed robbery reports. The data from the drones would not be uploaded to the shared drive. Sergeant Ron Hauser didn't want to rub salt in any wounds. Mainly his own since the fire marshal still had access to the computer drive. Hauser was glad to move on. It hadn't been his jurisdiction. His office wasn't in the business of conducting fire investigations. He didn't feel comfortable with this so-called "interagency cooperation." He hated the fact that this had cost his department time and money. And he didn't need Fire Marshal Tom Navarro snickering with his, "I told you so", attitude. It had been a complete waste of everyone's time.

CHAPTER
27

Elizabeth was in tears, having watched Michael walk out the door in the early morning hours. He had never left her behind in a hotel room before. She tried to convince herself that her hurt and anguish were based on the loss of a lucrative client and not heartbreak. She had narrowed her companions to just four over the years. Her preferred gentlemen. The select few with whom she wanted to share herself. She loathed her early "career" and the complications that had accompanied a larger clientele. Over time she had earned her way to financial freedom. Due in no small part to her most long term client and aging supporter, Richard. The fictitious attorney from the wealthy Manhattan family no longer needed his monetary support.

Her heart was broken. She had committed the cardinal sin of falling in love. Michael had let her go. She didn't like this type of freedom. Why had he done it? Women always wanted to know the why. She absolutely hated that part of her psyche. She wished to be indifferent, just as the fabricated persona of Elizabeth had been indifferent when her father screamed at her as a child.

Michael was lonely. He was scared. He was worn down from trying to keep two businesses in check. And, a demanding wife. So, why would he close the door on something simple and wonderful? Elizabeth was never troublesome. She was never needy. She was polished and confident. The epitome of her East Coast character. She never contacted him. She never asked. He shared only what he wanted. If he disappeared at times, she waited. He had the illusion of power. Elizabeth was always ready to please. And never, ever difficult. She was always what he wanted her to be. What he required her to be. Impeccable.

A distraction. That's what Elizabeth needed. She packed a few things in a duffle bag and purchased an Amtrak ticket online. She would unravel Elizabeth and remind herself that she was indeed Sarah. The girl from Pacific Grove. She missed her mother and the relaxed atmosphere of her coastal upbringing. Like Michael, she was worn out. Done.

Elizabeth departed from San Francisco's Montgomery Station. It was situated under Market Street, just three miles from her home, and served the area's financial district. The transit ride and subsequent bus transfer to Pacific Grove would take approximately four hours. Sarah had decided to surprise her mother, Lynda. She spent the afternoon watching the landscape speed by, trying not to think about what had transpired over the past few days. She would leave Elizabeth behind in San Francisco. As the miles passed, Sarah reemerged.

It was early September. Tourists were withdrawing from California's beaches for their return to suburban life. It was the perfect time to leave the City behind. Sarah hadn't told herself for how long. Her mother would be concerned about her daughter's well-being if she were away from her job for more than a few days. It was Friday afternoon, so that would make sense. But Sarah wanted to squeeze in a few extra days, to reconnect with herself. To be distracted by her mother and her authentic childhood memories. She'd work on her story before she arrived.

She reached the Monterey Transit Station just before 5:00 p.m. and boarded a local city bus for the quick ride to Pacific Grove. She would never take an Uber. Sarah was wholly unlike Elizabeth. Sarah was frugal and practical, splurging only now and again for the things which she felt mattered. An experience. An opportunity. Not material things. She shopped at Old Navy. She was the kind of person who would have had dinner with the girls a couple of times a month, but because Sarah would have shared a San Francisco apartment with a roommate, it wouldn't have made sense to waste an hour's pay on a luxury ride.

Elizabeth had vanished for the time being, and Sarah had re-surfaced. She was excited to see her mom. It had been a while. Too long. Almost six months. Of course, Sarah called Lynda regularly. They had a close relationship; as intimate as a daughter leading two divergent lives could share. Sarah was no longer dating so-and-so, but she'd had a promotion at work and was now leading a group of administrative staff members. This had been her excuse not to see her mom. She had been busy in her new role. Lynda understood. She was so proud of her daughter.

The bus dropped Sarah two blocks from her mother's apartment complex. After Sarah had moved to San Francisco, Lynda had decided to both upgrade and downsize her living conditions. She had moved from a two-bedroom to a smaller one-bedroom place. But it was in a better area of Pacific Grove, with modern amenities. Ten years had passed now. The area was still lovely, and the apartment manager kept the units updated. But the weather and time had aged the building.

Sarah often felt badly that Elizabeth had so much money but didn't share more of it with Lynda to help with her day-to-day living expenses. How could she? Her mother would have become immediately suspicious. Instead, Ivy League educated Elizabeth had established a money market account for Lynda. It had grown substantially over the past decade. It would be given to Lynda in twelve equal increments, beginning on her mother's 55th birthday, though the mechanism had not yet been decided. A long lost relative. Some sort of class action settlement that her mother has been unaware of until the first check arrived? Maybe. It was still two years off. Sarah brought her mother presents, telling her mom that the items had been gifted to her by friends. She had also secretly paid off her mother's car note, explaining it away by saying that the original payment schedule had been incorrect. Lynda happily accepted what she was told and rarely asked probing questions.

Sarah had a key to her mom's place. She walked the flight of stairs to the second floor, reached for her keys from her cloth shoulder tote, and let herself inside. She knew Lynda wouldn't be home for another hour. The place was spotless. Her mom had photographs of her daughter strategically placed on bookcase shelves in the main living room. Hanging on the hallway wall were three large black and white photos of mother and daughter taken over the years.

It sometimes surprised Sarah that her mother could be so happy living alone. She could understand her mother not wanting to be married. Sarah, and most especially Elizabeth, longed for a nurturing relationship but did not want to ever be Mrs. Anyone. Lynda, on the other hand, didn't care if anyone showed an interest in her as a friend, or romantically. She was settled. Lynda didn't clutter her life with objects or regrets. She moved forward and was grateful for her health, her daughter, and the role she had earned as supervisor over the entire housekeeping staff at Spanish Bay. Mother was in sharp contrast to daughter who had cluttered her life with an entirely different persona. Perhaps it was time to simply be Sarah again.

She knew her mother would be tired when she got home. Sarah scrolled through her phone and decided to order dinner. She selected a nearby café frequented by the locals. It was a little farm to fork place. Sarah chose the restaurant, not for its tomato bruschetta, honey garlic chicken, or grilled street corn. She craved the desserts. Chocolate lava cake. Vanilla brownies infused with dark chocolate. Whipped cream-filled cannelloni. French apple tarts. Sarah ordered them all. Elizabeth rarely ate dessert. Maybe a bite of cheesecake once in a great while, but usually if a sweet confection were placed in front of her at dinner or some lavish affair, she would politely move her fork through the plate so that it would appear as though she had sampled the dessert.

Sarah had ordered far too much food, which meant there would be leftovers for days. She timed the delivery to be within a few minutes of her mother's arrival. She opened a kitchen drawer and located placemats and flatware. She poured them each a glass of water then sat down on the sofa and waited. For the first time in weeks, her heart was full.

Like clockwork, Lynda walked through her apartment door at 6:35 p.m. She was startled to see Sarah sitting on the couch and a feast laid out on the kitchen table.

"Sweetheart, you're here," Lynda said gleefully. She was so thankful to see her daughter. "What have you done? Did you bring friends with you? There's so much food."

Sarah jumped up from the sofa to meet her mother's hug. The two women embraced for several seconds before pulling away.

"Let me look at you," said Lynda. "You look so happy."

Sarah was thankful that, in this moment, she *was* happy. Somehow, Lynda always seemed to know when Sarah felt any type of strain. For now, she was at peace just standing in her mother's apartment with the smell of food swirling around them.

"Come on, mom. Let's eat before it gets cold."

The two women sat at the table for hours. Sarah talked about her fictional job and friends. She assured her mother that she would begin dating again, as soon as she felt more secure in her new position at work. The promotion came with a salaried paycheck. Lynda was delighted to know that her one-and-only daughter had a promising hold in her workplace. Lynda told Sarah about the summer guests. Preparations were already underway for the TaylorMade Invitational, the only golf tournament in which players from the PGA, LPGA, the Champions, and the Nationwide Tours competed together. It was held annually in November on several local, prestigious golf courses. Although, it was not played at Spanish Bay, the players and spectators overflowed into every available space. The rooms at the Inn had long ago been reserved. It was one of the area's busiest weekends of the year.

It was after 10:00 p.m. before Sarah stood up from the table. She cleared their plates and set about preserving the remaining food. The refrigerator was filled. Lynda offered her daughter the bedroom, but Sarah wouldn't hear of it. Besides, the sofa converted into a bed. Sarah took a quick shower, kissed her mother goodnight, and got between the sheets on the pull out. She was home.

CHAPTER
28

Laura found herself snooping around her own house. So odd, she thought to herself. She wasn't very familiar with her city residence. The furniture had been selected by her personally many years ago even though she only slept there, now and again. Although she had her own office upstairs, it never felt like home. She needed the name of the insurance company which held the PFV Winery policies. Why was this so hard? Laura knew why. It was the one piece of her company where she had given up control.

It was becoming clear that there wasn't any paperwork to find in the house. It had to be at Michael's office. She had several options. One, ask her CFO, Rachel, to call Michael and get the information. Two, make a trip in the middle of the night to Mason Recruiting. She hadn't visited the high rise in years. But then what? Rummage through files? It wasn't the 80s. Everything would be stored on a computer database. Three, just ask her husband. He would have no choice but to acquiesce.

Michael was aware that Laura had planned to come into the City. She had told him as much. He wouldn't rush home. They had no security cameras, so Michael wouldn't be certain just what time she would arrive. He did know her well enough to surmise that she would make the distance over the bridge before the traffic settled into its daily grinding halt. He would guess that she would be at home no later than 2:30 that afternoon.

Michael liked to arrive around dinner time, giving Laura a chance to look around uninterrupted. She was thrilled to see Aiden when he walked through the front door after school. Mother and son sat at the kitchen island together. She asked about his start to the new academic year, if he had friends in his classes, and how he liked his teachers. He had her undivided attention. The chef arrived at 4:30 p.m. to prepare dinner. Aiden headed upstairs to tackle his homework. Laura climbed two flights and found shelter in her small office just off the primary bedroom. She looked through her desk drawers but found nothing. The room was filled with light, and yet it seemed so somber. It had no life because she never used the space anymore.

Dinner was set out on the kitchen table at 6:00 p.m., precisely the moment that Michael arrived home. She had predicted it perfectly. Mother, father, and son enjoyed the quiet evening, with Aiden occupying much of the conversation. Aiden had homework to finish. He carried his plate to the sink and then disappeared back upstairs. Michael stood up and began to clear the remaining plates. Laura walked over to the sink, turned on the faucet, and allowed the water to settle onto the dishes. For a brief moment, they felt like a normal family. Laura knew this was her opportunity to ask about the insurance policy. She tried her best to be casual about it all. But too many years of marriage had passed between them, and nothing about her was casual.

Michael was caught. He would have to tell his wife the truth eventually. She wanted to know the name of the company for a reason. He had already told her about his initial phone call with the agent. Clearly, that had not been good enough for his wife. He stood in the middle of the kitchen doing his best to disclose the insurance carrier's name nonchalantly. He guessed Laura wanted to know when she might receive funding to begin construction. She was unaware of the gross insufficiency of coverage. That would soon change.

"I suppose you'll have Rachel give them a call to see if she can get the ball rolling on the claim," Michael said.

"Yes, of course. I want to start the new build as soon as possible, said Laura in response. I know you said the insurance agent won't move forward without the fire marshal's report. But, I can't believe that there isn't *something* I can do to speed things up. I've never been very good at sitting on my hands waiting for others to fix my problems."

Yet another example of his wife believing she was special. It was so frustrating. Michael had been honest about the reaction from the insurance company, the very morning following the fire. It would all be placed on hold. What did Laura expect? The seas would part and a big, fat check would be in the winery's mailbox within a few days? She had unrealistic expectations. Laura's CFO probably knew that she would be wasting her time with a phone call to the insurance company. But Laura was her boss, so she would do as she had been told and make the call.

The series of events played out the following morning just as Michael had expected. Laura called to complain. The agent had told the winery's CFO that the insurance company was not able to do anything yet. Michael just shook his head. He wondered if Laura could feel his judgement through the phone. She had an uncanny sixth sense at times. Michael placated his wife, telling her how much he understood the frustration she must be feeling. Blaming the insurance company.

CHAPTER
29

The fire marshal had finally made his announcement. He was handing over the investigation to law enforcement. Trouble was, Fire Marshal Tom Navarro had no idea that the sheriff's department had decided to do some investigating on its own after initially being told to stand down.

Worse, the drone experiment had come up completely empty. Mrs. Laura Palmer-Mason had been given the attention she craved, but now she had gone radio silent. As far as anyone knew, she hadn't contacted Alameda, Napa, or San Francisco officials for a couple of weeks. Of course, Michael understood that despite Laura's calm demeanor, she was most assuredly upset. She needed a definitive answer. He held his breath, wondering when his wife would blow up.

It seemed like everyone had been waiting on the lab results. Laura and Michael Mason. The PFV Board of Directors. The company which insured the winery. Michael's CFO, not to mention the two detectives who had been given on again, off again assignments. Today, they were off, and their supervisors were about to come clean to the fire marshal that a fair amount of technical investigative work had been completed behind his back.

The Napa Valley and Alameda County sheriffs were both furious. It was total bullshit that the fire marshal would dump the case in their laps, after having been so certain any wrongdoing would be made clear once the lab results were returned. The only thing Fire Marshal Tom Navarro had managed to do was to get the results back in record time. He was hiding behind a fucked-up report and his ego. Elected officials didn't take things lying down. This was not going to become the problem of *either* sheriff's office. Navarro had no authority over law enforcement. The two counties were done wasting money and precious officer resources on a winery fire. Call it an Act of God, but there was no goddamned way this business was going to continue.

A heated meeting was held at the Napa Valley Sheriff's Office the following day. It had been "closed door," but there wasn't a person in the building that didn't catch the gist of the edict handed down by the sheriffs for both counties. There were over 12,000 fire marshals in the US. Navarro could easily be replaced. The back-and-forth crap that Navarro had served up was unprecedented. Administrative shit aside, many hours and dollars had been spent to use drone technology to take up where the fire marshal seemed not only to have left off, but to have not cared. It didn't concern the sheriffs that nothing had been discovered, but rather that the fire marshal's office had dismissed the process from the get-go.

The two sheriffs and their entourage emerged from the conference room 17 minutes after having entered the building. They headed straight for the front doors to their waiting cars. There would be no further investigation. Doctor up the report. Delete the paragraph regarding law enforcement. The fire marshal was going to do whatever he had to do to put a stop to this. End of story.

Sergeant Hauser walked out to his vehicle and slammed the door. He would make the phone call. To her. To Mrs. Laura Palmer-Mason. He needed to rip off the Band Aid. It was over. The fire marshal would update his report following the "internal briefing" which had just occurred. It wasn't unusual. These things often got reviewed before a final report was released.

The phone conversation was concise. She responded with three, "I sees." She thanked the sergeant for his commitment and hung up. She then called her CFO, Rachel. The final fire report would be released within 24 hours. Laura wanted a copy placed directly into the hands of the insurance agent. She wanted the construction of her new offices to begin as quickly as possible. She wanted life to return to normal. Whatever that meant.

CHAPTER
30

The crashing waves were in perfect harmony with the sand. Sarah felt in perfect harmony with her soul. She didn't miss Elizabeth. Or the City. Or Michael.

She had stayed for an entire week, telling her mother that she had worked so much overtime in her new position that she had been given several days of administrative leave. Lynda went to her job, while Sarah shopped and made meals. She also took some time to visit the owners of the restaurant where she had served customers through-out high school and junior college. Sarah tried to make a habit of visiting them every time she was in Pacific Grove. The husband and wife restauranteurs were always glad to see her and would joke that a hostess job was waiting for her. A new chef was now in charge of the menu, but the place remained as popular as ever.

Sarah knew it was time to release Elizabeth from the bonds of make-believe. She no longer wished to be Ms. Elizabeth Catherine Stevens. Ever again. She was through pretending. Being what others wanted her to be, so that she might have her own twisted sense of importance and success. She packed her things, kissed her mother goodbye, and told herself that the next time she put her toes in the Pacific Grove sand, it would be for good.

The return trip to San Francisco was excruciating. Sarah spent her mental energy thinking about how quickly she could untangle her counterfeit life. She would need to spend time with her remaining three clients, informing each that she was returning to New York. A simple enough task to accomplish. More difficult would be to sell her home. It had appreciated tremendously in value over the past 10 years, but the market had softened. She wouldn't want it to languish for months, but she also wanted a fair price. Richard had been so kind in paying for it all. She would approach him and ask for his help. He would enjoy it, she knew. One last thing he might do for his Elizabeth to make himself feel strong.

Funny, thought Elizabeth as she turned the key in the lock on her California Street home that evening. It wasn't that complicated. She didn't have a single friend in her made-up world. She had a banker who would take care of any financial concerns. She didn't "go to work" as an attorney. She would be unrestrained.

It was the weekend, so Elizabeth wouldn't be able to contact her financial advisor. That would have to wait. She had never called a client. But she couldn't be certain that the three men would be in touch anytime soon. Sometimes days would pass before one of her gentlemen called, sometimes only hours since a previous engagement. Elizabeth would need to speak with all three and make arrangements to meet with each. She would wait one week. None of the men had called while she had been in Pacific Grove. They were all due and were rarely mysterious in making contact. None were of the "every Tuesday at 7:00 p.m." sort, but none had been as exhausting as Michael. All three called with some regularity. If Elizabeth heard nothing from them in these next several days, she would reach out.

She felt a sudden panic that her wanting to return to her life as Sarah could no longer wait. Not weeks. She needed it to be now. Richard would be first. She would ask him to handle the sale of her property. She would offer it to him first. She knew he would refuse. She had to be delicate. There was a fine line between flattery and insult, and at his age, he would need to feel he was taking care of his love.

In actuality, the sale of the home would be taking care of Elizabeth, or rather Sarah, and her mother for many years. Yes, this would be the first step. Her other men had simply provided entertainment and expenses, as if she were a $1,000 an hour attorney from her made up Manhattan firm. She had earned a great deal but given up so much more. She was re-claiming it all. It had been decided on that train ride back into the City.

As for Michael, he was the only man in her life who actually had control. Now, he had decided that his relationship with Elizabeth was over. She tried to tell herself that he would call. That he would come back. Like so many times before, when she wouldn't hear for days, or weeks, or maybe an entire month. They would share amazing moments, or sometimes simply a series of texts while each sat at home watching a basketball game. Then, he would suddenly, and without warning, shut down. In the beginning, she didn't care. It was amusing. He always reached back out. But over the past year, as she had grown to care more deeply for him, it all mattered. It made her sick inside when he disappeared or grew cold. His behavior hadn't changed, but her reaction to it had.

She had developed genuine feelings, breaking her number one rule. It wasn't fun anymore. No longer safe from her own emotions. She felt like the proverbial hamster running on a wheel. Trying to stay calm, while his power over her grew. With every encounter, she had to be sweet and void of any meaningful attachment. She was bottled up inside.

The life she had presented to him had nearly no truth. For the first three years, it had been businesslike. But no longer. She couldn't know for sure if Michael was aware of her feelings. But it *had* been different this last time, when he left her alone in the hotel room at 1:00 a.m. He seemed sad. He didn't want a permanent relationship with Elizabeth. He didn't want his wife anymore, either. Elizabeth could feel it. Michael would be a father to his boys, in particular, Aiden. He would work and figure out a way to help his wife continue with her family's winery. He didn't want to have a happily ever after with

Elizabeth. Or with anyone. He would turn his attention to ensuring Mason Recruiting International was successful so that he could give his sons everything they could ever need. He would take his power and give it over to them. Just as his own father had done.

The world had become a solitary place. People stayed at home. If they socialized, it was for the drama of it all. Sincere connections were rarely made. Or valued. Move on to the next. Life was something to be endured with a side of pleasure, now and then. Everyone was inside their own head and seldom looked outward.

It was decided. Elizabeth was gone. Sarah had a real mother and a real home. She hadn't had a fancy education, but she was well educated. She was only 34 years old and had grown up in one of the most beautiful places on earth. She could still reconnect and be herself and stop listening to the noise from the outside world that she needed to be anything other than herself. She was enough.

CHAPTER
31

No. Further. Investigation. What the fuck did that mean, Michael Mason asked himself as he hung with the Napa Valley Sheriff. Michael didn't know the sheriff well. It was his wife who rubbed elbows with local and statewide leaders. Frankly, the call had caught Michael completely off guard. He couldn't believe he wasn't hearing the news second hand, from Laura. This was good news, he decided. The fire marshal's report would be made final. It would be passed along to the insurance company. Michael needed to come clean with his wife, before a random insurance representative did. It would be a difficult conversation, but he would have it with her soon.

Laura had retreated to the ranch and, of course, to the winery. Visitors didn't seem to mind looking at the temporary buildings and fencing. They simply walked into the tasting room, leaving with a bottle of wine or two for home. Laura and her CFO had not allowed the fire to interfere with their Costco business dealings. The contract which had already been set in motion was now winding its way through red tape and appeared to be near finalization. Palmer Family Vineyard would distribute two reds and one white to Costco's West Coast locations, hitting the market just prior to the holidays. If sales went well, Costco would become the main purchaser of their wine in the new year.

Even Michael had been impressed. This would lift the winery from its financial hole, minus the office rebuild.

Laura was moving forward. She was not looking back at the cause of the fire. She no longer seemed to care. Strange, thought Michael. Especially for such a controlling woman. Why didn't this matter to her? It bothered him and occupied his mind. Her new partnership with the fifth largest retailer in the world was more than a distraction. It was grace. Still, her offices had burned to the ground in the middle of the night. There would never be any closure, unless rebuilding was all the closure she needed. Move forward. Always.

He would drive out to the ranch and give her the news about the insurance. He wasn't going to involve his CFO, Dennis Smith-Hodges. He was simply going to tell her the honest-to-God truth. The insurance company would pay out what he had insured the buildings for, Michael guessed. He wasn't certain how he would make up the difference. At least, the process to find a contractor and an architect could get underway.

He made a quick call to Laura. It went straight to voicemail. He simply left her a message that he would be coming out to the ranch for the weekend. Aiden didn't have a game, so they could ride out together. It would save her a trip into the City. He didn't give a specific reason. Since it was a rare occurrence, he knew her interest would be piqued. They would both play it cool for their son's sake. Michael would wait for an opportune moment to break the news, but he would do so without drama, and he definitely wasn't going to drag it out all weekend. He would tell her Saturday morning.

As it happened, Aiden didn't want to go out to the ranch. He had been invited by some friends to go to the beach at Half Moon Bay. Michael decided rather than drive to the Valley on Friday evening, he would get up early and head over on Saturday morning. No need to spend any more time away from the home he loved than necessary. In fact, he could probably make a day trip of it, and be back in his own bed on Saturday night.

For a brief moment, he thought about her. Elizabeth. He had closed the book on it. He couldn't do it anymore. He could feel her wanting more. She thought she had hidden her feelings well, but over the past six months, he sensed her wanting to grow close in a new way. He couldn't do it. He was tired of marriage. He was tired of sharing himself with anyone other than his children. He had forgotten how to be himself. Except with her. Even then, he wasn't completely himself. He was the best of himself, but he didn't really know Elizabeth. Only the pieces that she shared to be perfect for him. That's what he had paid her to do. To be perfect. Their relationship was an exchange. Period. End of sentence.

Michael walked down the hall to his CFO's office mid-morning on Friday. Dennis was already aware that the report on the winery fire was being finalized. Michael stuck his head into Dennis's office. He could see that his numbers guy was on the phone. Dennis motioned his boss into the room. Michael took a seat near the desk. The conversation was short. Michael would go out to the ranch in the morning and tell his wife the truth about the insurance. Dennis agreed that it was the right thing to do. It was only a matter of a few days before Laura's own CFO would hear the news, as the insurance company was now working directly with PFV. Dennis wished his friend good luck. The two men decided they would have dinner together on Sunday.

It was a gorgeous morning when Michael pulled out of the driveway and headed for Napa Valley. He wouldn't rehearse the conversation with his wife in his head. Early on in his marriage, he had prepared dialogues when he wanted to talk about something of substance with her, just as he would if he were giving a presentation on behalf of his own firm. But over time, he had come to expect the unexpected from Laura. He had stopped second guessing her long ago. No, he would just lay it out spontaneously. Quickly. And wait.

Michael pulled up to the driveway of his second home just before 8:00 a.m. The sun was bright. The front door was locked. He had half expected Laura to be waiting on the porch. He used his key and could see through the glass in the door that his wife was sitting at the island in the kitchen with a cup of coffee in her hand. She looked up and saw him as he put the key into the lock. She didn't rise, but she wasn't rude either as he crossed from the living room into the wide open kitchen.

"Good morning," he said politely. "I think I'll get myself one of those," motioning toward her coffee cup.

"There's plenty. And cream in the fridge," Laura responded. She was lovely. She had her hair pulled back in a ponytail and was wearing jeans and a green t-shirt. She actually looked relaxed, Michael thought to himself.

He walked over and poured himself a cup of coffee. A loaf of bread was sitting on the counter next to the toaster.

"Want a piece," he asked.

"No. I've already had two but help yourself." Michael popped a couple of pieces of bread into the machine and waited. He took a plate from a stack on a shelf, put some butter on the toast, then carried the plate and his cup of coffee over to the island and sat down beside his wife.

"So, what's this about," Laura asked. "You hate it here."

"That's not true," said Michael. And it wasn't. Once upon a time he had loved the place. "I guess this has become more your home, and the house in the City is more mine."

"That's probably true," Laura admitted. "Do you mind the separation?"

Michael was taken aback. Laura rarely asked Michael anything that wasn't transactional. He thought about her question for a second before answering.

"You know what. I don't. It works for us." Laura nodded her head in agreement. It was unspoken that while they no longer had a marriage, they would probably never dissolve it on paper. It was easier not to. They were comfortable.

"I need to talk to you about the insurance for the winery," Michael said flatly. "You and your CFO are going to hear this soon enough, now that the fire marshal's ridiculous non-report is being finalized." Michael took a breath. Laura simply stared at him.

"PFV is underinsured."

There. He had said it. Not dramatically. Not defensively. Just plainly. He wanted Laura to hear his words before giving any sort of explanation.

Laura just stared at her husband in disbelief.

"I'm not sure I understand," she responded. "I signed a stack of documents. And I know the insurance company has been working with you, and now Rachel."

"Yes. You did. And yes, they have. But we don't have a policy large enough to cover the reconstruction costs for the offices. I undervalued the buildings, in fact, all of the buildings to save the winery hundreds of thousands of dollars this past year."

Laura said nothing. The color in her face drained. She set her cup of coffee on the marble countertop and waited.

"I don't know what your reconstruction costs are going to look like, but I suspect it will be triple what the insurance is going to pay out," Michael confessed. He was finished. He would wait and listen to her response. She wasn't likely to scream. She was more likely to be disappointed, and that was the worst feeling he could imagine. Michael held his breath.

Laura pushed her counter stool away from the island and stood up. She said nothing. She walked toward the French doors leading to the patio. She opened one of the doors and stepped outside into the morning. Michael decided to leave her alone with her thoughts. He got up and poured himself a second cup of coffee. He was too sick inside to eat the toast. Laura had left the door open. He could hear a set of wind chimes in the breeze. The setting was peaceful. It didn't feel as though he had just dropped a bomb in his wife's lap.

Michael returned to the stool at the kitchen island. He watched his wife pull out a patio chair and sit down. Finally, he saw her glance back at him. It was her signal for Michael to join her outside. He obliged, walking out to the deck and sitting in the chair opposite hers. He put his coffee cup down on the patio table.

"I'm not sure what to say," Laura began. "I've always trusted you and Dennis when it comes to business. I guess I never even looked at the papers you had me sign."

"I know," Michael said. He had decided he wasn't going to defend his actions. He'd had an entire month since the fire to know that there was no point in taking up a defensive position.

"So, you did this to save money, that's what you're telling me."

"It is," Michael said.

"I understand. I don't like it, but I understand." It was Michael's turn to listen.

"So, where will we get the money to rebuild?" she asked.

"I don't know," Michael said truthfully. "We'll have to wait and see what you receive from the insurance company, but it won't be enough to replace what you had."

Laura didn't show any signs of being angry. Rather, she seemed hurt. She had been lied to by her husband. Maybe deceived was a better choice of words. She understood why Michael had done it. The winery had been bleeding money for the past couple of years. Mason Recruiting had been supporting her family business. But this decision had left them vulnerable, and now their worst case scenario was playing out.

"Well, we have our new partnership," Laura finally stated. "I don't have a check in hand yet, but it's promising. I guess I'll have to work with the money we receive from the insurance company and move forward a piece at a time."

Laura stood up and walked back into the house. Michael remained seated outside, listening to the wind chimes. It had been an adult conversation. And now, it was over. It was *all* over. He would live the remainder of his life married to someone he didn't love in the name of convenience. The feeling of loneliness deepened within him. He had experienced isolation for several years, but this was different.

Michael waited a few minutes then walked back into the house. His wife had disappeared. He picked up his plate and threw the toast in the trash. He set the plate and cup in the kitchen sink then walked across the living room and out the front door. He got back into his Range Rover, started the engine, and drove off. He would spend the weekend at home. Alone. It would be okay.

CHAPTER
32

Detectives Philipson and Sufford had not been surprised by the reaction of their sheriffs to the fire marshal's report. They were, however, both a little shocked at just how quickly the fire marshal had responded to the blowback. Rumor had it that the draft report would be revised, wrapped up, tied with a pretty bow, and finalized within 48 hours. The initial report had been uploaded to the shared server, but it was a moot point now. The two detectives had not spoken to each other for a couple of weeks. There had been no need after the drone search had come up empty. Still, each could see that the other had gone into the files and at the very least, opened the fire marshal's most recent draft.

Jeff had considered picking up the phone to call Danielle several times. Each time, he would run through the conversation in his head. However, he had nothing pertinent to say. "Hey there, did you hear?" Well of course, she had heard. Everyone in both the Napa and Alameda County Sheriff's Offices had heard. Even San Francisco was aware. About the meeting. About the explosive tone used by the two sheriffs when they learned that the fire marshal wanted to pass the buck.

It had been a month since that first encounter, when the two detectives had been assigned to look into the winery fire. And three weeks since they had initiated the drone project, which ultimately yielded no useful results. Jeff needed an excuse to contact Danielle. He couldn't believe that a fire of that size was going to be labeled inconclusive, however it wasn't unprecedented. Certainly, he had investigated many crimes which were never solved. He also understood that a large fire didn't automatically equal a crime. Still, as an officer of the law, that's where his mind almost always landed. Jeff was not aware of any additional phone calls made to law enforcement by Mrs. Mason either. For a woman who had pushed so hard for action, she had now gone radio silent. There was probably nothing to it, but detectives were always suspicious. It was too quiet.

Detective Danielle Philipson had opened the fire marshal's report within hours of it being uploaded onto the shared drive. First, she read it on her desktop computer at the office. Then, she printed it and took it home for a more thorough going over. The report was not lengthy. The lab exhibits, however, went on for some 40 pages. That's what happens when you collected every piece of ash at a scene, thought Danielle as she reviewed the attachments. It was a rather incredible amount of paperwork. Then again, she and Jeff had worked with the Napa Valley drone team to create a significant amount of data themselves. It had been interesting but had led nowhere. What a colossal waste of time that had been.

Danielle decided it was now or never. She was going to call. She had nothing to lose. She knew Jeff had opened the files. She could see it on the server. But she wondered how much attention he had given the draft. Probably some.

It was Friday afternoon. If she didn't reach out now, she would have to wait for the weekend to pass. The final report would probably be released on Monday. It would be another chance to contact the detective, but she wanted to take this opportunity sitting in front of her before there would be nothing to discuss.

Rather than use her cell, she picked up the office phone on her desk and dialed. Jeff answered on the second ring.

"Detective Jeff Sufford, Napa Valley Sheriff's Office," he said into the receiver. Danielle grinned. She knew he could see from the caller ID that it was her office calling.

"Hello, Detective Jeff," she smiled as she responded. "It's your friendly counterpart out here in the City. How are you?"

Now it was Jeff's turn to smile. He knew full well that Danielle was on the other end of the line. He also knew that she knew that he knew. It was amusing.

"Hi there, long lost partner. I'm fine. Fighting crime for our community."

Danielle laughed.

"Good to know. Hey, listen, I'm sure you heard about the meeting between the sheriffs and the fire marshal, right," she asked.

"Ha," responded Jeff. "I think everybody's heard."

"Right? I guess it was brutal," Danielle said. "But honestly, I don't blame them. Kind of a shit show."

"Yeah. I mean throwing out an inconclusive report and then basically ordering us to take over. The fire marshal doesn't have that kind of authority."

"No. Let's face it. The only way we would have stayed involved would have been if the drones had found something," said Danielle.

"Yeah," said Jeff. "Did you read the draft report?"

"You know I did," said Danielle. She then confessed that she had printed a copy of the report including the 40 pages of lab results and studied it at home.

"I was hoping to discover something," Danielle told Jeff, "but, I didn't. It was a large fire. The building burned quickly. Nobody got hurt. It doesn't feel like it should be the end of the story, but I think it is, unless you've found something."

"No," responded Jeff. "Actually, I read the draft, but I didn't look too closely at the lab results. I trust them. You?"

"I actually do. I think this was just one of those things. The fire, I mean. There doesn't seem to be an obvious cause. At least there were no injuries."

Jeff agreed. He needed to say something else, otherwise this conversation was rapidly coming to an end.

"I don't suppose Laura Mason reached back out," asked Jeff.

"Not that I'm aware. I think if she'd called my sergeant, I would've heard about it. You know, it's funny that a woman with multiple sheriffs on her contact list suddenly went dark," said Danielle.

"Maybe," said Jeff. "Or maybe she realized that everyone bent over backwards for her and now she's trying to save face."

"I never thought about that, but you could be right. Better to slink away after making such a stink."

"I don't guess there's any point in reviewing the lab results together," said Jeff, half asking. He held his breath for her response.

"Probably not," said Danielle. She wanted to be honest. "I don't think there's anything here. Like your drone footage."

"Yeah, okay. Well, I guess I'll save a tree and not print it all out then."

Danielle laughed out loud. She suddenly realized she had blown an easy opportunity to see Jeff. But if he wanted to get together, he should just ask. He was maybe a little too polite. Red flag, she thought. She liked polite, but infused with assertiveness for God's sake. They weren't in high school. They were both grown ass adults.

"I suspect we'll read the final document when it's posted. I think it will be released on Monday, " said Jeff, stating the obvious. He was mad at himself that he hadn't pulled the trigger and asked her to dinner. Coward. But it had still been a pleasant conversation. The pair hung up. They would both be reading the final report on Monday.

CHAPTER
33

Just as Elizabeth had expected, Richard called. Always so kind and sincere. He wondered if she was available for dinner on Monday evening. Elizabeth knew she should agree even though she was physically and mentally exhausted. She wanted forward progress. She needed to talk with him sooner rather than later. About selling the house. And, to say goodbye.

He wanted to meet at the Ritz. It had been "their" place, where Richard felt most comfortable. She never felt at ease there but endured it because he was the client and he paid her very well. Truthfully, too well. She would dress simply in black. Head to toe. The dress, heels, and signature scarf around her head. She knew which handbag she would select to complete the ensemble. She thought about conducting some research regarding the real estate market, but decided she need not concern herself with those details. Richard would maneuver through it all in a show of affection and power. He would take care of everything. He would take care of her.

Elizabeth wasn't a phone watcher, but over the remainder of the weekend, she checked again and again to see if she had any messages from her two remaining clients. She did not. She really hadn't needed to check. She received automated notifications. She hated how nervous she felt inside. She wasn't obligated to speak with them at all.

She owed them nothing. They could be abandoned. But that wasn't Elizabeth's style, and she wanted them to believe her story. She was returning to New York. It would prevent them from searching, not that they would. They could each find a new Elizabeth. Or maybe even someone completely dissimilar. She didn't care.

The San Francisco weather was lovely. Elizabeth wanted to soak up her City by the Bay one last time. Before she said goodbye. She would never return. She would visit her favorite spots, and maybe do some shopping. This time at the places where Sarah would spend her money. She needed to slowly return to herself. She wasn't going back to Pacific Grove carrying Louis Vuitton luggage filled with Chanel and Hermes. Well, maybe a few of her most favored pieces. No, she needed jeans and some effortless pencil skirts. A couple of pairs of sensible heels, a pair or two of sneakers, and definitely some flip flops. A half dozen sweatshirts and plenty of tees. She walked into the afternoon air. She wanted to take her mind off her remaining clients. She knew she could complete her shopping quickly.

It was just after 4:00 p.m. when Elizabeth headed home, multiple handle bags on her arms. She was tired, but cheery. She walked through the front door, carried the bags directly upstairs, and placed them on her Italian linen bedding. She found a pair of scissors in a pale blush porcelain cup sitting on the nearby desk. She carefully removed every price tag, and in some cases, sizing stickers running in a vertical strip down the front of her newly purchased clothing. She thought it best to launder everything. Some things, more than once. She especially didn't want the sweatshirts or tees to look brand new. They needed to appear worn. It became a project of sorts on Sunday evening and well into Monday.

Richard had wanted a late dinner, giving Elizabeth ample time to shower, dry her hair, and carefully apply her make-up. For him, late meant 6:30 p.m. She dressed as she had decided the previous afternoon, in black. She added red lipstick for drama. She owed it to Richard. Her nails matched her lips. She gave the illusion of a 1950s Chanel model. He would be impressed. Her look would also confirm for him, what Elizabeth suspected Richard already knew. This was goodbye.

Richard didn't want to meet at the bar this evening. He had reserved The San Francisco Suite. The hotel had more expensive accommodations, but they were fairly modern. He preferred the navy and cream color scheme of the room named for his city. It was peaceful and sensible. Classic.

As had always been the case, Elizabeth arrived first. She approached the concierge, rather than the reservation associate. He handed her a white envelope which contained the room key. She felt special tonight. She was delighted with her choice of clothing. She was pretty. She didn't want to break his heart. He was a like a grandfather to Elizabeth, something Sarah couldn't understand. She had only ever known mother and daughter.

Elizabeth could see the champagne chilling on ice from the doorway. She stepped inside, removed her black cashmere coat, and placed it over the edge of the plush navy velvet sofa which looked out over the windows of a main interior space. A set of doors offered a glimpse of the separate bedroom, which would not be used tonight. It was understood that Elizabeth should pour a glass of Veuve Clicquot and enjoy it. A tray filled with cheeses and crackers and dried fruits sat on a glass coffee table. It wouldn't be touched.

Twenty minutes passed before Richard gave a gentle knock. She could hear the card key release the lock. He took one look at her, and his face changed. He had an idea of what he would confront, but it was now real. Elizabeth gave Richard a gentle smile. He placed his coat directly on top of hers, then sat down. She reached over and poured him his own glass of champagne. No scotch tonight, as was his custom. They stared at each other with a special fondness and knowing. The conversation was almost sympathetic. As Elizabeth guessed, Richard would have the house sold and the money deposited into an account of her choosing. He would insist on an all cash purchase. He felt he could complete the transaction within a couple of weeks.

They held each other's hands and sat in silence. Finally, she reached over and kissed his cheek. It was her signal. He stood up, took his coat, and walked through the hotel room door.

CHAPTER
34

Laura was on the phone to her CFO within seconds of Michael's departure from the ranch. The winery was underinsured. This news was difficult to share. It was equally difficult to process, especially coming from her husband, the man she had trusted, but not loved. Anymore. Thanks to his betrayal, there was no way to design and build a 10,000 square-foot office complex comparable to what had originally stood. The two women discussed a strategy. The conversation was brief. In the name of the environment, the new structure would be smaller, more energy efficient, and more reflective of PFV's public tasting room. Half the size. Maybe smaller. That could work. It made sense.

Rachel, Laura's CFO, had established a relationship with the insurance company shortly after the fire, at Laura's request. She would be involved with the inner workings of the payout. Michael had signed documents in agreement. He wanted out of the situation which he had created. With a "lack of cause" final report issued by the fire marshal in hand, the insurance company was now reviewing the policy and establishing its own documentation with regard to the reimbursement for the PFV Winery. It was fairly straightforward. More difficult would be the policy renewal process. The cost would undoubtedly be much higher, following a claim of this size. Laura, Michael, and Rachel all understood this would be the case.

The contractor who had originally built the Palmer Family Vineyard structures 20 years ago was now retired. At Laura's request, he provided the names of two builders whom he believed would deliver an exceptional product. Each had their favorite architect. Michael was standing down completely from the decision-making. Laura, her CFO, and the entire Board of Directors would all take part. It sounded like a grueling proposition to Michael. He would have never allowed more than three executive officers to be involved. However, Laura was the sort of person who liked window dressing. Give everyone a voice, even though in the end, she would lay down the law. It would be a waste of resources, but in Laura's mind, she was doing everyone a favor by keeping them involved.

For now, her executive staff all coexisted in three portable office units. The Costco agreement had been signed and was fully executed. It was not only something to be celebrated, but it would also be transformative for PFV. Costco Wholesale Corporation's business model was based on offering only 3,000 products at its locations at any given time, allowing for steep customer discounts. This was in stark contrast to the average grocery store which carried 40,000. To be among such an elite group of vendors was impressive. PFV Winery was now running 24/7 to fulfill purchase orders.

The wine itself was readily available, but the bottling and distribution processes were onerous. The Palmer Family Vineyard had been offered two options by their new partner. First, bottle PFV wine under Costco's in-house brand, Kirkland. Second, bottle PFV wines under their own label. Laura, unsurprisingly, had chosen the latter. The wine and its shipping methodology both had to meet packaging standards set by Costco, which exceeded those of the Alcohol and Tobacco Tax and Trade Bureau, better known as the TTB. Costco was a warehouse operation. Products were moved daily. Hundreds of people touched their merchandise. Safety measures were high, to coincide with the high cost of their liability insurance. It took a lot of effort to step up to these superior standards. However, the financial gain for PFV would be profound. Still, Laura was disciplined. She knew better than to borrow money against the gains or to use the funding directly to offset the underpayment of the insurance for the new building. Her business was fragile, and she needed a cash reserve to feel more secure. She did not need a 10,000-square-foot office space anymore.

The insurance company disbursed the payout in mid-September. For Laura, it had felt like a lifetime. Anyone else would have disagreed. To have a check less than two months following such a devastating event, was lightning fast. A new premium was set to insure the entire property, its buildings, and the employees. The cost was going to rise more than 40 percent. Laura would use some of the funds from her new contract to cover the costs. It wasn't a fun way to spend money, but it was necessary. Without insurance and the Costco venture, her family business would be finished.

She had stayed awake many nights thinking about the prospect of having to sell off the land. Her grandfather's legacy. The idea made her physically sick to her stomach. She was beside herself with joy that she didn't have to think about that for now, but she was acutely aware that Costco held the future of her company in the palm of its hands. She could not rely on that business long-term. She would need to rebuild and at the same time look to additional distributors. It crossed her mind that she might finally have to succumb to the trendy alcoholic beverage market, but that would be only as a last resort. She wanted to stay true to the label. Not to a tall, skinny Gen Z aluminum can.

CHAPTER
35

Michael had all but disappeared from Laura's life. He kept himself busy with his own firm and did his best to be at home in the early evening to share time with Aiden. He had made a couple of international trips. First to London, and then to China. It was not unheard of for these countries to reach out to Americans. Michael Mason had a stellar reputation for keeping things discreet when a company or agency needed help. Of course, there was a steep price to pay for this level of discretion.

Fall had fully settled into California. The fog in San Francisco had cleared. Michael still thought about Elizabeth, but he told himself it was better this way. Completely alone. He knew Elizabeth had fallen in love with him, and he just couldn't see himself in a long-term, complicated relationship. Still, he missed her very much. He thought he had seen her in the middle of Union Square with several shopping bags, but he would have never approached his Elizabeth on the street. She appeared so different. Casual, relaxed. But also, not so pulled together, which was surprising to him. He thought of her only as he demanded. Even his version of casual was expensive. It never occurred to him that she would live a different life outside of their relationship.

In fact, the scene had actually bothered him. Something inside him festered. So much so that he finally picked up the phone and called his CFO, Dennis. He needed some investigative work. Against his better judgement, Michael Mason wanted to know how Elizabeth Stevens spent her time, and her money. And who she was spending it with. The firm had several private investigative agencies on retainer. These organizations were used to vet potential senior executives for their clients. At one time, Mason Recruiting had its own internal investigation unit. But it was cost prohibitive, especially when the services weren't required on a daily, or even weekly basis. It made more sense to have options, both in the States and abroad. Dennis would know who to call. Michael didn't want to waste time on a background check. It was a bit late for that. He wanted eyes on her.

Dennis arranged for a private investigator to begin surveilling Ms. Stevens immediately. First though, the agency would need to uncover her home address. The investigator assured the CFO that it would only take a matter of minutes. Property ownership was a matter of public record. As long as Ms. Stevens had purchased her home, the lookup would be a simple matter. The investigator would then report on her whereabouts, contacts, and general habits. She was to be watched around the clock, which meant several shifts. It wouldn't be a single person keeping track of Elizabeth. All reports were to be made directly to Dennis. He decided it would be best to serve as a filter between the findings and his boss, just as he did in their work lives. Until Dennis knew how Elizabeth spent her time, and with whom, he wasn't going to allow Michael to be made aware of every detail. It could be unpleasant, to say the least, depending on what his boss did or didn't want to know.

For some reason, Michael had never discussed Elizabeth with Dennis. Not once. Until now. She had only been to the office a few times. She was listed as a lawyer and consultant. Although Dennis was the CFO, he didn't get into the weeds when it came to paying Mason Recruiting invoices, unless the totals were in the high six figures or more. The company had a rather extensive accounting department which took care of the day-to-day operations. Michael knew he could trust Dennis. He came close to telling him about the relationship with Elizabeth over dinner a few times. But frankly, Michael wanted Elizabeth all to himself. He had never wanted to know if Elizabeth had other men. She always seemed available. It was his ego which wouldn't allow him to believe she had others.

Michael felt ashamed about his decision. It would have both startled and saddened Elizabeth to know that he would choose to have her followed. She would have felt betrayed and misunderstood. It would have frightened her, as well. Speculating about his intensions would have been intriguing, but being stalked would have unnerved her.

* * * * *

A silver Toyota Rav4 was the vehicle of choice for the first shift. The investigator pulled into a parking space on the street about four homes down from Elizabeth's. Thankfully, the spots were along a vertical row, headlights to taillights. The diagonal spots, which had become necessary with the influx of electric charging stations, made it difficult to see anything. Even more difficult, cars were not allowed to park in those spaces for any length of time. It was exactly 9:00 p.m. The night sky was dark. A bit late to begin a Monday evening surveillance, but the investigator had only received the call three hours ago. Remote microscopic Wi-Fi cameras and microphones would be placed around her home when the first opportunity arose. Elizabeth didn't appear to have a car, so there was nothing to be done in that regard.

The investigator could see several lights on in the two-story building. Actually, the house was three stories, as were many homes in San Francisco proper. Ground floors served as garages, and most of the time, offered no living space. Elizabeth's home had a large bay window stretching across the front of its creamy white plaster façade. A double wide garage door sat below the window. It was painted a pure white. There were no blinds or sheers covering the window glass. It always seemed strange to this particular investigator that people didn't want more privacy. He could look straight into the living room and see

Elizabeth. She was propped up on a butterscotch colored leather sofa with a laptop appearing to serve as a TV. He couldn't make out what she was watching. But he had a good view of her shapely legs. She was wearing white shorts and thick gray socks. It appeared she was eating corn nuts from a black ceramic mixing bowl. He had no idea that only 30 minutes prior, she had returned from her appointment and last goodbye with Richard. He missed the beautiful woman exiting a cab, wearing a black cashmere coat and polished heels. Instead, he was looking at a 30-something woman in a sweatshirt and socks.

At precisely 10:00 p.m., Elizabeth got up off the sofa, turned out the lights in the living room, and headed upstairs. Another light came on momentarily, but this time the watchman couldn't see inside. The two windows on the top floor were shuttered. Within a few minutes, the glow from the upstairs lights was gone. The home's interior was dark. Ms. Stevens was down for the evening. It would be a long night for the investigator sitting in his car. He was familiar with what it took to be patient, to accept the long hours. He was a retired cop.

CHAPTER
36

Jeff Sufford was on the phone, leaning as far back as his black office chair could withstand, when his lieutenant walked over and motioned for him. Jeff held up a hand, signaling he would meet his boss in his office. He just needed five minutes to get off the call. Despite the hierarchy, cops respected each other and their work.

Jeff finished his call, then walked down the hall, straight into the lieutenant's office, situating himself in one of two empty chairs.

"What's up," Jeff asked his senior supervisor. He crossed his legs and waited.

It was a bit unusual to be called into the lieutenant's office. Usually, detectives reported to a sergeant, but it wasn't completely unheard of either. The lieutenant was responsible for a large portion of the Napa Valley Sheriff's Office staff, including Jeff's unit. The majority of law officers and administrators had cooperative and casual relationships. They didn't take themselves too seriously. It was Napa Valley after all, not New York City. The office wasn't large, but not small either. Jeff didn't know everyone, but he had a broad circle of friends at the office.

"Just wanted to let you know that the fire marshal's final report has been uploaded to the shared drive," his boss responded. "I know you've been keeping up on it all, but there hasn't been anything new submitted since the release of the draft report and the marshal's attempt to dump all the work onto us. I figured you'd want to know."

"Yeah, thanks. I checked over the weekend, actually. I thought maybe that the final report would be posted within hours after Navarro was chewed out by our illustrious sheriff. But I guess the fire marshal wanted to do it on his own timeline," said Jeff. "Still, it's pretty quick."

"Well, you've got my permission to spend some time on it. Then get back to me. I'm curious, but not curious enough to read the damned thing myself."

Jeff laughed. He would finish up some paperwork and take a look. It crossed his mind that Danielle had probably already seen it. He would know if she'd at least opened the document when he logged into the system. Jeff wanted to play it cool. He didn't want to seem overanxious to review the report, just because he had been given permission. He wanted it to appear as though he didn't care too much. Of course, he had just given away the fact that he'd been in the system the day before. Jeff was pretty sure that his boss was already aware of that fact. Danielle probably was, as well.

About an hour later, Jeff logged into the shared drive. Sure enough, Detective Philipson had opened the file that morning. It was now smack dab in the middle of the day. She hadn't called Jeff. His ego was bruised. Maybe she had been interrupted and hadn't finished her review. Or maybe she was finished with it all. Final was final, and for the second time, law enforcement was no longer involved. This was definitely the end of any shared work.

The final version of the fire marshal's report was largely the same as the draft, with the exception that any reference or suggestion that law enforcement conduct an independent review had been removed. The report detailed countless lab results and had dozens of photographs listed as attachments. Ultimately, the key finding read simply, "Inconclusive." The fire marshal laid blame on no one. That was that.

Both the Napa Valley and the Alameda county sheriffs were satisfied. They did not need or want any further involvement by their staff.

Money had been spent on officers, detectives, a drone search, and administrators. Enough was enough no matter how much money Laura Palmer-Mason and her fine friends contributed to their campaigns. It was an unfortunate event. The majority of the Palmer Family Vineyard and its assets remained standing. Most importantly, there had been no injuries.

Jeff Sufford remained impressed with the exhibits presented in the report. He and the Napa Valley sheriff's drone team had produced similar work over a much larger area. They were all proud. It had been an interesting exercise to use the technology over a relatively large area that was difficult to maneuver. It would also now serve as a data reference.

Should he pick up the phone and call her? Jeff thought about it for a few minutes. It was pushing 4:00 p.m. on Monday afternoon. Danielle had probably had a busy start to her week, rationalized Jeff. If he didn't call her office now, he might miss her. Then again, it wasn't like he didn't have her cell number. The thing was, they were both on the clock. If he waited much longer, it would be after hours. If there was such a thing for a sheriff's detective. Jeff picked up his desk phone and dialed. One ring, two, three. It went to voicemail.

"Hey there. It's Jeff Sufford. Just wondered if you'd had a chance to look at the final report on the PFV fire thing. It's pretty straightforward." He took a breath. "Anyways, give me a call when you've got a moment."

He hung up. He hoped he hadn't sounded desperate. "Give me a call," Jeff thought to himself. It was too late. The message had been left. He was probably overthinking it. She'd call him back. He hoped.

CHAPTER
37

Elizabeth's missing gentlemen had finally called. The first, on Tuesday morning. The second, on Tuesday at precisely noon. She was relieved. She knew that contacting either would have immediately resulted in red flags for both. She was thankful that she had narrowed her client list to four. Elizabeth had made certain that each man felt as though he were the only one. Richard most certainly knew better, but he played along. Michael assumed there was no one else. The other two weren't needy or big thinkers. But they were big spenders, and that's why they were Elizabeth's clients.

David, the first to call, simply wanted to fuck. She would connect with him at his place along the Pacific Coast Highway on Tuesday night. It wasn't much notice, but she didn't care. The sooner the conversation was put to rest, the better. The waterfront property was where they usually spent their time. Only on rare occasions had they shared a meal together in a public place. She didn't mind. The PCH house felt safe. Their encounters were rather repetitive, but it was his money, and he spent it freely.

The routine was always the same. Elizabeth would use an Uber. David would have a meal prepared. They would chat about sports and celebrities. Then they'd sit on the oversized couch in near darkness, until they had undressed each other. He would lead her into the bedroom. He was a good lover. Gentle. Always holding her face in his soft hands. He was physically fit. In much better shape than Michael, but he was also 15 years younger. She appreciated his incredible upper body and the work which resulted in his defined arms and chest.

Elizabeth's favorite part of her evenings with David was the quietness under the bedding. After. He was never in a hurry to gather up his clothes. They would lay together, sometimes for an hour, lightly sleeping in each other's warmth. He would then call a car, and she would disappear. Until the next time. Elizabeth would not, however, be sleeping with him one last time. She didn't have an attachment to him, so it was best to just be done. A clean break. The conversation would be brief. She would keep the Uber waiting.

Her second gentleman, Colton, asked Elizabeth to attend a business dinner at Atelier Crenn on Fillmore Street the same week, on Thursday night. The restaurant had three Michelin stars; Elizabeth recalled. She was annoyed. Certainly, he had been invited to dinner prior to his Tuesday afternoon phone call. A-list celebrities were the only people who got reservations on short notice. Even politicians and sports figures had to wait their turn. He was asking her to accompany him with only two days' notice. She would have to sit through a lengthy meal with strangers before breaking the news about her move. She wasn't going to let him go before dinner. That would be tacky. She had more class than that.

Colton would deposit the funds for their time together into her business account, prior to the evening. He always did. It was a bit presumptuous that there would never be a change in plans. However, Elizabeth had learned long ago that if her client list was to remain consistent, she needed to be available. Always. She never cancelled. It was understood though, that should his plans change, the money would remain in her account. For the first time, Elizabeth would return his money. She wanted it that way. It would be more hours than she wished to share with him. Still, the encounter was welcomed. She would close the door forever on this portion of her entirely made-up life. It would all be over soon.

Elizabeth had packed her new, but carefully curated wardrobe for Sarah, into two nondescript duffle bags. She conscientiously selected only three Hermes scarves and one small Chanel bag to keep, placing them at the bottom of one of the duffels. She would leave everything else behind. The things she once coveted no longer held value. The only thing that mattered to her now was returning to Pacific Grove, to her mother, and to the place she called home.

She hadn't heard anything from Richard about the sale of the house. It had only been a day. It would take time. She would need to be patient.

Elizabeth placed the two duffle bags on the floor inside the guest bedroom closet down the hall from the main ensuite. Other than a couple of wool blankets on a shelf, the closet was empty. Nobody had ever slept in the room. Not even Elizabeth. Not once. She didn't need to hide the bags. It wasn't as if anyone would be visiting, but she wanted them out of her way, for now.

She showered, then looked at the rows of clothing hanging in her closet, deciding what to wear. She had actually created a spreadsheet to keep track of with whom she had worn a particular outfit. She never wanted to wear anything twice with a client unless they specifically requested it. It would be cool along the coast tonight, Elizabeth thought to herself. Not that she would be spending any time outside. She selected a pair of black slacks and a black turtleneck sweater. Elegant casual. Her panties and bra were always a set. Black tonight. Not that anyone was going to see them. No jewelry, except for a pair of diamond stud earrings. Her hair hung in waves below her shoulders. Her shoes were simple, but very expensive loafers. Patent leather.

The Uber arrived at 5:49 p.m. The drive would be about 40 minutes. She should find herself in the driveway at just about 6:30 p.m., unless there was traffic. She always erred on the side of caution. Better to be early and have the driver pull in someplace a couple of miles up the road, than to be late. She had paid drivers extra on more than one occasion. She wasn't expected until 6:45 or 7:00 p.m., so she would be fine. She'd made this trip many times but had never had the same

Uber driver. Funny, she thought. Then again, San Francisco was a big city, and oftentimes drivers would come from other areas to make the big fares. They could actually see the estimated fee before saying "yes" to a ride. It made sense.

The journey was uneventful. For such an expensive address, the PCH was rather loud. Just like Newport and Malibu, many of the homes sat feet, or sometimes inches, from the road. She looked out the window as they passed trees and homes and cars. She wasn't nervous. She was grateful. She wanted it to be over. No drama. No big explanation. A sincere conversation. She would end it with a gentle kiss, this time his face in her hands.

Elizabeth arrived at her destination sooner than expected. She asked the driver to continue past the address to a nearby lookout. The two sat in silence, the windows rolled down, enjoying the breeze. At precisely 6:50 p.m., she had him turn the car around and drop her off, asking him to wait. He agreed. Ten minutes at the most, she promised. He watched her as she opened a small gate on the righthand side of the garage and disappear.

As Elizabeth had anticipated, the talk was brief. David pretended he understood. She could see his eyes flinch. His head gave a subtle nod backward. His face seemed to flush. As she guessed, he didn't ask a lot of questions. Even now, he needed a last shred of control. And dignity, perhaps. He looked deeply into Elizabeth's eyes, catching her gaze one last time. He held her hands in his and leaned in to kiss her warm, wet mouth. She allowed it. She knew he was disappointed. Hurt. Probably a bit sad. And then, they moved away from each other.

That was it. She would return the money. She didn't need to. He would have gladly permitted her to keep it. As a final gift. Elizabeth felt his hand on her shoulder as she was leaving. He turned her so they were facing each other. This time, they embraced fully and shared one last kiss. She did not hold his face in her hands.

* * * * *

It had been fewer than 10 minutes when the private investigator saw Elizabeth return to the car. He was certain that his dark blue Honda Accord which had been following them hadn't been noticed. The entire incident was curious. "Who the hell takes an Uber all the way out here then turns right around and leaves," he wondered out loud. He jotted down the car's license plate and the address of the house. It would take minutes to determine the owner of both, but cell service was spotty at best out along the coast. He would have to wait until they were back in the City to look up the details. He'd go to the county records for the house, and to the DOJ for the car. The navy Honda followed the Uber back to California Street. Elizabeth got out of the car and headed straight into her house.

The investigator watched as Elizabeth removed her shoes. He couldn't see the kitchen through the bay window. It was apparently in the back of the house, but just a few minutes later Elizabeth was settling into her leather sofa with what looked like a chicken pot pie. That was unexpected. No salad? No plate of veggies and tofu? It was before 9:00 p.m. when she turned out the downstairs lights and headed upstairs. Just as the investigator had witnessed the prior evening, a glow from an upstairs light remained on for a bit, and then the house went dark. But this night was different. He had something to report. A suspicious rendezvous.

CHAPTER
38

It was Wednesday morning before Detective Philipson returned Detective Sufford's call. She told herself she was playing hard to get. It was dumb. Who was she kidding? She had nothing going on in her personal life.

The thing was, she didn't have anything interesting to contribute to a conversation. The fire marshal's report was concise. It wasn't a surprise that the punt to law enforcement had been removed. That had been expected. Danielle had spent Monday evening and a large portion of Tuesday thinking about her response. She didn't want it to be a 30-second phone call. She wanted him to ask her out for Christ's sake. She took the phone's receiver in her hand and dialed his number. It was just before 10:00 a.m.; maybe he wouldn't pick up.

"Detective Jeff Sufford, Napa County Sheriff's Office," he answered on the second ring.

"Hey there, it's Danielle," she replied, in her most casual voice.

"Hey yourself. Thanks for returning my call." Jeff said. He didn't wait for a response. "I was just curious if you'd given the fire marshal's final report a once over."

Danielle knew that at a minimum, Jeff could see she had accessed the files. To be fair though, he had no way of knowing if she'd spent five minutes or five hours reviewing the report.

"I did," she said. "I saw that it had been posted on Monday morning. I printed it out and read it at home yesterday. Sorry I didn't get back to you sooner."

"I mean, you do have other work," Jeff replied. "Not much there."

"Agreed. Nothing surprising. Basically, the same as the draft, only with all references to getting us removed, just like our bosses wanted."

"I don't know," said Jeff, trying to prolong what should really have only been a two-minute call. "It just seems a bit too neat and tidy."

"I guess," was Danielle's response. "I mean, for an inconclusive report."

"Yeah, you got me there," said Jeff, feeling immediately stupid. "It happens."

"It does," she said quickly in agreement. "Happens all the time around here."

"Listen, it was great to work with you," Jeff told Danielle. "I know it was short-lived, but I enjoyed getting to know you. Do you think we could grab a beer sometime?" There. He had asked her out. Sort of. The question hadn't been very specific.

Danielle decided it was time to take charge. "Well, I don't have any plans this Friday night."

Danielle could hear the shift in Jeff's voice. He sounded relaxed. Completely. He probably hadn't minded her taking charge of the situation. At all. She wasn't forward. She was confident.

"Friday works. I can come into Berkeley, or do you want to meet up somewhere around the halfway mark?"

"I have a better idea." she announced. "You owe me a burger. How 'bout late afternoon? We can grab an early bite."

It was perfect, the two detectives both thought to themselves.

"Great, if you're sure you don't mind driving all the way out here," said Jeff.

"Of course not. But this burger better be worth it," Danielle laughed. Jeff knew she was kidding.

The two officers hung up. Both had smiles on their faces. Finally, they would spend some time together which had nothing to do with work. It didn't happen often. It would be fun.

CHAPTER
39

Michael's CFO, Dennis Smith-Hodges, had the private investor's most recent findings in front of him. It all seemed so Tom Clancy. He wondered if anyone under 30 knew or read Clancy? At least half the office was under 40, he guessed, still thinking to himself. Hell, did anyone born after 1990 even read? Dennis quickly brought his thoughts back to the report.

Apparently, Ms. Elizabeth Stevens had some unusual extracurricular activities. Driving out to a random house on the Pacific Coast Highway, only to turn around and come straight home? What the hell, thought Dennis. According to the notes, the house belonged to a wealthy 40 something-year-old lawyer. But, it wasn't his primary residence. In fact, he lived in Sacramento. That was a good two-hour plus drive from the Bay without traffic. Distance was never measured in miles when you lived in California. It was calculated in time spent on the road.

The report detailed that the lawyer was married with an eight year-old daughter. He was a partner in a large firm, a registered republican in a blue state, and the owner of a brand new fully electric Porsche. He went to Cal for undergraduate school, then University of Chicago law. He was originally from Sacramento, probably the reason he had returned, thought Dennis. The wife was a lobbyist for the dental industry. The couple had no credit card debt. They didn't have so much as a parking ticket between them. And that was all the information the investigator had gathered. For now. A deeper dive could be done, but Dennis hadn't authorized it. Not yet, anyway.

The car which carried Elizabeth Stevens along the PCH was a nondescript Uber. Nothing there. Why in the world would a Mason Recruiting consultant be wasting an hour and a half in a car for an exchange taking fewer than 10 minutes, Dennis questioned silently. On the books, Ms. Stevens was a lawyer. But Dennis knew better at this point. Honestly, having her followed had been the tipoff from his boss. Sure, maybe she *was* a lawyer, but Dennis was certain his boss was also sleeping with her. Or maybe he was contemplating an intimate relationship if she checked out. Honestly, good for you Michael, Dennis said to himself.

Mr. and Mrs. Michael Mason were not a happy couple. It was obvious the marriage was dead. They lived in separate homes. They both worked excessive hours. The couple never vacationed together. Hell, they didn't even go to a movie together. The only time Michael and Laura were seen together was for the obligatory winery function which Laura deemed "essential" for Michael to attend. Occasionally, she drove into the City to watch one of the boys compete in a sporting activity. But the older the kids got, the less Laura was involved. She was never around when Dennis came over to the San Francisco house to watch a game with Michael. There were few signs of a woman even living in the house. Michael had never complained, but Dennis was fully aware that his boss had been living the life of a bachelor for a half-dozen years. Dennis couldn't be completely certain that Michael was seeing Elizabeth, but he wouldn't blame his boss for wanting someone in his life.

Dennis was getting lost in his thoughts again. He turned his attention to the words of the private investigator. If the retired cop following Elizabeth had seen her carry in a pile of documents or a file or even a briefcase, it might have made sense. This didn't. Two lawyers having an encounter at a coastal retreat? This was definitely beginning to sound like a Tom Clancy novel. The investigator had wanted to retrieve the phone records of both attorneys, but that would be expensive and require a subpoena to be legal. That meant Elizabeth would be alerted to the investigation. Dennis declined. Following Michael's mystery woman was one thing. Paying to illegally obtain records, so she wouldn't be tipped off, was another. It wasn't worth the risk. Besides, this pair was probably smart enough to use burner phones. Dennis put his feet up on his desk and mulled over everything he'd learned for the next several minutes. He wasn't going to tell Michael any of this. It just brought up more questions than answers. Elizabeth hadn't spent the night with the guy. Hell, she hadn't spent 15 minutes.

The investigator would continue to send his team out to monitor her activities, though he suggested that maybe two evening shifts might suffice. Elizabeth didn't seem to do anything particularly unusual during the day. She jogged. She got coffee. She picked up a few groceries. Besides, video cameras and microphones had been placed around the house on Tuesday while Elizabeth had been galavanting out along the PCH. It was now Thursday morning. And nothing. This woman didn't seem to have any friends. She didn't make phone calls. Other than her three-mile morning jog, she hadn't left the house all day Wednesday. She had cooked. She had watched TV. She had done an at-home yoga workout. Her movements had been unremarkable.

Out of some strange level of respect, there were no cameras placed inside the bathrooms. The investigator told Dennis he had standards. So, unless she was making calls from inside her shower, Elizabeth was in essence a recluse. Except for the fact that she had taken some sort of joy ride out along the coast for a private meeting, this woman appeared to be nearly invisible. Of course, what Dennis and the investigators didn't know was that they had just missed the calls from Elizabeth's clients. The men had set up their meetings with her only hours before the recording equipment had been installed.

Dennis agreed to call off the daytime surveillance. Elizabeth's movements, or lack thereof, spoke volumes, he thought to himself. If Ms. Stevens were a high-priced attorney, Michael's relationship or activities aside, she would be going to work. At a minimum, she would be making calls and holding online meetings. It was crickets. He wasn't going to put in any effort, or pay anyone else, to discover whether or not Elizabeth was an attorney from New York. That was absolutely not the point. His boss wanted to know what she was up to, and it wasn't the CFO's place to ask the proverbial "why." He would wait until the end of the week to give Michael a report. All of it. Maybe some additional pieces of information would come together to help the puzzle make sense. A good numbers guy was never in a hurry to over share news. Numbers made sense. People, not so much.

* * * * *

Michael had made himself scarce and hid out in his office. He took unnecessary meetings and generally kept himself busy. He had tried not to think about her. However, the manufactured distractions had been pointless. He was back in it. He missed Elizabeth. Seeing her. Conversing with her. Being intimate with her. It had been more difficult to shut it down in his head than he had anticipated. She would never call. She never had. He couldn't pick up the phone. Where would that end? So instead, he had spent money to have her followed. It felt so primitive. Really? Having her followed? Not once in four years. It would have been a simple matter. His confidence was all he had needed to assure himself that she was exclusively his. This was *his* fault. Allowing an emotional connection had cost him the relationship. He sensed a growing attachment over the past two years. But when he understood that she had fallen in love, it had to be over.

Michael wondered when he would get an update from Dennis. He didn't want to appear eager. Michael guessed that his CFO knew he was in a personal relationship with Elizabeth. However, Dennis would never ask, and Michael wasn't about to share. For now, he had resigned himself to his work and spending time with Aiden. They were buddies. His wife? He didn't care anymore. They would stay married on paper, unless she asked for a divorce. He would give it to her, he decided, without any questions. He knew that would kill Laura. If asked, it would be because she wanted a fight. A fight would suggest that he was still invested and willing to do damage control. He wasn't. As long as they lived separate lives, he could go on like this forever. He would stay married, for Aiden.

Michael wanted Elizabeth back in his life. He considered calling her. That had been his only means to connect with her over these past four years. They didn't have a secret meeting place. He had never thought to lease a hotel room, or condo. Because his ego had gotten in the way. It wasn't his job to protect her. It was her job to entertain him. Somehow, the lines had blurred, and he had started to lose control. He certainly didn't have any right now. Jesus.

He wasn't being honest with himself. He needed her more than he cared to admit. Not because he had fallen out of love with Laura. He had compartmentalized the two relationships a long time ago. He had been with other women, but he had never felt any significant emotional attachment. Until Elizabeth. The walls he'd built up around his heart were well fortified. He loathed appearing weak. Now, he was in the dark.

CHAPTER
40

Finally. A text message. Detective Danielle Philipson's brother had broken his silence after what he deemed was nearly unforgivable behavior from his older, and cherished, sister. The text simply read: "Let's move on."

It had been forever since the brother and sister had shared a text, let alone a phone conversation. It was killing Danielle; however, she knew better than to reach out to her younger brother before he was ready. She had walked out of the Ninth Circuit Court of Appeals, on the biggest day in his career, for what had turned out to be nothing. A fire, where she had been jerked around as to her involvement.

Now, Peter had opened the door. However, she was smart enough to know that her brother's text hadn't exactly been an invitation to pretend nothing had happened between them. She would wait a few hours before she responded. They were both busy. But they admired and loved one another very much. It would all be okay. Eventually.

About the only positive thing that had come from the whole experience was meeting Jeff Sufford. He was a nice guy. A good detective. He was detail oriented. And now, they were going out for what he claimed was the best burger in town. Danielle admitted to herself that she was excited. In fact, she'd been thinking about what to wear for their date. And it *was* a date. It wasn't couched in a working dinner, or to rehash the information from the fire marshal's report. Nope. Both detectives had agreed that there were no anomalies in the report, or its attachments. Or even law enforcement's own drone work. The heat from the fire had been so intense that there was nothing left to investigate. It was funny, thought Danielle. Most people incorrectly assumed that all investigations had a beginning, middle, and an end. But some cases never had an ending. Investigators were left hanging. No closure.

CHAPTER 41

Elizabeth removed her thick, white robe, placing it on a hook opposite the shower. Steam filled the space. This was it. The last time she would share an evening with her client, Colton. Or, any client. She felt as though she were washing the weight of the past 10 years off her body and down the drain literally. She understood that she would be obligated to speaking with Richard a time or two regarding the sale of her home, but even so, she would minimize the contact. She would just need to be kind if he called. She wanted her home sold quickly, quietly, and neatly. Richard was the only person she would trust to do that for her.

The bathroom's heated marble floor met Elizabeth's feet as she stepped from the hot water. One of the small luxuries she would miss when she returned to Pacific Grove. Nothing in comparison to missing her life as Sarah in the quaint oceanside town where she and her mother had raised each other not so long ago.

A Michelin-starred restaurant would never have been Elizabeth's choice for her final encounter to close the book on this life. So public. And such a long evening ahead. Still, it would all be over in a matter of hours. As she prepared for their dinner date, Colton was completely unaware of what lay ahead. No doubt, he was looking forward to showing her off to a group of people who were about to have an excruciatingly expensive meal.

Elizabeth selected an emerald green dress. It was silk and sleeveless. It clung to every curve of her body. The hem fell perfectly, a few inches below her knees. Rather than her signature black heels, tonight she slid a pair of Jimmy Choo nude pumps onto her feet. She had decided to wear her hair down, allowing the light curls to cascade across her back. She looked elegant. She felt pretty.

"Hello gorgeous," Elizabeth whispered the words aloud as she glanced at her mirrored reflection, fastening a diamond pendant around her neck.

* * * * *

The private investigator sat straight up in the seat of his car the moment he saw the black sedan pull up. He had been listening to the start of the night's NFL game. The Denver Broncos versus the Kansas City Chiefs. The Broncos were going to get killed. The Lincoln Town Car barely fit into the drive. An elegant man dressed in a signature black suit, white dress shirt, and black tie got out of the vehicle and headed straight for Elizabeth's front door, ringing the bell. This evening's surveillance was being conducted by the same retired cop who had wandered the PCH with her only two evenings prior, on what seemed like a pointless trip. Of course, the investigator knew better. You didn't follow the innocent.

The door opened. There stood Elizabeth Stevens in a stunning green dress. Her legs appeared to be a mile long, thought the cop. Wherever she was headed, she was in stark contrast to her buttoned up professional look two nights ago. This was going to be interesting, thought the on-looker. At least this outing had potential.

Elizabeth was guided into the sedan by the chauffeur. She carefully placed her legs into the back seat. The driver closed her door, then got into the car. He backed out of the driveway and headed into traffic, oblivious of the sedan following two cars behind. The trip was quick.

Fewer than 15 minutes. Whatever she was up to, she wasn't taking a long drive, thought the investigator. The black car doubled parked in front of Atelier Crenn on Fillmore Street. Their tail had no choice but to continue up the street. He glanced back and forth across the road, looking for a place to put his car. He saw someone pulling out about half a block up the street. He made an illegal U-turn and grabbed the empty spot. This was going to be tricky.

The PI didn't have direct access to the restaurant's front door, let alone an opportunity to get inside the place. This was clearly a very posh restaurant. Fortunately, there was a Starbucks just diagonal from Atelier Crenn. He'd start his surveillance from there and see how the night progressed. The black Town Car pulled away just as Elizabeth entered the establishment. The cop had no idea if she had been greeted by someone. He walked into the coffee shop, ordered a double espresso, then found a counter stool at a window facing the restaurant. He could see clearly into the establishment through its decorative windows using a small pair of Steiner binoculars.

Elizabeth joined a table for six, where five people were already seated. A man stood up and gave her a kiss on the cheek. He then pulled out her chair, signaling Elizabeth to sit down. This wasn't a business dinner. It appeared as if three couples were sharing an evening of fine dining, and probably boring conversation, thought the voyeur. Elizabeth outshone the other two women. She was with a well-dressed man. Probably late 40s. Good looking. Nah, handsome the investigator thought. All three couples were easy on the eyes. This was going to go on for hours, he thought to himself. He knew the Starbucks closed at 8:00 p.m., so he would have to find a new place from where he could continue watching.

At five minutes to closing, the investigator walked out of the Starbucks. He used their bathroom first. The three couples were still chatting away. Fortunately, dessert and coffee were being served. He was surprised. An early evening for such an expensive place. He was grateful. Watching people eat wasn't exactly riveting stuff. A sports bar next to the Starbucks was still open. There was only a partial view of the fancy joint across the street, but it was better than nothing. The PI ducked inside, sat at the edge of the bar, and ordered a grilled cheese sandwich with a side of fries and a beer. The beer was ordered just for show. He'd never drink on the job. From his vantage point, he could just make out the doors of the restaurant across the street. He couldn't pull out his binoculars for a closer look. There were too many people around. But as long as he could watch the couples exit, he felt comfortable.

It was another 40 minutes before the dinner party finally broke up. The investigator had polished off his food and paid the bill. He got off the barstool when he saw Elizabeth and her mystery man walk out onto the sidewalk. She took the man's hand and motioned up the street. They were going for a walk. Jesus Christ, thought the PI. Now what?

It was cold and dark. Mystery man took off his suit jacket and placed it around Elizabeth's shoulders. The investigator followed them from about 20 yards back. The great thing about cities like San Francisco was that there were always people around. It was fairly easy to go unnoticed. It wasn't New York City's Times Square, but San Francisco was a vibrant place. The investigator was impressed that Elizabeth was able to walk gracefully up the street in her heels. The couple came to the same corner where he had made the illegal U-turn in his car hours earlier. Elizabeth and her companion crossed the street. The retired cop did the same. It was impossible to tell if the pair were friends, or something more. And the conversation would remain between the two of them. Forever. They stopped in front of the now dimly lit Starbucks. She gave the gentleman a kiss on the cheek, then removed the borrowed jacket from around her shoulders, handing it back to him ever so gently. He took the jacket from her, then stood looking at her for a moment before he headed up the block. He hadn't rushed off, but he hadn't given her a hug either, and her kiss hadn't been reciprocated.

Elizabeth pulled her cell phone from her handbag and made a call. Within two minutes, the black sedan had reappeared. She was headed for home, the PI assumed. Still, he needed to confirm his suspicions. He got back into his own vehicle, which was parked only feet from the Starbucks and followed the Town Car. As suspected, it took her home. The driver got out of the sedan and accompanied Ms. Steven to her front door. She used a key to let herself inside. The black Town Car pulled away from the house and into the night.

The retired officer found a place down the street to park. He'd taken a lot of notes. However, the license plate of the black sedan was the only hard piece of evidence from which he could obtain solid facts. Random people at dinner. Conversation he couldn't hear. He might be able to go back to the restaurant and tip enough to get the name on the reservation, but that was probably about as far as he could go with it. Honestly, most restaurants of that caliber wouldn't hand over the details regardless of the cash placed in a pocket. It was their reputation at stake, and it wasn't worth it. Besides, the patrons tipped well enough to ensure flawless service, and privacy. The investigator sat and watched Elizabeth's home. The football game had ended. As predicted, the Chiefs had crushed the Broncos. Just as Elizabeth had done on Tuesday evening, the lights upstairs were on briefly, and then the house went dark.

CHAPTER
42

It was a glorious Friday morning Danielle Philipson concluded, as she pushed back the bedroom's white sheers. It was only 6:00 a.m. It would be hours before she met Detective Jeff Sufford for that burger. With traffic, she'd need to leave no later than 3:30 p.m. She had already told her boss that she would only be working a half-day. She was hoping he'd tell her to spend her time on the international drug bust files from home. He did not. She would have to drive into Dublin, but she would leave by noon. She wouldn't go on this date looking like she'd just come off a shift. Jeff had already seen that look, and frankly, it wasn't Danielle's favorite. Sure, some women felt best in a suit and heels. And they looked good in them. Danielle was more comfortable in jeans and sneakers. She owned two pairs of dress shoes, but more than a dozen pairs of rubber-soled footwear.

She stood in front of her closet. Unlike some of her friends who might have gone out and purchased something new to wear, Danielle was practical. Anything she wore would be new to Jeff. In addition to her sneaker collection, Danielle had quite the array of jeans. Dark rinse, light rinse, high rise, skinny, wide leg. It was a little ridiculous. She pulled out a favorite pair of button up fronts and a gray turtleneck sweater; they would be ideal for the occasion. It was cooler now. And getting dark much earlier in the evenings. She selected an understated pair of New Balance, if there was such a thing. New Balance shoes were no longer for fitness training. Sure, some people still ran in the brand, but celebrities had turned the tide and New Balance had shifted a large portion of its inventory with a focus toward fashion. White with charcoal suede logos adorning the sides. Perfect. She'd be back to take a shower and change before making the drive.

It was still early when Danielle finished her second cup of coffee. She headed out the door and across the street to her county assigned SUV. She was thankful she had plenty of work to take her mind off things. Besides Jeff, that "other thing" was her brother. They had exchanged a text or two, but she hadn't seen him in weeks. It seemed too early to call, but she decided that there was no time like the present. He could let it go to voicemail. She assumed he'd hear it later that morning. She scrolled to his contact information on her cell and hit the number as she pulled away from the curb.

Her brother's familiar voice came on the line.

"Hello. Thank you for calling. Please leave a message."

It was the most nondescript voicemail ever, thought Danielle. The only thing less personal would have been the automated bot message. Jesus, she thought. Always, always so conservative.

"Hi there. It's me," Danielle spoke. She was on speaker, so she hoped her voice would be clear. "Just thinking about you. Want to grab dinner this weekend? Let me know. Bye." Danielle ended the call. She knew she sounded a little desperate. She should. Her brother was still hurt.

The drive into the Alameda County Sheriff's Dublin location took about 50 minutes. Danielle pulled into the office parking lot just before 8:00 a.m. The office was quiet. She entered through the back door using her key card, then walked down the corridor to her office. She threw her backpack into the still sticking bottom desk drawer. She *really* needed to get that fixed. The remainder of the morning was spent with her colleagues finalizing files for the district attorney's office. Danielle and her fellow officers were literally taking bets on how many of the defendants would actually go to trial. The four assistant district attorneys working round the clock on the case were not amused when they learned what their colleagues were doing. Really, they were upset with themselves for not getting in on the action. The rumor was that the prize pool had grown to $600. One of the officers joked that the money should go into a savings account so that it could earn interest. With so many pending cases, it would be a while before anyone collected the cash.

Danielle removed her backpack from her desk drawer at precisely noon. A pulled pork food truck was outside in the parking lot. She thought about a sandwich for a minute but changed her mind. She'd be eating a burger and fries later. Better to eat a PowerBar and skip lunch. She got into her SVU and headed home. Traffic was light. She eyed her gym bag in the backseat of her vehicle. She definitely had time for a workout. It seemed dumb to belong to a gym when the sheriff's department had a well-equipped facility. But Danielle wasn't always in the mood to work out alongside fellow officers. Additionally, there was the fact that she didn't live near the office. The gym was only five minutes up the road from her condo. It provided fewer excuses to skip weight training. It was just about 1:00 p.m. when Danielle drove into the gym's parking lot. The place looked empty. It was a different story at 5:00 a.m. or 6:00 p.m. She could grab a run on the treadmill, do some chest and back work, and still have plenty of time before she needed to leave for the Valley.

An hour later, Danielle was headed back to her place. She pulled her SUV into its usual spot across the street from her complex, then headed into the house. Still no call back from her brother. Ugh! When was this going to end? The holidays were approaching. They had to kiss and make-up or their parents would be crushed.

At 3:32 p.m., Danielle was back in her vehicle. She had turned Hits1 up full volume. She loved what she was wearing. Simple, Casual. Perfect for a burger and fries. It was a Friday afternoon, and as she had expected, traffic was picking up. It didn't matter. Nothing was going to spoil her mood. Nothing. Post Malone, Rihanna, and Chris Stapleton accompanied her for the drive. She had seen the first two in concert, but not Chris. He was on her list. That was the beauty of living in the Bay Area. There were several concert venues within an hour's drive. Top performers always seemed to be in town. The problem was that ticket prices had become outrageous. It was difficult to justify hundreds of dollars for a couple of hours' worth of entertainment. It wasn't even the price of the tickets that bothered Danielle. It was the crazy tacked on service fees, and for what? Everything was electronic. It wasn't like tickets were printed on paper and people were working a box office. You simply punched in your credit card info and your entry was downloaded to your phone. Still, Danielle and her friends would pay the fees a few times a year for someone they really wanted to see.

The same applied to sporting events. The Niners actually played their home games in Santa Clara, not San Francisco. Everyone in the Bay thought it was funny that the NFL would show live images of the Bay Bridge or the Golden Gate, even though Levi Stadium was some 45 miles off in the distance. Additionally, the Bay Area was blessed with major league baseball and NBA basketball. They also had two professional soccer teams. And then, there were the college sports. Stanford, Cal, San Francisco and San Jose State, Santa Clara, and Saint Mary's were all in the region. Usually a concert or two, a football game, and a baseball afternoon made the annual list of events for her group of friends. Two were married. One was divorced. Danielle was the only one who hadn't walked down the aisle. They had been friends since their early days as uniformed officers. They understood each other. And they were all forces to be reckoned with at the gun range.

* * * * *

It was 4:25 p.m., and Jeff Sufford was still at the office. There had been a rash of burglaries over the past two weeks. It was only a matter of time before they caught the guys. There was plenty of CCTV footage now circulating. The stories had been all over the news and social media. Still, each new victim meant another case file for Detective

Sufford. Tourism usually slowed in the fall. These crimes, however, were perpetrated against Napa residents. It was unfortunate. When caught, this group of three would be looking at serving hard time, not six-month jail sentences or 300 hours of community service. If the detective, and the District Attorney, could prove it was the same assholes hitting the houses, they could end up doing two to six years for each first degree burglary conviction. Uniformed patrols had been beefed up over the past week. Jeff's experience had taught him that criminal minds didn't stop to think. They laughed all the way to the pawn shops. These guys weren't going to laugh when they got shoved into the back of a black and white in handcuffs, Jeff thought to himself.

At 4:35 p.m., Jeff got up from his desk and headed out to his government issued sedan. He was wearing jeans and a blue button down shirt. He had grabbed a navy sweater from a drawer before going into the office that morning. He reached for it across the front seat of his car and put it on. He pushed his hair off his forehead with his fingers, straightened what little bit of shirt collar he could see peeking out from underneath the sweater, gave himself a final look in the rearview mirror, popped a breath mint, and pulled out onto the street. The burger joint was a few miles up the road. He'd be there before their designated meeting time of 5:00 p.m.. He was excited, but not nervous. He and Detective Danielle Philipson hadn't seen each other in several weeks. He would do his best not to talk shop, but it was tough. It's what they had in common. For now.

Jeff and Danielle spotted each other as they headed toward the restaurant. He was coming from one direction, she the other. She waved first. So far so good, he thought as he waved back. The parking lot was busier than he had expected. It was still early. But it *was* a Friday evening. The place looked like it needed a paint job. It was a sort of sky blue wood structure. But it had a large and welcoming outdoor patio. The tables were round and covered with red and white checked tablecloths. Jeff loved how very country it looked. Completely out of character for Napa Valley, with its stark white table linens, olive oil bottles, and leather bound menus. No, this place was relaxed. It had a ranching feel which was also part of the Valley, though most people didn't associate Napa with cows.

Danielle exited her SUV first and headed straight toward the restaurant's entrance. She stood and waited for Jeff to join her. He was wearing cowboy boots. She loved the look, but she kept that opinion to herself.

"Hi," Jeff said as he approached his date. "It's good to see you." He went in for a hug. Danielle gave him a friendly hug in return.

"Thanks for the invitation," Danielle replied. "I'm looking forward to tasting this *amazing* burger of yours."

"Trust me," he responded. "You won't be disappointed. Do you want to go inside or sit out here," he asked motioning to the patio area.

"Let's sit outside. It's nice," she said.

Jeff motioned for Danielle to select a table. The patio overlooked a large, grassy area away from the parking lot. It wasn't a million dollar view, but it was pretty. The sun wouldn't set for about an hour. Jeff watched as Danielle noticed the lights strung across the covered patio. He knew it would be romantic once the lights came on. Jeff left Danielle momentarily, going inside to let the hostess know that they would be dining on the patio.

"Someone will be right out with menus," he shared when he came back to the table. "But you won't need a menu. Have the burger."

"I'm having the burger," she replied and laughed.

A server brought the menus and two glasses of water. Jeff ordered identical meals for the two officers, now on an official date. They both ordered beers. His was a Corona. Hers, a Miller Light. They made small talk while waiting for their food. More and more people poured into the restaurant. Jeff was glad that he had suggested an early dinner. He hated to wait. And, he knew she would have an hour-plus drive home. Both did their best not to talk about work but they finally succumbed after their enormous burgers and a mountain of fries were brought to the table.

"Wow, you weren't kidding," said Danielle as the server put the plate in front of her, then walked away. "This is huge!"

"I told you. Now try it."

Danielle took a bite, as juice from the beef began to cover her fingers. It *was* amazing. Jeff grabbed a handful of paper napkins and handed them to her.

"Guess I should have warned you about that part. They are kind of messy."

Danielle just laughed. She seemed lighthearted and happy. She took the napkins from Jeff and wiped her hands. They plowed into the fries which were equally delicious. No ketchup necessary.

Jeff was surprised that Danielle hadn't brought up the fire. Then again, they had gone over the files several times. Instead, she talked about the international drug cases. He shared information about the burglaries. The patio lights came on at about 6:30 p.m. The place was packed. Country music came over a series of speakers. They were each working on a second beer, to keep the evening going. It was still early.

"What do you like to do for fun," Jeff asked.

"You know, I work a lot. I work out. I spend time with a few friends. We'll go to a concert or a Niners game. I guess that's about it. You?"

"Same. Well, except for the Niners. I'm a baseball guy all the way. I'll go to watch the Giants lose whenever I get a chance."

They both laughed. The Giants were pretty up and down. But their fans were second to none. They cheered no matter how far out of the playoffs they were.

With their beers finished and the small talk winding down, Danielle made the first move.

"Thanks so much for such a fun night," she said. "I think I should be getting back."

"Of course," Jeff responded. He was bummed, but then again, they had met at 5:00 p.m. and this was only their first date. It wasn't going to go into the early morning hours. Besides, they were in a tucked away location away from Napa's downtown. It wasn't like they were going to walk up the street to a bar.

"Thanks for meeting me out here," Jeff said politely. "So, was it the best burger you've ever had?"

"You know what? It was," Danielle said winking at him. "Come on, walk me to my car."

They got up from the table and headed to the gravel parking lot. It was just after 8:00 p.m. and there were no signs that the restaurant would be clearing out. They stood awkwardly at her SUV for a few seconds."

"Thanks again. I had a great time," Danielle said.

"Me too," answered Jeff.

They gave each other a hug goodbye. Danielle unlocked her vehicle and got inside. Jeff walked off to his car. It had been a perfect first date. Danielle was fairly certain that Jeff would be calling again. If only her brother would.

CHAPTER
43

Dennis Smith-Hodges received the phone call from the private investigator at 9:00 a.m. Friday. Mason Recruiting International's CFO was annoyed. He hated taking calls before 10:00 a.m. Unless it was his boss. Even then, he still hated it. The owner of the agency he'd hired was on the line. Dennis would have preferred to hear any news directly from those who had done the actual investigating, or more accurately, cloak and dagger following, but he understood. There were at least three people involved in the surveillance, and the agency's owner probably wanted the glory of reporting out.

Turns out, Ms. Elizabeth Stevens had not stayed home the prior evening. Not only had she put on a beautiful dress, but she'd had dinner with five other people at a lavish restaurant. The sidewalk tour with a mystery man following dinner was intriguing, but without a name, it was a dead end. Dennis questioned why the investigator hadn't gotten a plate number off the guy's car. In response, he was told that the investigator had been tasked with watching Elizabeth and the black Town Car.

So, this was where it ended, unless Michael Mason wanted to continue to have her followed. Except for one final detail. Apparently, Ms. Stevens had put her house on the market only a couple of days prior, and it was already in escrow. It was record time by any account, no matter how hot the real estate market. And it definitely wasn't hot like it had been a few years ago. Elizabeth Stevens was moving. The CFO did his best not to raise his voice or sound surprised. He was a good poker player. Instead, he told the lead investigator that he'd get back to him with regard to any continued surveillance.

Now, Dennis had to decide what to tell Michael. The truth. Simple enough. He played out the dialogue in his mind. "Hey boss. Your contractor slash lawyer friend likes to drive the PCH for ten minute meetings. She also enjoys dressing up and dining at ostentatious restaurants with other couples. And, oh yeah, in her spare time, she's selling her home."

That was not going to go over well. Michael Mason would immediately ask questions. Anybody would, with such random details. And there were no real answers. Better to pull the trigger and let him know right away. Dennis was still at home. He could either go into the office and have a face-to-face or make a call. He decided to talk to Michael in person. He grabbed the keys to his silver Mercedes off the top of the bedroom dresser and headed downstairs. Dennis's wife was sitting at a small square table in the breakfast nook reading the paper. She was the only one, he thought. Nobody read a hard copy of *The Chronicle* anymore, did they? He walked over and gave her a kiss on the lips. He and his wife were still in love after 30 years of marriage. They'd never had kids. They both had careers. She was an oncologist at the University of California San Francisco. She loved her patients. She loved her students. His wife looked up from her paper momentarily, as Dennis walked out of the room and headed for the garage. He could almost walk to the office, but he preferred the car. He used the time to gather his thoughts. Plus, he didn't want to sweat in one of his Italian suits.

Dennis arrived at the building quickly. He decided to head straight for his own office for a couple of minutes before checking if Michael was available. The staff were all busy, especially considering it was a Friday, he thought to himself. Business was good. Thankfully. He stopped in the break room and picked up a bagel. He wasn't in bad shape, but he knew he should hit the gym more often. His boss was in great shape. That guy probably never ate a carb.

Dennis asked his assistant to see if Michael had a few minutes. She returned two minutes later and announced that Mr. Mason had time at 10:30 a.m. Perfect. Dennis could eat his breakfast in peace.

The CFO walked across the floor to meet with his boss at exactly 10:30 a.m. Michael's assistant nodded for Dennis to go on into the office. Dennis grabbed hold of one of the handles on the set of double doors and entered. The view never got old.

Michael was seated on the sofa. He appeared to be looking over a set of papers. Dennis knew better. His boss had set the scene so as not to appear anxious. Or nervous. He looked up from his "work" and greeted his numbers guy.

"Let's have it," Michael said flatly, inviting Dennis to sit in one of the adjacent club chairs. "What did they find?"

Dennis's boss wasn't pulling any punches. He knew why his CFO was in his office. He wanted to hear how Elizabeth was spending her time. He hoped she was going to an office, or making calls, or hell, sitting around her house eating ice cream from a Blue Bunny container.

After taking a seat, Dennis began sharing the details. Elizabeth had used an Uber to go out to a home along the PCH, where she met someone for fewer than 15 minutes. It turned out the home belonged to a lawyer up in Sacramento. Michael listened. He didn't say a word. She'd stayed in all day Wednesday. No calls. No visitors. And then, Dennis shared the story about her outing the prior night. In a green dress. The elegant restaurant. The dinner where she was part of three couples who talked, ate, and appeared to enjoy each other's company. He continued with the unusual fact that following dinner, Elizabeth and a mystery gentleman had exited the restaurant and then walked up a half block, crossed the street and walked back. She'd then called for the black Town Car and proceeded home. Alone. That was it. And the fact that her home was in escrow, and it appeared she would be moving soon. The entire synopsis took less than five minutes. Michael didn't ask any questions. He knew that if his CFO had additional information, he would have shared it.

The men spent a couple of minutes in silence, just staring at the view out the office windows. Finally, Michael spoke.

"I wonder if she is moving back to New York."

"Could be," responded Dennis. "I suppose until a moving truck pulls up, there's no way to know. It's possible she's decided on a new place in the City somewhere."

Both men had no idea what to do with the details regarding Elizabeth's movements that week. Michael felt somewhat at ease knowing she hadn't gone home with either of the men. But it was unsettling to think she was out and about and yet didn't seem to be working. The sale of the house caught him off guard. On one hand, if Michael wanted her gone, it seemed he might get his wish. But clearly, he didn't want to be finished. Otherwise, he wouldn't be having her followed. Michael knew that he would need to take action if he wanted to see her again. Elizabeth wasn't going to reach out. Hell, he was sure he had hurt her that night when he left the hotel room. She probably wouldn't take his call. The only thing he could do was to go to her home. He wasn't sure he had the stomach for it.

"Okay, that's it," said Michael finally, breaking the room's silence. "There's no point in following her any more. I'm sure you've figured out that we were in a relationship. But I ended it a couple of weeks ago. She was getting emotionally attached, and that wasn't good for me."

Dennis wasn't sure how to respond.

"It's none of my business," he answered. "You know I'm always here for you. Whatever you need."

"I know. And I appreciate it. My marriage has been dead for years. I've still got my boys. Well, at least Aiden. For now," said Michael.

"I think I'd better leave it all alone with Elizabeth," he continued. "Whatever she's doing and wherever she's going, it's none of my business since I'm the one that broke it off."

Dennis sat and listened to his friend. It was hard to watch some-one he admired, and more importantly, cared about be so conflicted. Sometimes, Michael was too practical.

"Do you love her?" Dennis asked.

"What?"

"Do you *love* her," Dennis repeated the question. "Look, maybe you don't love her. But if you care about her, then hell, either pick up the phone or go see her. If she rejects you, then you can close the door. If she doesn't, well it might be what you both need. Each other."

"It's not that simple," Michael was quick to respond. "Starting over again."

"Maybe you don't start over. Maybe you go along as you have been. Just enjoy each other."

Michael wasn't about to tell Dennis that he had been *paying* Elizabeth for her company. He'd been stupid for ending it. He had been good at compartmentalizing their relationship. Things began changing for him a couple of years ago. She started to mean more to him. Too much. And he recognized that her feelings for him had been intensifying for a while. They never spoke about their emotions or intentions. They could have left it that way, but his need for control had caused him to intervene. His fucking ego had gotten in the way. Again.

"Yeah, maybe," Michael said to his friend.

Dennis took it as a sign that their discussion had ended. He would go back to his office and call off the investigation. Michael didn't want to know any more. He knew enough. He had lost Elizabeth.

CHAPTER
44

Danielle's brother finally decided to pick up the phone and call. It was Saturday morning. The sun was high in the sky and the air was crisp.

Her cell phone rang. Once. Twice. Answer it, he thought to himself. He wasn't going to leave a message. She picked up on the third ring.

She knew who it was before she answered. She was nervous. And grateful.

"Hello," Danielle said. Peter was on the other end of the line. It was about time!

"Good morning," he responded. And then in his best lawyer tone, he said, "Listen, I'm sorry I ghosted you. It was immature. I know you wouldn't have left me at the Ninth Circuit, if it hadn't been for a good reason."

"Hey, I'm sorry I…."

"Let me finish, Danny," responded her brother, calling Danielle by her nickname. "I don't need to know what pulled you away. I think I let my pride get in the way. I miss you. Let's cut the crap and be brother and sister again."

Danielle agreed. She didn't want to go five rounds. She had apologized. He was apologizing in his own way.

"Fair. Do you want to get dinner tonight?"

"I've got a better idea. I have tickets to the game tomorrow. Want to go?"

Danielle knew her brother was talking football. It was perfect. They could spend time together, but they would also have a distraction in case things got awkward.

"Uh, yeah. Seriously? That would be great."

The two made plans. He would pick her up for the afternoon game. He had great seats. Danielle ended the call with a happy heart. Her date with Jeff Sufford had gone well. Her brother was speaking to her again. Her files on the drug case were almost complete. It felt like a scoop of ice cream kind of day. Maybe two.

She wasn't on call for the weekend, so she could truly relax. Danielle thought about what had brought her and Jeff together. She wondered to herself if she should take one last look at the files on the server before they were archived. No, she decided. There was no smoking gun. Only smoke. Mrs. Laura Mason and the PFV Winery were in her rear view. Maybe if she and Jeff started dating in earnest, they would go wine tasting. Or maybe they could go to the shooting range. One thing was certain. She needed to get a cat.

CHAPTER
45

The sun was beginning to rise across the Sunday morning sky as Michael rounded the corner onto California Street. He found himself staring at Elizabeth's home. "What the fuck," he uttered under his breath. He was being ridiculous. He could feel the knot in his stomach move into his throat. He had parked a couple of blocks over and walked up a side street. The sidewalks were cracked. The slopes, steep. Too steep to be wearing his signature loafers. This game of hide and seek hadn't been necessary. He was fairly certain that she had no idea what type of vehicle he drove.

California Street was better described as a boulevard or avenue. It ran in a nearly straight line for some five miles from the Financial District to Lincoln Park. Its iconic 54 blocks included such famous landmarks and neighborhoods as the Embarcadero Center, Chinatown, and Nob Hill. Skyscrapers intermingled with freestanding homes and tiny businesses. Historic architecture stood next to the nondescript modern. Michael thought about all of the reasons why Elizabeth would live here as he continued to observe the house. There were absolutely no signs of life inside. What was he doing? He was going to screw this up. He already had.

He checked his watch. For the third time. It was 6:32 a.m. The only people up this early on a Sunday were the damn runners training for their next marathon. And maybe a few dog walkers. Why would he expect Elizabeth to be awake and roaming the house? It was a beautiful home, Michael said to himself. A huge bay window greeted visitors. The cream and white exterior was subtle. Pretty. A small patch of grass on either side of the front walkway was expertly manicured. Large black clay pots near the entry were in sharp contrast to the cascading white roses which they held. Elegant. Like Elizabeth. Michael imagined an interior covered in floor to ceiling moulding. From the street, he could see into the main living space, where she had selected a butterscotch leather sofa. The walls were a shade of white. A camel throw was folded over the top of a pale blue chair. It looked comfortable and fresh. Her home wasn't as large as his, but he had raised a family in his place. She was alone. He hoped.

Michael continued to linger, pacing slowly back and forth, until nearly 7:00 a.m. He decided that he had punished himself long enough. He certainly couldn't "casually" run into her as she headed to her morning coffee spot. It was a three-mile jog from her place, according to the private investigator's report, and nowhere near his home or office. Michael would have absolutely no reason to be anywhere in the vicinity. For a moment he played out the idea of crossing the street and ringing her doorbell. He envisioned Elizabeth greeting him excitedly, ushering him inside as she gave him a passionate kiss. Shit, he should have brought flowers if that had been his intention. It wasn't going to happen.

Just as Michael was about to give up and head back to his car, Elizabeth suddenly opened the front door. It took him a second to process the unexpected scene. She had large, mis-matched duffle bags in each hand and some sort of farmer's market tote slung over her right shoulder. She was dressed plainly. A faded pink sweatshirt, ripped jeans, and sneakers. Her hair was pulled back into a tight ponytail. It wasn't a flattering look. Sloppy, Michael judged. She wasn't a college student. Sure, she didn't need to be in $5,000 worth of clothing with Gucci bags over each arm in order to meet his standards, but it appeared as though she was reaching for her inner youth. It reminded him of the day he thought he'd seen her near Union Square. He now realized that it *had* been her that afternoon. He knew his internal comments were shitty. He wasn't exactly runway-model gorgeous himself, but she was about one step away from sporting a couple of tattoos, he decided. He cringed. Who was she kidding? She was beautiful, but she wasn't 19 anymore.

California Street was wide. Michael wasn't overly concerned that Elizabeth would spot him. She was headed somewhere in a hurry. She moved rapidly down the front walk and headed left up the street. He followed her as she maintained a steady pace. One block soon became two, then three, and then four. She was making great time, especially for someone carrying two large bags which appeared to be very heavy. As his pursuit continued, Michael realized that his car was parked almost a mile away in the opposite direction. Still, he couldn't bring himself to turn around. He continued to pursue Elizabeth as she approached The Embarcadero. He was starting to break into a sweat when an underground BART station entrance came into view.

Michael was just a few yards behind her as she disappeared down the escalator. He was left with no choice but to make the same descent. He could see Elizabeth scan her way through the large bank of turnstiles. Michael rushed over to a Clipper vending machine and swiped his credit card. A ticket emerged from a slot. He raced to the turnstile area and crossed onto the other side, then realized he could relax. It was early Sunday morning, so the trains ran on an intermittent weekend schedule. He could see Elizabeth standing nearby, her duffle bags resting on a stone bench. She hadn't noticed him. Where was she headed? He was going to find out if it was the last thing he did.

CHAPTER
46

Michael kept an eye on Elizabeth from a distance. He was doing his best to blend in among the people who had filtered into the station, spreading themselves out behind the yellow curbs on the platform's concrete. Without warning, the screech of steel on steel suddenly filled the air. A train came roaring up the metal tracks, clamoring to a stop. The doors immediately slid open. After several passengers emerged, Elizabeth picked up her bags and got on. Michael followed, stepping into the adjacent car. He watched as she sat down. The train was headed across the Bay. That meant only one thing. They were speeding toward Emeryville, an Amtrak hub situated between Oakland and Berkeley.

It was nearing 9:00 a.m. when the train pulled into the station. Michael paid close attention as Elizabeth stepped off. This was a large connection point for Amtrak. She could be going anywhere from here. Michael had to choose. Either approach Elizabeth now or let her go. Forever. As he stood and debated with himself, he realized he had been distracted. He abruptly refocused his attention. He had lost sight of Elizabeth. In a panic, his eyes darted from side to side scanning the various platforms for any sign of her. That's when he saw it. Her cheap duffle bag. She was boarding the train two tracks over. His thoughts were frantic as he searched for a way to get to her. There were no God damned signs! How the hell had he let this happen?

He rushed down the nearest corridor which took passengers across to the various sets of tracks. He was relieved to find the correct platform entrance. He looked up at an electronic sign above. It read, "Salinas" and announced the departure time. Her train wasn't leaving for another 20 minutes. He could calm down. That's where she was going, he thought to himself. The Central Valley. Who the hell was in Salinas?

Michael could feel the jealousy rise up. He had to see this through to the end. He pulled his phone from his pocket, and within a matter of minutes had paid for and downloaded an e-ticket. It was about 100 miles to the Salinas Valley. Yet it seemed like a million from the Bay. He stayed on the platform until the last boarding announcement was made before finally committing to the ride.

As he made himself comfortable on the train, Michael started to beat himself up. This had become a cluster fuck. What the hell was he doing? Did he really think he was going to have a happily ever after with her? On his terms? If only he'd had the balls to approach her outside her home hours earlier. But that would have been *way* too easy, he admonished himself.

Michael tried to redirect his attention to the scenery. The journey was surprising pleasant. Salinas was a huge farming region just eight miles inland from the Pacific Ocean. It was artificially green from all the water used to irrigate the various crops. As the train neared its destination, he could almost smell the sea air. It was an incredible day. The sky was a perfect shade of blue. Soft white clouds caught his attention. It had been years since Michael had visited this area. When was the last time he'd noticed the clouds? He couldn't remember. What had this woman done to him?

Michael stayed lost in his thoughts until the Salinas station was in view. Its architecture was clearly Spanish. Red clay barrel tiles covered the roof of the depot's smooth concrete walls. Numerous people were standing around, waiting for passengers to disembark. The train had come to a grinding halt, but Michael remained in his seat. It didn't take long before he saw Elizabeth with her duffle bags in tow. He quickly moved from his position, down the railcar's steps, and out onto the platform. He could see Elizabeth casually walk into the station's main building.

Now what, Michael asked himself? He was tired. And ashamed. He was a grown man acting like a fucking teenager. He couldn't sneak around, following Elizabeth indefinitely. This was beyond ludicrous. In his head, he knew he should get on the next train back to the City. But in his heart, he couldn't let her go. He needed to look into her beautiful eyes. And apologize. For hurting her. For disappointing her. For leaving her. For never having admitted that he loved her.

CHAPTER
47

Michael took a deep breath, as he moved from the outdoor platform into the station building. He could see Elizabeth proceeding through the terminal toward the main exit. She seemed so incredibly happy.

He picked up his pace as he moved toward her. He couldn't believe he was about to do this. Confront her. In such a public place. He could almost touch her as he called out.

"Elizabeth!"

Sarah was startled. She immediately stopped. It took a moment before she recognized who had accosted her. And then… it was him. Her mouth dropped open, and her heart sank. She was both thrilled and scared to death. What was he doing here? How had he found her? How could he have so blatantly disrespected her privacy? Elizabeth was well aware that Michael had paid to have her followed in San Francisco. She had noted the series of unmarked cars parked across the street over the past week. She had been amused when she had allowed herself to be tailed from a distance along the PCH. Even the man sitting in the Starbucks using binoculars the night she wore her emerald dress had not gone unnoticed. She was the master when it came to being invisible. But this?

Michael had stalked her. She was shocked. And maybe a little impressed. But mostly, she was so very hurt. What did he want with her now? They had already said their goodbyes.

Michael had intruded into Sarah's escape. She had left Elizabeth's world behind. He didn't belong here. She didn't want him here. This was abusive. She looked intensely into Michael's eyes as they stood in the middle of the train station, inches apart.

"Michael," she said in a statement-like tone, doing her very best not to sound surprised. But he could hear her raised pitch. He could tell that he had caught her completely off guard and feeling vulnerable.

"I know," he paused. "I'm not here to hunt you down or frighten you," he said.

Now, Sarah was pissed. Of course, he was hunting her down. What else would you call it? Michael thought he could leave her and then return whenever he felt like it. Why? Because he had money and power? He had played with her emotions one too many times. She knew he loved her, but she wasn't going to let this man hurt her anymore. In his own cowardly fashion, he had made it clear that he no longer wanted to be together. Without using any words, he had let his feelings be known that last night in the Sausalito hotel room. So, she had left him alone. Moral of this story, she thought. Be careful what you wish for.

"You've done both," Sarah responded, sounding more like Elizabeth than the girl from the beachside town. She was proud of herself for staying calm. He had absolutely hunted her down, and she was definitely feeling frightened. But she wouldn't let him get the best of her. She was the one with the power now.

"I know this is going to sound wrong, but I'm not here to apologize to you, Elizabeth."

"Asshole," she whispered under her breath, bringing Sarah out again.

"Then what? I dare you to tell me the truth, Michael. Just once."

"The truth is, I want you in my life." There. He had said it. He hadn't given a full admission of his feelings, but he was close. He cared about her deeply, but he could never give himself to someone else completely again.

"I promise, if you don't want to be with me, I will turn around and you'll never see me again."

Sarah wasn't going to give Michael any satisfaction. He was a man who showed so little emotion, and yet she had allowed him to inflict such deep wounds. He would never hurt her physically. The pain he left her sitting in was strictly emotional. She stayed silent. If this was supposed to be his Hollywood ending, she wouldn't give it to him. She wasn't going to throw her arms around his neck and walk off into the sunset hand in hand with him, no matter how manipulative his words might be.

No one was paying any attention to the couple standing in the center of the terminal. Sarah was certain that this was not how Michael had imagined it. In a crowded train station. Desperate. No, he would have wanted one last private evening to win her over, on his terms. Always his terms. And that was the problem.

"I think you know how much I care about you. I think you've known for a while," said Michael. "But I've been too afraid to tell you, because I can't be what you want me to be. I want us to be in each other's lives. But I don't want to be married. I don't want more children. I want to spend time together, but I don't want to live together. And that's not what you want."

How dare he? Michael was telling her what she wanted for her life. He didn't know anything about her. And he never asked. She didn't care about marriage. She didn't want children. Michael had no idea that she had been masquerading as someone else these past four years. He could never imagine who was standing before him now. Her true self. And she wanted it to remain that way.

Sarah was no longer Elizabeth Catherine Stevens. She was not an attorney from New York, the daughter of a fearless lawyer with two brothers and a mother overly concerned about her social calendar. She wasn't the girl who was both punished and dearly loved by her father. Who had spent her summers running along the beaches of

Nantucket. She hadn't come from an Ivy League heritage. She didn't have a father who loathed his own father, and his father's father. Who stood watch as the First and the Second slithered away and died. No, she had earned her wealth, one man at a time. She had lived the past 10 years in a life of make believe.

"I need to tell you something," Michael said, staring down at his feet, too afraid to look directly at her. "You'll be able to hold this secret over me for the rest of my life."

Sarah was becoming exhausted. She didn't care. It was still all about *him*.

"I did it."

Did what, she wondered. Broke her heart? He had tried. She knew now that he hadn't succeeded.

"I set the winery fire," he declared, his voice quivering. "It was easy. I thought a fire would bring Laura to her knees. But it didn't. It only made her stronger."

Sarah continued to listen. What did the winery fire have to do with her? Nothing.

"I did it for us, so we could be together," Michael tried to explain. "I wanted Laura to hate me when she found out about the insurance. But she didn't. She became even more fierce. She will never give up her fucking winery, and she will never divorce me. That would mean admitting failure."

Sarah was more certain than ever that Michael didn't love Elizabeth. He only loved himself. And deep down, he probably still loved Laura. If he wanted to, he could divorce his wife. He didn't need her permission. But his ego wouldn't allow it. He didn't have the stomach for it.

Even in his perverted confession, his reason for setting the fire had nothing to do with Michael and Elizabeth's future together. He claimed to have done it in order to force Laura to end their marriage. She would have to leave him. He would never leave *her*. He was too selfish and weak.

He was also lying. Sarah was disgusted. She had practically begged him to tell the truth. But he was unwilling. Incapable.

"You're still lying, Michael," Sarah said flatly as he finished his confession.

Michael looked shocked.

"Why would I lie," he asked. "I'm risking everything."

"No, you're risking nothing. Except maybe your pride and what you believe is the power you have over me."

Michael's body tensed.

"Do you *really* think I'm going to race back into your arms, because you told me you set the fire for us?"

Michael continued to stand, motionless. Stunned.

"Even now. You can't tell me the truth."

Sarah chose her next words very carefully.

"I know you're lying, because I'm the one who set the fire."

Michael went white. He began to shake. She had caught him. She had given him one last chance to be honest. To utter "those three little words" telling her he wanted to be with her. To apologize for his behavior. His callousness. He hadn't set the fire. He seemed to believe that if he claimed responsibility, Elizabeth would accept this stunt as a proclamation of his love.

"You make me sick," Sarah said. "I caused the fire. I thought it would put an end to the two of you. Instead, you both just went on with your sad, stagnant lives of fancy parties, hating each other, and pretending to be a couple for your nearly grown children."

Michael said nothing. For the first time in his life, he was helpless. He had no response. How could his Elizabeth have done this to him? His eyes stared past hers.

And in that moment, she had no more doubts.

"I don't care about you anymore, Michael. Go home."

Sarah walked away. At peace. A suffocating weight lifted. Michael would never be the person she needed. It was freeing to leave him and the illusion of Elizabeth standing in the train station. Alone. Lost.

She knew he would keep her secret. The truth about setting the fire ultimately indicted him. Their lives would be forever intertwined.

From Elizabeth's ashes, Sarah had discovered herself. She had always been the girl from Pacific Grove. The girl who loved her mother, collecting seashells, eating chocolate lava cake, and greeting people at the quirky beachfront restaurant.

The Michaels of the world would never consider Sarah fitting for themselves. They would find her incapable of meeting their shallow standards. The Michaels of the world would only ever want Elizabeth.

* * * * *

Sarah Anne Jennings glanced in the reflective urn as she stepped into the ocean's icy surf. Impeccable. It was a word her mother had used often to describe her only child. Sarah gazed beyond her mother's dust as she scattered her remains. Thankful she had stopped pretending all those years ago. She smiled inside. Content.

THE END